Someone
I Wanted to Be

Someone
I Wanted to Be

AURELIA WILLS

CANDLEWICK PRESS

Copyright © 2016 by Aurelia Wills

First U.S. edition 2016

Library of Congress Catalog Card Number pending
ISBN 978-0-7636-8156-2

16 17 18 19 20 21 BVG 10 9 8 7 6 5 4 3 2 1

Printed in Berryville, VA, U.S.A.

This book was typeset in Adobe Caslon.

Candlewick Press
99 Dover Street
Somerville, Massachusetts 02144

visit us at www.candlewick.com

For Stew, Jess, and Miles

One

I talked to myself all the time. I pretended someone was listening and interested in my favorite color, what music I liked, and what I thought of Kristy. I told this listener, pulling thoughts and feelings out of the tangled mess inside me as I lay on my bed in my little room with puke-green walls decorated with posters of Bruno Mars, kittens, and puppies. Splotches of red dust grew on my window. Behind the yellowed glass were thick black bars and a window well full of garbage, dead leaves, and spiders.

I twirled the matchbook between my fingers. I opened the cover, smelled the peppery matches, and studied the name Kurt King and the number written inside in red ballpoint. His writing was small, tight, and jagged like lightning strokes. As he'd handed it to me, he'd said, "Tell her to call me."

I opened my phone and slowly pushed in the numbers, then held it to my cheek and stared up at a basket of black kittens with tiny pink tongues. I listened to the phone ring and waited in a cloud of nothingness, paper kittens, and an endless ringing. Then it stopped and a man with a hoarse voice said, "Yeah?"

The phone felt like a little bomb.

"Who is this?" he said.

TWO

Corinne and I went to Kristy's to get ready. Kristy's house had silky beige carpet like cocker spaniel fur. Seedpods and dried grass stuck out of a brown jug, and a shellacked wooden cross hung over the gas fireplace. Orange light shone through the smudged picture window that looked out on a cedar fence. Beyond the fence were the roofs of a hundred houses, every single house with a mountain view.

Kristy's dad sat in his recliner with his thick fingers curled under his chin. He tilted his head and stared dreamily at a cooking show on the flat-screen TV. He'd taken off his work clothes and wore a ribbed undershirt that stretched over his big soft belly. He was always tired—he worked at some job in the office park by the mall. "Kristy, Pastor Steve is coming in twenty minutes. Do you want to come in and pray with us?"

"Um, Dad, I think we'll be gone by then. Sorry!" said Kristy, widening her eyes at Corinne.

Mrs. Baker hung on to the kitchen counter with both hands. She was wearing her footed toddler PJs with the zipper up the front. She looked like a giant baby chicken with a few tufts of gray hair like wilted feathers. "Girls, can I get you juice? We have flaxseed cookies."

Kristy rolled her eyes. "Mom, those cookies are disgusting." She shook out her hair, pressed her head against Corinne's, and whispered something. They ran laughing down the hallway.

Mrs. Baker wobbled over and put her arm around my waist. "How's my girl?"

"Oh, you know, I'm OK. What about you?" Her arm felt like a little branch, her hand like a leaf. She was the sickest person I'd ever known.

Mrs. Baker, this medicine will make you feel very sick for a few weeks, but afterward you will completely recover, I imagined telling her. I wanted to be a doctor but hadn't told anyone.

"Don't you worry about me." She weakly squeezed me with her leaf hand. Her eyes were so bright in that gray skinny face.

"Leah, get your big butt down here!"

Mrs. Baker wrinkled her forehead and raised her

eyebrows, or the skin where her eyebrows used to be. I could suddenly smell the cold, sharp medicines. She shook her almost-bald head. "She's a pistol."

"See you later, Mrs. Baker."

She squeezed my shoulder with her little trembling hand. "You call me Mom."

The walls of the hallway were covered with framed photographs of Kristy. Eight-by-ten school portraits in wooden frames, a baby Kristy surrounded by floating toys and bubbles in a blue bath, Kristy doing the splits in a leotard before she quit gymnastics, Kristy on her dad's shoulders at Disneyland, the towers of the Magic Kingdom glowing in the weird black light behind them. Her dad, squashed beneath her, grinned and hung on to her ankles while she stuck out her chin and bared her teeth.

Kristy slammed her bedroom door shut behind me, then slid down it until she sat cross-legged on the carpet. She pulled her hair out from behind her and patted it like it was a pet. "Damn, those people wear me out. God! I can't believe my dad asked me to pray with them." She flipped open her laptop.

Corinne and I sat at the foot of her twin beds. Kristy's parents had given her the master bedroom. The floor was covered in soft pink carpet. The comforters, curtains, and the skirt around the vanity were all done in matching fabric—a white background filled with fat roses. Kristy had taped up pictures of models and a giant poster of Lil Wayne, though she didn't even listen to his music. Kristy's nose almost touched the computer screen. She typed something super fast and laughed.

Corinne pulled off her shoes and squinted at her toenails. "I don't mean to be rude, but there's something different about your mom's face."

I said, "God, Corinne, rude. Just rude." I would never have said anything.

"Her eyebrows fell off. Chemo." Kristy's eyes darted back and forth as she scrolled down the screen.

"Oh. Wow," Corinne said, and we both solemnly nodded. As a doctor, I would have to get used to this stuff.

Kristy looked up. She raised her own white eyebrow and dug her pinkie into the corner of her eye. She smiled savagely. "She's so skinny now, her butt's all wrinkled."

I felt a little sick at the thought. The waistband of my jeans was cutting into my stomach.

Kristy uncrossed her ankles and jumped to her feet. "I get first shower." She always got first shower in her pink-carpeted bathroom. Even the toilet lid had a fuzzy pink cover.

Corinne pulled the laptop over. She brought up a picture of her and Kristy with their heads tilted, mouths open, fingers pointing at their chins — gangsters. She rolled onto her back and yelled, "Kristy, that night was so awesome!"

I picked up an old *Seventeen*. On the cover was a picture of a girl with big shiny eyes and long shining hair and long skinny legs like flower stems. A girl like a flower, but flowers couldn't talk. Flowers were quiet like me. The girl on the cover looked so happy, as if being perfect was all it took.

Kristy turned on the water, ripped the shower curtain down the pole, and started screeching a Beyoncé song.

Kristy was my girl—we'd been friends since junior high—but something white-hot like hatred for her ran through me like a nerve. Except for her mom being sick, she had a life like in a magazine. Her parents were still married, and they adored her. They bought her diamond earrings for her thirteenth birthday and a barely used red Civic when she turned sixteen. She lived in a house with ten huge rooms. It was practically a mansion. She had everything you could possibly want, but she still wanted more.

Kristy was beautiful, though she wasn't even pretty if you dissected her. She had squinty eyes with stubby white lashes and wore so much mascara that it clumped and flaked onto her cheeks. When she smiled, shiny pink gums showed above her teeth. She'd gotten her invisible braces off the year before.

She had a little face the size of a saucer, but her nose was substantial, a full-grown Italian-lady nose. She claimed to have a deviated septum, which would require a nose job when she turned eighteen. I could do a scarily good imitation of her whiny voice.

She wore little padded push-up bras and had red bumps, baby acne, on her skinny arms. But Kristy was tiny as a fairy, and she had long, curly, white-blond hair. That hair did it every time. She'd get out of the car with that hair floating around her, and the boys were instantly drugged. I loved her and I hated her. She annihilated me. When she walked in the room, I disappeared.

I always told Corinne, "You're so much prettier than Kristy." And Corinne was, with her round cheeks and deep dimples. She streaked her brown hair, hid her freckles under orangey foundation, and wore green heart-shaped studs that brought out the color of her eyes. But there were a million Corinnes in the world, and Corinne knew it. This knowledge was like an arrowhead buried deep in her heart. It gave her eyes an icy glint and was the best part about her.

"Movie-star eyes and a movie-star mouth," Mrs. Baker always said about me. But I had rolls on my stomach and gigantic pale thighs. My hair and feet were OK, but it was like an erupting volcano of blubber in between.

I was like a princess trapped in a spell of fat. I was in love with Damien Rogers, a junior at Arapahoe High School. He was tall and dark-haired with a dimpled chin. We saw him almost every weekend we went down to Torrance Park. I'd talked to him once. I said, "Hi," and was almost positive that he heard me.

The bathroom door opened and Kristy burst out in a white terry robe with her hair in a pink turban. "Go!" she said. Corinne slowly got to her feet. Kristy's ironed size-zero jeans lay on her bed. She'd let the silk conditioner in her hair soak for fifteen minutes.

Kristy grabbed her phone and leaned back against her lace-covered pillow. I sat on the floor. I leaned against the foot of her bed and stretched. "Can I use your laptop?"

Kristy said, "No. Chubs, you got to start waxing those arms."

I glared at her. She wasn't even looking at me. I pulled on my hoodie and thought about how his voice sounded. Kurt King. He slowed way down. He said, "I want to talk to you." His voice had gotten into my head like smoke, like a cat, and curled around me.

When we walked back through the living room, Pastor Steve was on his knees in front of the couch. He held Mr. and Mrs. Baker's hands, and they all had their eyes closed.

Three

Kristy pulled into the 7-Eleven parking lot.

"He's here."

He was standing out front, leaning against the brick wall. He was smoking and had one cowboy boot kicked back against the bricks. I was skewered, pinned to the seat by the sight of him.

He had long streaked hair with bangs that made him look boyish, green eyes, sharp cheekbones, and a mouth that looked like he'd just finished kissing someone. I wanted to put my hands around his narrow hips. He wore jeans torn at the knees and the corduroy jacket with the cheesy leather collar that he'd been wearing the first time we saw him. Corinne called him Mr. Corduroy. I was the only one who knew his real name. Kurt King.

Kristy ran her car into the curb, and we all jerked against our seat belts. One of the oldest kids in our grade, she'd gotten the Civic in September but was still a bad driver. By law she could only have one other kid in the car. She usually had two.

He took one last drag off his cigarette and flicked it across the parking lot. I was in the backseat. I always rode in the backseat when Corinne was with us.

"He's heading over," said Corinne in a singsong. She pulled the sleeves of her hoodie down over her hands and jammed her fists in her armpits.

Kristy unbuckled, lowered her window, sat up straight, and stuck out her chest. Her face was framed by a cloud of white ringlets. She was wearing giant silver hoop earrings and a tight lacy top she'd bought at the mall that afternoon. "Do we need cigarettes?" she said, when there were two packs sitting on the dash in front of her. She turned down the radio.

"He's here," Corinne said under her breath.

He stood outside Kristy's door with his arms crossed. He tilted his head to the side and squinted as if she were a car he was thinking about buying.

"Hey," he said with a crooked smile. He sucked in his cheeks like he had a mouthful of sugar.

Kristy spun around. Her mouth hung open in fake surprise. "Oh! Hey."

He braced himself against the door and leaned down until he filled Kristy's window. His streaky bangs fell into his eyes, and he shook them back. His hands were brown and smooth except for the veins that ran like little snakes under the skin. His corduroy sleeves smelled like cigarettes and wind. His lower lip was swollen; his upper lip was thin and curved with a little dip in the middle. His eyes were dark-lashed. He was older than us, in his twenties at least. His face belonged on a magazine cover. He was the kind of guy you couldn't look away from — you'd try to look somewhere else, and your head would slowly turn back. I was the fat girl with huge thighs.

He said, "What's going on?" His scratchy voice made me feel strange and secret. I was barely breathing.

Kristy's shoulders swayed in a little circle to the song on the radio. Rihanna. She laughed for no reason. "Not much," she said.

He grinned as if she'd said something of incredible wit.

"Did you call me?" He pulled back a little and squinted at her. "Was that you who called me the other night?"

I was invisible. It was like being in a movie theater watching Kristy's life on the big screen.

"Uh, no," said Kristy, as she tried to shush Corinne. Corinne was poking Kristy with her elbow and whispering.

"Hey, would you do us a favor?" said Kristy. She twirled her hair around her fingers and widened her eyes. "I remember seeing you here last weekend. Would you maybe buy us some beer?"

Kurt King sighed, stood up, and stared across the
ing lot. He slowly ran his tongue across his front
He looked down at Kristy, then cocked his head. "Man, I
hate it when kids ask me to do that. But I'll do it for you,
sweetheart."

"I've got money," said Kristy. She stretched to get the
twenty out of her back pocket, and Kurt King just looked her
over and drank her in. It was kind of sick, and exactly the
way I'd imagined Damien Rogers staring at me.

He crumpled the money into his fist. He had huge nails
rimmed with dirt. "Pull around to the back by the Dumpster.
What do you want?"

Corinne leaned over Kristy's lap. "Whatever's cheap. And
get us a pack of Marlboro reds. OK, sweetheart?"

He gave Corinne a glassy-eyed stare, rolled back his
shoulders, and swaggered over to the door. He jerked it
open. For a minute, we watched him inside in the yellow
light. Kristy started up the engine, and the Civic shot backward. She drove the car around the back of the store and
pulled up next to the Dumpster. She yanked down the rearview mirror, smeared on some lip gloss, then looked back to
see if he was coming just as I leaned forward. She whipped
me in the eyes with her hair. "How old do you think he is?"

"Kristy, you like him?" said Corinne with a little shriek.
"He's old! He wears a stupid-looking corduroy jacket! He

has dirty hands! He highlights his hair! Mr. Corduroy is disgusting."

"Corinne, shut up," I said. "Mr. Corduroy's coming. He's right here."

He walked up to Kristy's window. He was wearing a belt with a big brass belt buckle engraved with a picture of a bucking horse. He scuffed his boot against the pavement and let us look at his bulky crotch and bucking-bronco belt buckle for a long minute. Then he shoved the case of beer through the window and tossed the cigarettes onto Corinne's lap.

"There you go. Here's your change. Now. How you going to thank me?" His face was still and serious.

Corinne set the case on the floor under her feet. There was a big light by the store's back door, but by the Dumpster it was all shadows. Big blooming shadows like a garden of shadows, layers of shadows, all the different colors of shadow. Kristy sat motionless as a rabbit. She was shivering, maybe because Kurt King was drawing circles on her bare arm with his finger.

"What's your name?"

Corinne jabbed Kristy's side. Kristy put the car in reverse and the car rolled backward. Kurt King hung on to Kristy's window and walked alongside.

"Girl, what's your name?" he said. "I know it was you who called."

"I got to go," said Kristy. When she turned her head, I

could see her nose and her thin, glossy mouth through her hair. She was shaking with laughter.

"Thanks a million, Mr. Corduroy," sang Corinne. She put her feet up on the dash and stuck her elbow out the window.

Kristy drove slowly around the store to the street. Kurt King walked beside the car, still hanging on to her window. His boots crunched against the asphalt. "I'm not letting you go," he said, "until you tell me your name." Kristy leaned back, laughed, and chewed her gum. Her eyes gleamed. I watched her in the rearview mirror.

Kristy stopped the car before she turned onto Tenth. "We got to go, dude." She smiled to herself and pretended to look for something in her purse. "We got to go." She shook out her hair.

Kurt King let go of Kristy's window and leaned into mine. His big fingertips pinched the door. "Hey, quiet girl. What's her name?"

His eyes, just a few inches away, looked steadily into mine. Warm breath blew against my cheek; it smelled like cigarettes and beer and something minty and dark and hot. I could have gotten drunk on his breath.

"Ashley." That was the name I'd always wanted.

He put his big, dry hand around my chin. "Thanks, sweetheart." My mouth brushed his palm as we pulled away.

Kristy and Corinne grabbed each other's arms and shrieked with laughter. The car shot forward, spraying gravel, and Mr. Corduroy jumped back. He yelled, "I'll be seeing you, Ashley!"

Kristy and Corinne laughed the whole way to Torrance Park. Besides the mall and the mountains, there was nowhere else to go in Hilton, Colorado.

Four

We drove down Torrance Avenue through Hilton's dinky downtown: brick buildings, a scabby park, one little skyscraper. Past downtown, the avenue widened into a four-lane road lined with lumberyards, warehouses, junkyards, fastfood restaurants, a couple of gas stations. The park was at the end, right before the road turned into a highway. Torrance Park had a concrete-block recreation center that was never open and a tiny basketball court with bent hoops. Other than that, there was just a stretch of weedy, thorny grass and a huge parking lot hidden from the road by a line of dark pines.

Kristy pulled into the parking lot, checked to see who was there, then backed into a space on the east side, where West High kids hung out. She sat sideways in her seat and started drinking Mr. Corduroy's beer. She was so small, like a kid in a blond wig, but she could really put it away. She chugged a can and cupped a hand under her chin so the beer wouldn't run down her neck. Corinne curled in her seat, sipped beer, and watched the boys.

I sat in the backseat and played it all back in my head. How his voice had sounded when he said, "Thanks, sweetheart." I could still feel his hand against my mouth. Kristy twisted around and stared at me, then squawked with laughter and blew yellow streams of beer out her nose.

Some boys strolled up to Corinne's window. She lowered it and handed out cans of beer. "Dudes, we don't have that many! OK, one more." Corinne loved it when boys crowded around her like that. And the boys would gaze sweetly down at her—she was exactly what they had in mind for the night, just the ticket.

Then they'd look farther in and see Kristy and her hair, and they'd start to bristle and shove each other. And me? Their eyes would slide right over me and my thunder thighs all squashed in the backseat. That was fine. Nothing could touch me that night. I was in love with Damien Rogers, and a guy whose face belonged on a magazine cover had touched my cheek.

Kristy got out of the car and headed across the parking lot. Boys called to her and followed her like a swarm of bees. Some boy would say, "Hey, Kristy!" She'd turn around and yell, "What the hell do you want?" Then she'd stumble over, and he'd put his arm around her and hold his cigarette or whatever he was drinking to her mouth, and she'd take a puff or a sip, protected in the curve of his arm.

Corinne and I got out and sat on the hood of Kristy's car. We lit cigarettes, unzipped our jackets to show off our tops. I crossed my legs so my thighs would look smaller. Our hair, perfumed by shampoo, hung in silky curtains around our faces. We both wore Kristy's rose-petal lip gloss and smoky mauve eye shadow. The night boiled with possibilities.

West High kids on the east side of the parking lot, East High kids on the west side, and Arapahoe on the south. In the nucleus of the parking lot, rich kids, athletes, and the extremely good-looking from all three schools partied. They laughed the loudest. Ray Ramirez, quarterback of our football team, was there without LaTeisha. LaTeisha Morgan would never hang out in a parking lot. LaTeisha got invited to house parties, where she drank Sprite and left early enough so that she could get up for church. Corinne, Kristy, and I were in the middle, but without them, I would have been punted to the dark edges of the parking lot where the stoners partied.

I wasn't wasted like Kristy, just drunk enough for everything to fall away—the long dead hours in the apartment, homework, the insults and degradations of school. Nothing existed but the night, beautiful shadows, laughter, boys, songs thumping from car windows. Corinne and I sat on the hood of the Civic like beauty queens on a float. Corinne shouted to guys she knew. I kept watch for Damien Rogers. He was out there somewhere in the rippling crowd half lit by the smeary light from the streetlamps.

A Jeep pulled into the parking lot. Kelsey Parker whistled from the passenger window. "Corinne!"

Corinne grabbed my hand and made me walk over with her. The captain of the boys' swim team was in the driver's seat. He had a mean face and a bleached-out buzz cut. Both he and Kelsey were wasted. "Can I borrow ten bucks, Corinne? I lost my wallet, and Dean doesn't have enough money. We're starving."

"Sure," said Corinne. I stood behind her, breathed exhaust, and smiled stupidly. Kelsey and the swim team captain didn't look at me.

Corinne handed over the money. "Thanks, sweetheart," said Kelsey, already turning away. "OK, Dean. Let's get out of here." The Jeep backed up, then bumped over the curb into the street.

We walked back, weaving around groups of kids. Corinne and I had just sat down on the hood of Kristy's Civic again when a boy said, "Oh, man!" and jumped back. Kristy had thrown up a big chunky puddle on the ground and plopped down next to it. Corinne and I slid off the car.

A football player with a shaved head squatted down next to Kristy. He put his arm around her and said he'd forgive her if she came with him and his friends. She looked up at him through her hair and nodded. She was drooling.

Corinne pushed through the boys. "No way. She's coming with us."

We crouched next to Kristy. "Kristy. Kristy? Come on."

The football player stood up and stretched. "Dumb bitches," he said.

Kristy sat with her knees up by her face. She looked confused, like a toddler just woken up from a nap. I found a hamburger wrapper on the ground and wiped puke off her chin. Corinne grabbed up handfuls of her hair and wound it into a bun.

We each took an elbow and hoisted Kristy to her feet. She was wearing flip-flops, and her toes had puke on them. I stepped in the puddle and got vomit on my Vans. We steered her to her car and pushed her into the backseat.

Corinne tossed Kristy's cushion into the back, got into the driver's seat, and dug through Kristy's purse for her keys. Corinne could drive a stick shift, though she didn't have a license. "Damn it. She always does this."

As we left the parking lot, Corinne's head swung around. "Damien Rogers was in that truck."

"What? Where? Do a U-turn, Corinne. Go back!"

Kristy groaned and hiccuped in the backseat.

"We can't. She's going to barf again."

But Kristy didn't barf on the drive home. She just lay in

the backseat, looking sweaty and sick. Her hair came out of the bun and stuck to her face.

We drove down Torrance Avenue through downtown, up into the foothills, past the spotlights at the entrance to Mountain View Estates, and down the smooth black streets. Corinne pulled to a stop in front of Kristy's house.

"I'd have her sleep over, but Derrick would go ballistic." Corinne's stepfather, Derrick, shouted all the time because he had too many kids. He wouldn't let Corinne go out for softball. He had a grizzled double chin and wasn't nice to her mom.

We tugged Kristy out of the car and led her across the sheet of lawn turned white by the streetlight. Kristy shrieked, shook us off, got down on her knees, then flopped on the ground and rolled onto her back. She lay on the grass with her earrings tangled in her vomity hair. She twisted from side to side and screamed, "No! No! Leave me alone, bitches!"

The front door swung open. Kristy's dad came out in his boxer shorts. His legs were like Popsicle sticks covered with dark hair, but he had a monstrous pale stomach with a huge belly button like a Cyclops's eye. His face was creased and red, and his hair was crazy like he'd just pulled his head out of a washing machine.

He marched across the lawn, got down on one knee, and shoveled Kristy up in his arms. She cried and hammered on his chest with her fists. He held her still with one of his big hands. He kissed her forehead. "Shhh, shhh. It's OK, baby doll."

Mr. Baker turned to us. "Leah, you're spending the night, aren't you? Corinne, do you want to stay over? No? Are you sure? Can you make it home safely?" He was calm and unembarrassed as a king as he stood there in his underwear with Kristy moaning and twisting in his arms.

I followed them up the steps into the bright light. In the kitchen, Mrs. Baker stood with her hands folded under her chin like she was praying. Mr. Baker set Kristy on a chair in the circle of light from a purple glass lamp. Kristy curled up in a ball with her arms wrapped around her knees. She rubbed her eyes against her kneecaps and made mewling sounds like a sick cat. Her makeup was smeared all over her face.

Her mom wet a towel, toddled over, and dabbed at Kristy's eyes and cheeks. Her dad pulled a leaf out of her hair. He tucked a strand behind her ear.

"Now, Kristy," said Kristy's mom. Her upper lip quivered like she was about to sneeze. "We're not angry—we're just concerned."

"I'll just go back to Kristy's room," I said softly behind them.

"Brian, do you think . . . ?" said Mrs. Baker. She clutched the edge of the table and wobbled. They had forgotten that I was standing in the kitchen behind them.

I walked down the hallway to Kristy's dark room. I pulled

off my shoes and jacket and slipped between the clean sheets. My head sunk into the cool, squishy pillow. The pillows at my apartment were lumpy from washing and stained a dark yellow.

Kristy's dad carried her in and laid her on the other bed. Her mom unbuttoned her jeans, and her dad pulled them off by the bottoms. Her vomity feet with fuchsia toenails lay on the rose-covered comforter. They pulled the sheet and comforter over her, smoothed the blankets, then took turns laying their hands on her forehead. She groaned and whimpered and batted their hands away.

They tiptoed out and left the door open. A wedge of yellow light shone on the pink carpet. Her dad crept back in and left a silver bowl next to her bed. I'd read in a first-aid booklet what to do if she puked—turn her on her side so she wouldn't choke to death.

The hall light shone all night long. Hours later, the phone began to ring. In my dream, I was in a submarine and the phone was ringing on top of the water. I smelled Aquafresh, opened my eyes, and found a bulky body leaning over me.

I jerked up. Kristy's dad said, "Shhh. Leah, it's Mr. Baker. Connie and I are making a quick run to the emergency room. I just wanted you to know what was going on. We didn't want to wake Kristy. You stay here. I'll lock the door. You'll be fine. We should be back in a couple of hours."

When I woke up, the late sun was shining on the carpet.

Kristy was asleep, a pile of blond curls buried in roses. I opened her laptop and looked at pictures people had posted. The night before. Damien had been with a girl whose hair was the same color as mine. They didn't look serious. I shut down the computer, pulled on my shoes, found my jacket and purse under the bed, and tiptoed down the hallway.

There was no sign of an emergency, no blood, no bandages strewn on the orange carpet. Kristy's dad was crashed on the recliner, his chin rising and falling with his chest.

I crept up. His face was creased and pouchy and sad. I had a weird impulse to comb the thin brown hair strung across his spotted head. His forehead was lined like an accordion from worrying. He wore a big silver watch on his hairy wrist. His breathing and the watch's faint tick were the only sounds in the room.

"I'm going home, Mr. Baker. Thanks for having me," I whispered. He snored and turned his face away.

Five

I'd swiped a couple of cigarettes from Kristy's purse and lit up as I walked home in the bright April light. I had to walk in the street because there were no sidewalks in Mountain View Estates. The road was so black and clean, the curbs white, the grass thick and green. Every house had a two-car garage and a six-foot cedar fence.

It was cool but not cold. The mountain, blue-green with trees and craggy with red rocks, stuck into the sky. We moved to Colorado from Florida when I was ten, and I still wasn't used to it. Everyone else thought the mountain was magnificent, but to me it looked hulking and threatening, like it was going to keel over and crush me at any second. When we drove up to Denver, a blue wall of mountains lined the entire state.

A man in a silver helmet and spandex shorts shot past me on his bike. A woman in a purple jogging outfit eyed me from beneath her visor. Her Siberian husky freaked out and lunged at my leg—she yanked the dog away and glared at my cigarette. Families in SUVs drove to the late service at church.

I passed through the brick entrance gate, jogged across Pueblo Avenue, and headed down the hill to my neighborhood. Vargas Avenue was a mile and a half from Kristy's, right off Tenth. On my street, the little houses had drawn shades and tiny dirt yards surrounded by chain-link fences. My building had chunks of yellow stucco falling off the walls. Every second-story apartment had a miniature balcony where people stored empty beer cans and bags of cat litter. It was an embarrassing and depressing address to have. Davidson's Bail Bonds was two blocks down.

Our building was called the Belmont Manor. The front door slammed shut behind me. Except for the sizzle from the lights, it was silent, as if everyone in the building had died. I headed down the stairs to the basement. A gray path led down the middle of the orange hallway carpet. Nauseating odors swarmed through the stale air. The gold had worn off the door handles. Half of the door numbers hung crookedly by one nail.

I unlocked the door to #3. On the TV, a man in a suit shouted, "Praise! Praise! Praise Jesus!" The wedding wineglass and a saucer of pretzels were on the coffee table. The wineglass was the only wedding present left from Cindy's marriage to my dead father that hadn't been broken in one of our moves. The disgusting pink-and-blue blanket we never washed dragged off the couch onto the floor. I turned off the preacher and tried Cindy's doorknob.

My mother's arms were flung out as if she'd fallen from the top of a building and landed on the bed. Her small white face tipped back toward the maple headboard. She had purple dents under her eyes, and her hair was sweaty and flat. I crept over and held my hand over her mouth until I felt a puff of air. She smelled like Chardonnay, and a little sour like milk that had gone bad.

When Cindy was passed out, she reminded me of an old Barbie. A Barbie you find in the back of a closet or at the bottom of a box, a Barbie you haven't seen since you were four. Her head's twisted backward, her hair is a fuzzy mess and half of it's gone, and she's marked all over with ballpoint pen and permanent marker. Nothing is sadder than an old Barbie with her tiny hard feet and her faded eyebrows and blue eyes.

Home. I stripped down, changed into sweats, microwaved four pieces of French toast, put slabs of margarine between them, and poured half a bottle of Karo syrup over it all. I pulled down the flyers and coupons we kept stacked on top of the refrigerator, sat at the sticky wooden table jammed between the stove and refrigerator, and began to stuff my mouth and swallow as fast as I could without choking.

I put a fifth piece of French toast in the microwave, poured a big glass of milk, and looked through the coupons again—coupons for bathroom cleanser, tampons, frozen french fries, spaghetti sauce, peanut butter, a new kind of toilet cleanser that foamed. *Lose 30 pounds in one month without being hungry and get the body you DESERVE to have!!!!* I took another bite and started to feel sick. I chewed slowly and studied the expiration dates and the pictures of women with straight shiny hair and apple cheeks who joyfully held up sponges and scrub brushes. The moms.

My phone vibrated. Kurt King's number lit up the little screen. I set the phone back on the table and looked at it. The phone went silent and dark, then vibrated again. I opened it. "Hello?"

"Is this Ashley?"

Sometimes I had the feeling that I did exist, that I had a life and would have a life in the years to come. I'd lose weight and become a doctor. Everything would unfold for me. But lots of times, there was nothing inside me but huge billowing emptiness, or sadness, or clouds. Like an atom: 99.99 percent emptiness. When you're nothing, you can be anything you want to be. I closed my eyes.

"Yeah."

He said in a slow voice, "What's going on, Ashley?"

I got up from the table and left the last bite of French toast floating in a puddle of syrup. I lay down on the couch. "I'm really tired. I was out late. . . ."

I talked softly through my nose in my Kristy voice. It was easy. It was like floating above the world.

Six

Monday morning, I smoked and waited for Kristy to pick me up. The sky was a smoggy blue. Old cigarette butts were mashed between the little sticks of grass. The night before, I'd had a dream that I was lying on my back in tall thick grass next to Damien Rogers. It was dark, and I couldn't see him through the grass but I knew it was him. He was pointing out the constellations.

That morning I felt like a girl in a movie, as if cameras were pointing at me. My first real phone conversation with a guy, Kurt King, had lasted fifteen minutes. He said, "I'm gonna call you again tomorrow, little girl." I wore a new pair of jeans with iridescent stitching on the back pockets that made me look skinnier, and the gold hoop earrings that

Cindy let me have, though I wasn't supposed to wear them to school.

A plant with fuzzy leaves was growing by the curb. The sunlight flashed, birds chirped, little baby leaves unfolded on the tree branches. A block away, my bus pulled to a stop and flashed its lights. Three kids climbed on, and the bus roared off. Fifteen minutes passed. Since Kristy had gotten her car, she'd driven me and Corinne to school every day. She'd never been late before.

Maybe her mom had died. The gigantic nature of this possibility made my head feel like it was full of helium. I texted and texted, but she didn't text back. Kristy was never late. At seven thirty, when the last bell rang, I started walking.

I walked down Vargas Avenue, and the sidewalks glistened with little bits of mica. Lit in the orange sunlight, my neighborhood looked like a stage set. I barged in front of a woman loading Amway boxes into her car trunk. She stepped back with her boxes and glared at me. I glared back; she had no idea what was going on in my life.

Mrs. Baker was dying and maybe actually dead. Her heart might have stopped. They might have taken her off a respirator. My throat throbbed. I forced the thought of Mrs. Baker out of my mind and considered instead my complicated love life—I was still pretty much in love with Damien Rogers, but the memory of Kurt King's scratchy voice made me woozy. He was calling later. The windows of the

7-Eleven, the Safeway, the check-cashing place, the car wash, and EZPAWN all shone like gold in the morning sun.

On the corner of Santa Fe Street and Tenth Avenue, a lilac bush covered with cones of tiny purple flowers hung over the sidewalk. The air reeked of lilacs. Every spring, Kelsey Parker and her friends walked to school with armfuls of lilacs like they were beauty queens in a pageant. I had never walked to school with an armful of lilacs before. I reached into the bush and twisted off a branch. I walked the rest of the way with my mouth buried in cool, purple flowers.

Seven

I left the flowers on the steps as a memorial to Mrs. Baker. Above the doors stretched a new red-and-white Coke banner with WEST HIGH SCHOOL in small white letters. I climbed the rest of the steps and entered the building at ten after eight. Duct tape covered a new sunburst of cracks in the front window.

I said good morning to the cop who stood by the door all day with a Taser, club, and gun strapped under his belly. He was heavily armed but a sweet old guy who'd never squash a fly. The back of his spotted, bald head flattened into his neck; the kids called him the Iguana. "Good morning, Sergeant Motts."

"Morning, Leah," he said in a low croaky voice; he'd smoked way too many cigarettes. I walked into the office and waited for the office lady to look up.

"I need a pass, please. My ride didn't show." I was calm and sad. Soon my role in the tragedy would be revealed.

"Can a parent or guardian vouch for that?" The office lady drew her eyebrows on with an orange pencil. She wore silver and turquoise bracelets on her skinny freckled arms.

"My mom's at work. I can only call if it's an emergency." I tried to be patient with this old lady; she didn't realize that I was part of something bigger than her little day.

She rolled her chair to the computer. "Who was supposed to be your ride?"

"Kristy Baker." I tried to assume an appropriate solemn expression. The only dead people I'd known were my aunt Peg, whom I'd met once, and my dad, but I was two years old when he died.

She scrolled down the screen. "Kristy Baker is not absent today. You, not Kristy Baker, are responsible for getting yourself to school on time." She scribbled on a pad. "Here's your pass. Automatic detention after school."

I got to my locker just as the bell rang. Kids burst out the doors and flooded the hallway. Kristy, Corinne, and a girl named Victoria pushed through the crowd without looking at me. Kristy's arm was hooked through Victoria's. Two days before, Kristy had said that Victoria Miller was an incredibly stupid, diseased skank.

Corinne hung on to Kristy's shoulder with one hand. When they were farther down the hall, Corinne looked back and mouthed, "Call me."

In chemistry, second period, Victoria sat in my seat next to Kristy. Mrs. McCleary called me to the front. She blinked slowly like a cow and explained that she'd decided to switch a few lab partners around. I would be working with Carl Lancaster.

I walked to my new seat with humiliating flames on my cheeks. Some guy said, "Porker," as I passed him. Lard-Ass, Porker, Cow, Fat Pig. It usually sounded like the chirping of crickets, but that morning it felt like a sharp blade aimed and thrown hard.

"Hello, Leah," Carl Lancaster whispered. "I'm glad we get to work together." Mrs. McCleary was fiddling with the laptop and overhead projector, trying to get them to work.

"Whatever."

Carl had what Cindy called excellent bone structure. His cheekbones were covered with a mash of light-brown freckles and a little acne. He had thick, brushy hair the color of an old penny. His breath smelled like tangerines.

He glanced at Mrs. McCleary. She bent over, checking plugs and swearing under her breath. He said, "Our sink doesn't work, but Andrew and Kevin said that we were welcome to use their sink when we need to." The laminated LAB SAFETY poster behind him had holes in it from being splattered with acid. Carl leaned over to get a pen out of his backpack and poked me in the boob with his elbow. He closed his eyes and said in his low voice, "Oh God. Pardon me."

We were starting a new section in chemistry: Acids, Bases, and Solutions. Mrs. McCleary dimmed the lights and turned on the overhead. "OK, heads up, key vocab for this section: *Solution. Solute. Solvent. Solubility. Insoluble.* Can anyone give me a clear working definition of the term *solution?*"

Carl glanced around the room, waited ten seconds, then raised his hand.

"Carl!"

"A solution is a homogeneous mixture of . . ." Carl leaned forward and answered Mrs. McCleary in his deep man voice. He was famous around the school. In December, he'd played classical music on the school piano at an assembly for a South Korean official. No one had forgotten or forgiven him, and people still tripped him in the hallways. At least once a day, a little paper football ricocheted off his back or neck.

Just then a paper football flew across the room and hit him in the shoulder. He didn't flinch.

"Carl, can you tell us the definition of *solute?*"

"Yeah. A solute is the substance that gets dissolved. . . ."

I looked back. Kristy and Victoria Miller slouched on their stools and stared at me.

Eight

My favorite teacher—everyone's favorite teacher, Mr. Calvino, language arts—was even more depressed than usual. He was young and would have been good-looking except for the black pits from insomnia under his eyes. He was addicted to Diet Coke. Though he never said it out loud, I suspected he cursed himself for having left New Jersey.

For the first few minutes of class, he sat on the edge of his desk and stared out the window at the mountain. Suddenly, he clapped and scared the crap out of us. "So, kids! What standards do you think we should meet today? Any competencies you feel like working on?"

LaTeisha Morgan laughed from her front-row seat. "Mr. Calvino, you're a trip."

He shook the Diet Coke cans on his desk until he found one that swished. He tipped back his head and poured the brown liquid straight down his throat.

Mr. Calvino wiped soda off his chin. "OK," he said. "Let's get started. First, did anyone do the extra-credit assignment? Just one page, imagining your life in ten years, your educational and career paths, relationships, travels, technological changes, shifts in society? It was worth ten points! Anyone? LaTeisha? Wonderful! Leah?" I shook my head.

LaTeisha and I were Mr. Calvino's best students. We were the only ones who paid attention. LaTeisha should have been in AP. She was even bigger than me, but she didn't seem to know it. She moved around like a queen. She had straightened hair with bangs, dark eyes and skin that glowed with vitamins and happiness, and a huge, fantastic smile. She wore shiny red lip gloss. Her dad was a minister, and she was Ray Ramirez's longtime girlfriend. They got dressed up and went to church together.

Mr. Calvino liked LaTeisha for obvious reasons, and for some reason, he liked me. He would look for me in the crowd of faces. He'd smile when he handed back my papers. He'd gaze at me in the middle of class, shake his head, and say, "Leah, you belong in AP." Me and LaTeisha. LaTeisha was moving up the next year, but Cindy wouldn't let me. She said, "Don't fly too high. You'll crash. It's better to get good grades in normal classes." I was also the only kid in the school without a smartphone or Internet—Cindy wouldn't pay for them, and Cindy wouldn't let me get a job until I turned sixteen. Cindy was deranged.

On the way out of the room, I stopped at Mr. Calvino's bookshelf, his famous lending library. He'd been called in front of the school board twice by Christian parent groups because he lent out books about being gay. He lent out all kinds of books, not just fiction, because he said literature was about the world and being alive. I'd borrowed a couple books from him about becoming a doctor.

There were new books on the top shelf, but the titles blurred. "Go on, Leah. Take something," he said behind me.

"Nah." I didn't look back and walked out of the room.

I hadn't been feeling very well. I couldn't concentrate. I forced myself through my homework but, other than that, only felt like reading magazines and little-kid books. Simple things you could read in a kind of daze and not have to think or feel. How to lose ten pounds in four days on a raw-food diet. The hairstyle that is best for your face shape. What kind of personality do you have? *Little House on the Prairie*. Ma and Pa and poor blind Mary and Laura and Carrie, and *Farmer Boy* and all the cakes and pies and fried chicken Almanzo ate. I was apparently regressing. Not AP material, after all.

After third period, it was time for lunch.

I stood by the pop machine at the edge of the cafeteria. The windowless room was lit by long, thin rectangles of fluorescent lights. It was a sea of chewing, talking faces. There were a couple of tables of black kids, a third of the tables were Mexican kids, and the rest were white. With a few exceptions, each group sat together. At each table, everyone wore the same shoes, jeans, jackets, had the same hair and the same expressions on their faces. Everybody laughed on cue, especially if someone was being made fun of. The tables were like petri dishes of almost-indistinguishable bacteria.

The saddest thing about the cafeteria was that you pretty much knew where someone would be in five years just by their lunch table: jail, working at Walmart or the auto-parts store, community college, their parents' basement, state college, residential treatment for the fourth time, alone with two babies in a dirty apartment, private college, potentially Ivy League. The potentially Ivy League kids never ate school lunches. They brought homemade granola and Italian ham on focaccia in reusable lunch bags.

Victoria sat in my place at our table. A state-college table. Kristy and Victoria smushed their heads together and took pictures with Kristy's phone. I felt disoriented, like a planet that had been rudely kicked out of its solar system. I had a very brief fantasy of calling Cindy and saying, "I feel sick. Can you pick me up, Mom?"

LaTeisha Morgan would have let me sit at her table, where all the black girls sat, but it would have been too pathetic to ask. Especially since all the seats were taken. The girls laughed, stuffed their mouths with french fries, and played with their phones. LaTeisha smiled like a tolerant camp counselor, probably daydreaming about getting into Stanford. Ray Ramirez stopped by with his tray and kissed her cheek. The other girls squealed and beamed up at him. Ray looked like a tall Bruno Mars. His clothes were always ironed, his shirt tucked in. His dad was on city council and running for mayor. His big brother went to Boston College.

Kelsey Parker and her best friends—Kaylee, Brianna, Maya, and Alexis—arrived at the double doors. The five girls dressed identically in suede boots, black leggings, and black fleece jackets. Each had a blanket of long highlighted hair she'd curled that morning. They kicked two nerdy girls off a table and sat down with their phones, all of which had matching striped purple cases. Expensive private college.

I became self-conscious just standing there all alone, so I got in line. The pushing and shoving, the roaring voices, the smells of deodorant, acne cream, BO, aftershave, conditioner, and the heat from all the bodies almost made me throw up. The cafeteria lady snapped at me because I didn't hear when she asked if I wanted nachos or pizza. I was distracted by the black hairs growing above her upper lip—they also made me want to throw up. I bought nachos with extra cheese sauce and two chocolate milks and carried my tray to the end of a nearly empty nerd table.

Down from me, the tall, skinny guy known as Stork and his only friend, a boy with bright-red cheeks and a big stomach, hunched over their trays. Jamie Lopez sat down by himself at the end. Jamie had dark-blue eyes and caramel skin, and was by far the best-looking guy in our grade. He had shaggy, dyed-black emo hair and wore thick eyeliner. He'd been lifting weights and kept his arms curled like a boxer's. He was the only kid in our school who admitted that he was gay, and he'd been jumped six times.

I stared down at the greasy chips soaked in shiny yellow goo. It had started as a good day. I'd had a dream about Damien Rogers. The night before, I'd talked for fifteen minutes on the phone with a guy. On Saturday, Cindy had taken me to Marshalls and bought me three tops and a pair of jeans.

That morning as I pulled on my new top, I'd felt hopeful, as if good things were possible because of my new shirt. The week before, Kristy had worn the same shirt in a different color, but it didn't work on her—she was too skinny. The lacy neckline looked good on me, and the deep-blue color made me look thinner. I breathed in the brand-new chemical smell. Thrift store clothes smelled different—weird, like other people's gross laundry.

I was choking on a chip and coughing when Stork got up and stood next to me. Stork had freakishly long skinny legs. My eyes were level with a black belt pulled tightly through the belt loops of rumpled brown corduroys. He held out an unopened container of juice. His thumbnail was chewed halfway down.

"Do you want this?" he said. "I'm not going to drink it, if you want it."

Usually, I would have looked up and smiled. I'd have said, "No, thanks." Or I would have taken it just to be nice. But instead, I finished coughing and stared across the table. "No, Stork. Get away from me."

The person next to me vanished. And after a moment of shock, the shock of being a total jerk, I felt even worse, like I was full of broken ribs that were cutting into my heart. I forced myself to look over — Stork and his friend were carrying their trays to another table. Jamie Lopez considered me, picked up his tray, and headed for the garbage cans. There was a long stretch of shredded lettuce, wrappers, and milk puddles. I was sitting alone at an empty table in the middle of fourth-period lunch. Kelsey Parker and her friends were two tables over.

I began sweating on my forehead and in my armpits, and got chills up and down my back. My vision got fuzzy. I thought I'd lose consciousness when something black moved into my field of vision.

A girl wearing a black leather jacket stood holding her tray. We'd ridden the same bus before Kristy started driving.

The girl said, "OK if my friends and I sit with you?" She was followed by two thin girls dressed in black.

"I don't care."

The three girls sat down. I started to breathe again; my skin dried up; the buzzing went away. The cafeteria slowly came back into focus. The girl across from me had long hair dyed black, bangs that were cut in an angle across her eyes. She'd lined her eyes in black and wore three shades of purple shadow. She had a sharp, tan face. She looked at me and didn't smile, but not in an unfriendly way. We didn't have any classes togther but I knew her name was Anita Sotelo.

She shoved her tray into the middle of the table, opened a sketch pad, and hunched over it. As she drew, she held her bangs away from her face. The bell rang and I stood up with my tray. "You didn't even touch your lunch."

She looked up at me with calm brown eyes. "It's slop. Anyway, I'm vegan. If you want it, help yourself. I practically get it for free."

I walked away without answering. She was the only person I'd ever heard admit that they got a reduced-price lunch.

Nine

My last period was study hall in the library. I sat at a table and opened my chemistry text to the chapter "Acids, Bases, and Solutions." We were having our first quiz on Thursday. I couldn't concentrate. The words, formulas, and equations dissolved into black squiggles.

Across the room, Carl Lancaster sat alone at the end of a table. He leaned over his books and took notes in a notebook. Carl always wore cotton shirts that buttoned down the front, open at the throat, with button-down collars, very preppy. He had a pretty nice throat for a geek. Muscular, like a wrestler's throat.

I watched him for a long time. I picked up my books, walked over, and stood there.

Finally he looked up, startled, then not startled. He waited.

"Carl, can you explain the difference between molarity and molality? I'm sorry, but my brain's not working. . . ."

"Have a seat. It's really simple, Leah."

I sat down across from him.

After study hall, I had detention. Mr. Balke, the teacher on duty, ignored us and graded math tests. He scratched his scalp through his thin, frizzy hair as he stared with disgust at a test. He shoved his aviator glasses up with his thumb and madly marked the paper with a red pen. He wore a baggy gray sweater so big that the shoulders hung down to his elbows.

When I got tired of observing Mr. Balke, I doodled in my notebook. I wrote *Kristy is a bitch* fifty-eight times. I wrote *D and L* in different styles of handwriting. Very, very small, I wrote the name *Kurt King*. It sounded like the name of an actor.

Mr. Balke suddenly thundered, "Go home, future leaders of America!" Everyone jerked up from the desktops where they'd been sleeping or playing with their phones. Dan Manke yawned, lifted his leg, and farted.

Mr. Balke raised his eyebrows and smiled as if we'd lived up to his expectations. He put his hands behind his head and his feet up on the desk. He was wearing cheesy red-striped athletic shoes. As we filed out, he said good-bye to each of us by name. "Good afternoon, Mr. Manke. Good afternoon, Miss Lobermeir. . . ."

Stork, Carl Lancaster, and a few other boys were standing outside the biology room. Science Club had just let out. Stork was talking excitedly, but Carl Lancaster wasn't listening. He watched me walk down the hall.

I left the building at the same time as Dan Manke. Dan Manke had a flat freckled face and wore a cowboy hat and boots every day. He lived in Mountain View Estates and had never ridden a horse, as far as I knew.

As we left the building, Dan Manke shoved a pinch of dip under his lower lip. "See you later, Fat-Ass." The steel door slammed shut on my shoulder.

On the other side of a chain-link fence, the softball team, which consisted of Kelsey Parker and her friends, ran around the playing field in shorts, whistled, shouted, laughed, called to one another. It sounded like everyone in the whole world was on a team that I hadn't been picked for. Corinne was better at softball than any of them. A hideous shriek of laughter seemed directed at me, the fat girl walking alone in the weedy ditch that ran alongside the road. The road ran straight toward the mountain.

I took a detour toward 7-Eleven, hoping in a terrified way that Kurt King would be there — my new jeans and blue shirt had gone completely to waste so far that day — but no one was there except for some junior-high boys. The boys oinked when I pushed out the glass door with a jumbo bag of hot fries, and two bottles of Brisk. I also had gummy worms and a king-size Kit Kat bar that I'd swiped and stuffed into my backpack.

As I unlocked the door to #3, my phone vibrated. It was Kurt King's number. He said that he would call, and he called. It was like having a boyfriend. I shut the door, walked to the couch, and sat down. I put the drinks and snacks on the coffee table. I looked at the little glowing screen and held the phone to my ear.

"Ashley," he said. "How you doing, Ashley?"

"All right. I had kind of a bad day."

"Man, I'm sorry to hear that. A girl like you should never have a bad day. . . ."

"My mom's really sick," I said. "She might be dying."

He was talking to Ashley, and he was talking to me. Ashley and I became the same girl. I laughed at his jokes, and when he said again that a girl like me should never have bad days, something warmed up inside me for the first time since that morning, and I believed him.

I closed my eyes, and when I opened them, we'd talked for an hour. Our long phone calls were so old-school.

"Where'd you say you lived at?" he said.

Ten

After I hung up with Kurt King, I started eating and couldn't stop.

An hour later, I was curled under the blanket in front of a talk show. The pop, hot fries, gummy worms, and Kit Kat were gone. I felt sleepy and sick.

Cindy walked through the door, turned on all the lights, and set her purse on the kitchen table. Her pink polyester uniform was wilted. She yawned and glanced tiredly around the kitchenette. Even though she had dark lines crisscrossing her face and usually looked cranky, I thought she was beautiful, though I'd never tell her that. I called her Cindy instead of Mom because she was such a failure as a mother type, though she did wash my clothes every Sunday in the cobwebby laundry room.

She was skinny because she didn't eat. She lived on salads, pretzels, and white wine. She had small hands with pink fingers that were always damp from washing. She was obsessed with her nails. She worked as a receptionist for a discount dentist. Her dream was to become a hygienist because they made tons of money. The dentist required that all his employees let him bleach their teeth. It looked like Cindy had a piece of paper stuck inside her mouth.

Cindy took a deep breath and turned to me; I watched her force herself to do it. "Hi, Leah." She closed her eyes and put her hand on her forehead as if she was taking her own temperature. "Will you get yourself some dinner? I bought groceries yesterday."

"I'm not hungry."

She opened the cupboard doors and moved things around. She pulled out her "hope jar" and shook it. It was a mayonnaise jar she'd washed and decorated with sunburst stickers. It was about a third filled with coins, wadded-up dollar bills, and little strips of paper—every good fortune she'd ever gotten out of a cookie. Her boss, Dr. Dingle, had learned how to give Botox injections, and she was saving up. "Have you been in my jar? It's looking kind of skimpy."

"No."

Cindy crossed her arms and walked over to catch the last five minutes of the talk show. When the commercial came on, she turned to me. "Honey, you've got to eat something. . . ."

Then she saw the empty bag and wrappers, the bottles, and the big plastic cup of melting ice.

"Are you eating this crap again? I told you, no junk food on weekdays! God Almighty, Leah, you're going to get diabetes. That's the last thing we need." She picked up one of the plastic bottles and shook it at me. "Do you know what this stuff does to your teeth? I'm fed up with you! You're going to end up as big as a whale."

I covered my head with the velour pillow and breathed my own hot oxygen-depleted air. Cindy had bought the pillow at a garage sale and it smelled like cat pee.

"Please leave me alone. I beg you. I had kind of a horrible day," I said from beneath the pee pillow.

"Leah, do you think I want to spend my life"—a really loud commercial came on—"worn out from this constant battle? I give up! I'm turning it over to you. It's in your hands. I can't save you from yourself. . . . Damn it, Leah! You used half my ice!"

I pulled the pillow off my head, got off the couch, and walked down the short hallway to my room. I shut the door and threw myself down on the dirty sheets and ratty blankets.

I woke up in fuzzy darkness. My phone said it was nine thirty. My mouth was dry, sticky, and sour. Bacteria foamed on my teeth. I pulled off my jeans, crawled back into bed, and called Corinne.

She answered right away. "I thought you'd call earlier."

"I fell asleep. What is Kristy's problem? I had to walk to school and got detention."

"Sorry, Leah. After she picked me up, she drove straight to school. I go, 'Kristy, what about Leah? Is she sick?' She says, 'She's sick, all right.' Then I was kind of confused, but after second period, Kristy told me. Saturday night, when you stayed over, her dad told you that her mom had to go to the hospital. She just got out today. Kristy was pissed that you didn't wait and ask if her mom was OK. You just left."

I felt sick; I had just left. "I texted her twenty times Sunday. She never texted back. I didn't know how bad it was when I left. Kristy was asleep. Her dad was asleep. He said they were just making a quick trip to the emergency room. What's wrong with her mom?"

Corinne said, "She had to have blood transfusions or something—I don't know. I feel really bad, Leah, but I can't abandon Kristy. I need to be there for her because of her mom. She tweeted something kind of mean about you, but I'll get her to delete it."

Corinne hung up. I got out of bed and opened my door a crack. Cindy was asleep on the couch with her wineglass clutched under her chin. I pulled on my jeans and my shoes, then crept out of my room and tiptoed around her, turning off the TV and slowly detaching the glass from her hand. I covered her with the pink-and-blue blanket. She looked like she was getting a cold—her nostrils were flaky and red.

I locked the apartment door behind me and jogged down the hall and up the stairs. I pushed through the glass entryway door and was free in the cool black night. I'd gotten in the habit of walking in the dark after Cindy passed out.

Eleven

When I walked in the night, I felt like I was flying. I walked so fast, it was like being a bird gliding over clouds or a fish cutting through dark water. I dodged car lights because if it was the cops, they'd bust me for breaking curfew. If I heard footsteps or saw someone coming toward me, I hid behind a tree or bush in case it was a rapist. I was a kid again. I was playing hide-and-seek with the whole world.

Vargas Avenue was silent, its ugliness transformed into shadows, silvery light, the silhouettes of mysterious people behind yellow-lit shades. The streetlights looked like burning matches sticking out of the sidewalks.

Corinne lived six blocks over from Kristy. Every light in her split-level house was blazing. Corinne's stepdad sat at the kitchen table drinking beer; her mom was on the laptop.

The buzz-cut heads of Corinne's brothers bobbed through. Derrick, the stepdad, stood up and opened the refrigerator.

The light was off in Corinne's room, but there was a shifting blue glow. "I hope you're feeling bad," I whispered. "I hope you're feeling some guilt."

Farther down Rocky Mountain Lane, the houses got bigger and had skylights and huge windows facing the mountain. Every house had a trampoline and a tree house with a rainbow roof in the fenced backyard. The houses were lit up like department stores and were stuffed with matching furniture, potted plants, throw pillows, silver refrigerators, vases of dried vines. The women in the department-store houses all had weird geometrical haircuts and the men wore bike shorts. The people lay sacked out in front of their giant TVs. They were wiped out from working at the office park or their two-hour commute back from Denver.

Kristy's Civic and her dad's Suburban were parked side by side on the swept black driveway. The grass was cut and edged. The windows were lit from inside by a soft glow as if from firelight.

I sat on the grass next to a piney shrub, lit a cigarette, and stared at Kristy Baker's perfect house.

Twelve

All week, Kristy and Corinne blew me off. I sat in study hall with Carl Lancaster. We silently read about acids and bases and practiced molar conversions, then I'd hand him my notebook and he'd check my answers, and I'd check his. We quizzed each other. I got a B+ on the test. Outside of study hall and chemistry, we didn't talk.

Kurt King called every day, sometimes twice. Usually I answered, but sometimes I was too tired to be Ashley and just listened to his messages. I was like a fish that had been hooked; I felt a constant tug to check my phone, to listen to his voice again and again. When we talked, it was always the same. He'd say, "When can I see you?"

I'd say, "It's complicated. I have a boyfriend."

"Forget your boyfriend."

"But I kind of love him. . . ."

I'd always wondered what it would be like to have a boyfriend. Kurt King felt like my boyfriend. It was complicated. . . .

It was like trying on clothes that you love but can't afford, clothes that are totally inappropriate. I did that once with Corinne. When we were fourteen, her mom took us shopping in Denver. Corinne and I rode the escalator to the second floor of Macy's and tried on silvery two-hundred-dollar shirts. We made faces at ourselves and laughed like donkeys, though we were both half-serious about how beautiful we looked. The saleswoman stood outside the dressing room and rapped on the door. "How can I help you, girls?"

Kurt King wanted Ashley. "Girl, you are so beautiful," he said. "I think I'm fallin' in love. . . ." But he was talking to me.

I was the girl on the phone, and the girl trying to pull on too-tight size-fourteen jeans, and the beautiful girl in my head, and the girl who got a B+ on her test and was going to be a doctor, and the girl staring at a cracked puke-green ceiling as the refrigerator door opened and wine gushed out of the spigot into the wedding wineglass. Like a girl in a funhouse full of mirrors, but all the faces looking back were different.

In the school hallways, Kristy walked past me as if I didn't exist. She and Victoria were always shrieking over something.

Corinne went along with big sad eyes. Groups of boys, if they were bored, called me Mack Truck, Beached Whale, and the old standby, Fat-Ass. I floated away from it all and thought about what Kurt King had said to me the night before. He said, "I think about you all day, every day."

At lunch, I sat with the girl in the leather jacket again. Anita Sotelo.

Anita's eyes were tea-colored with stars of darker brown. Her left eye would squint and her mouth would open a little when she was confronted with stupidity. She had the calmness of an adult. She was skinny and always wore a black jacket and tight black jeans with black Keds knock-offs. She constantly combed her bangs back with her fingers. Sometimes she wore scarves wrapped around her head. She had Screamo band stickers all over her notebooks.

Anita was into manga and anime, and once, freshman year, she came to school dressed as a Japanese schoolgirl. Her friends Iris and Maria seemed to find that perfectly normal. Though there was something incredibly normal about Anita, in spite of her weird habits and appearance.

Iris and Maria both wore eyeliner and string bracelets on their tiny wrists. Iris had blond roots and a face like a cat's. Maria had sharp canines, looked like a Mexican Katy Perry, and sometimes came to school with a furry tail pinned to the back of her jeans. Maria and Iris finished each other's sentences and became silent and rigid if anyone popular came within two feet of them. They were obsessed with the TV show *My Little Pony*.

If I thought about it, I could not believe that I was sitting at this table. I had joined the nerd herd.

Anita picked a carrot off my tray, chewed it, and stared at me. "Why did you even hang around that chick Kristy Baker?"

I took a bite of the mushy chicken-particle sandwich and pretended to give her question some thought. "We've been hanging out since seventh grade. . . . We're old friends, I guess. I really love her mom and dad. They are both super sweet. Her mom has breast cancer."

I couldn't explain to Anita that hanging around Kristy was an addiction, sort of like smoking. Kristy had a normal teenage life. Her room was interior-decorated. She had a mom and a dad who adored her. She was skinny, and boys loved her and her long blond hair. It wasn't my life, but I could be near it. I could be inside the circle, even if I was on the very outside.

Anita raised her eyebrows. "Sad about her mom." She drew a person with spiky black hair on the back cover of her notebook. She tipped back her head and stuck the pencil between her teeth—the pencil was deeply indented with chew marks.

"Kristy Baker is still an incredible bitch," she said cheerfully, then set back to work on her drawing. "She's horrible! You're friends with the meanest girl I've ever met, and we've moved nine times and I've met thousands of people. . . ."

Iris and Maria cackled about a message Iris had gotten on her phone. Probably something to do with hair dye or anime or *My Little Pony* fan fiction. It made me sad how they hunched over their lunches, squinting over their shoulders like they were about to be attacked.

Anita looked at Iris's message, smiled, and returned to her drawing.

"I'm going to either be a screenwriter, an actor, or an anime illustrator," she said out of nowhere. She didn't even look up to see if I was listening. "What about you?"

"I want to be a doctor." It came out in a whisper.

"A what?"

"A doctor."

"What kind?" She kept drawing.

"Possibly an obstetrician or maybe an oncologist, but that would be really sad. I have no idea, actually. I haven't . . ."

"Have you wanted to be a doctor for a long time?"

"Yeah, I always wanted to, but like six months ago, I decided to actually try and do it. I have to get a good grade in chemistry if I want to go to med school. . . ."

Anita lifted her face and stared at me. She grabbed my wrist. "That is so cool. That is so, so cool. You got to do it."

Anita was the first person I'd ever told that I wanted to

be a doctor. She acted as if it was possible, real, like the most obvious thing I could do. I felt happy, like bells were ringing inside of me. "When I was in middle school, I always read this book called *Human Diseases and Conditions* during study hall. I used to watch this doctor show with my mom. We watched every episode twice. And since I was eleven, I've gotten my checkups from this woman doctor, and she's really nice and smart, and she always tells me I remind her of herself when she was my age. I read some books about being a doctor I borrowed from Mr. Calvino, and I just knew that's what I wanted to do. But I've got to get a good grade in chemistry."

Anita shrugged, dipped her head. "Yeah? So? You got to just do it. Get Carl Lancaster to help you. He's really good at chemistry."

Anita acted like this was all very workable and doable, and if I just put the time in, it would definitely happen. I would be a doctor.

"You think I could actually do it?"

"Duh. Obviously, yes! You are super smart."

"What? No, I'm not," I said. "By the way, my nickname for Kristy is Yertle. Like Yertle the Turtle? In Dr. Seuss? Yertle is the king turtle, and he sits on a throne of other turtles stacked on top of each other. . . ."

"Yeah, I'm familiar with the story." Anita shoved her hair behind her ear and studied her picture.

"If I'm really pissed, I call her scrawny bitch."

The eyebrows again. "That one's lame, but Yertle's not bad," she said. "You've got to have a plan, girl. You're gonna be a doc."

Kristy, Victoria, and Corinne sashayed by with their arms intertwined. They looked over at us like we were the display of jarred pig fetuses in the biology room. They put their heads together and almost choked on their amusement.

"Hey," said Anita. "Just ignore them. Ignore them, Leah."

I tried to ignore them, but the happy ringing inside me faded away.

Thirteen

The next day after study hall, Carl and I walked out of the library together by accident. We stood at the door for a second. He swallowed and started to say something. Before he could, I took off for my locker.

On the bus, Anita said, "I could hang out today."

I said, "Oh." Then a minute or two later, "Do you want to come over?" Corinne had been in my apartment a couple of times, but I had never allowed Kristy inside the building.

When we got to my building, Anita walked without any observable disgust through the entryway, down the stairs, and along the hideous orange carpet through all the weird smells. She came into #3 and didn't stare at the worn-out green carpet, the lumpy couch, Cindy's teacup collection, the ten-year-old TV, or the battered old Yahtzee box under the coffee table. She didn't ask to open the gray accordion curtains that covered the basement window above the couch.

I suddenly realized that the shiny beige paint was the color they used in lunatic-asylums and all the little bumps in the paint looked like zits. But Anita stood there like she was in a normal house, and not an apartment that was like a couple of boxes taped together.

"Do you want something to eat?"

"Sure," she said. "Got anything vegan?"

We went into the kitchenette. I pulled open the pink cupboard doors, which I suddenly realized were brown and sticky around the handles, and pushed around some boxes and cans, the blue cylinder of salt I'd labeled *NaCl* in first semester chemistry, and a bag of potato chip crumbs.

"What's that?" said Anita. She reached for the decorated mayonnaise jar full of change and tiny fortunes.

"My mom's hope jar. Don't ask."

I had to get her to step out so I could open the refrigerator. There was some milk, lettuce going black around the edges, and a dried-up pork chop on a plate. I checked the freezer — there was a half a can of orange juice concentrate sprinkled with crumbs. "I forgot — we're going shopping tonight. I thought we had waffles. Do you want a bowl of cereal? I could make some Kool-Aid."

"I'm fine." She turned off the light.

I bumped into her as we stepped around the kitchen table

into the living room. Anita did a twirl by the couch, and all the fringy things on her jacket swirled around her.

I said, "I don't want to be mean and that leather jacket is cool, but do you think you should wear the same thing every day? People say stuff."

She said, "Whatever, Leah. You don't think the lemmings like it? This jacket is vintage seventies. It's leather, but it was my mom's, so I can't throw it out."

She came to the door of my tiny room and acted as if a cardboard bookshelf and boxes of clothes were just what you'd expect to find in a teenage girl's bedroom.

"It's kind of a dungeon." I opened the blue polka-dot curtains so we'd have some light, saw the spiderwebs, garbage, and black bars, and closed them again.

She sat on the end of my bed—which was, in fact, just a squishy mattress on a metal frame—and looked at the two newspaper photos of Damien Rogers playing basketball that I'd taped to the wall. After a minute, she said, "He looks very athletic."

"Oh, yeah. That's Damien Rogers. He goes to Arapahoe. He's kind of a friend—more like an acquaintance, I guess—but he's a super-nice guy and I thought those were really good pictures."

"Ah." Anita lifted my laptop off the floor. "Can I check my e-mail?"

"Uh . . . I don't have Internet. It's just for writing papers."

I had the laptop and an iPod that Cindy bought at the EZPAWN for my fifteenth birthday, but no Internet. It was like an online party I wasn't invited to. In the library or whenever I could borrow Kristy's or Corinne's phone, I checked to see what Damien Rogers's had posted. He constantly shared stats from his games and was tagged in pictures from parties. He always had a different girl under his arm. He wasn't serious about any of them.

"Me neither. It sucks," Anita said.

"Yeah." I sat at the top of my bed on the pillow. "But you kind of get used to it."

"True." She smiled and set the computer back on the floor. She pulled *Oh, the Places You'll Go!* off my bookshelf. "I love Dr. Seuss," she said.

I leaned against the wall and opened an old *Glamour* I'd pulled out of someone's garbage. "God, I'm fat."

"Shut up! Don't talk about yourself like that." Anita flipped through one of the picture books. "I'd love to live there." She pointed at a tiny crooked house hanging off a precipice. "Where's your mom?" she asked.

"Work."

"Do you have any brothers or sisters?"

"Nope."

"What about your dad?"

"He died when I was two."

"Oh. Sorry. My mom died six years ago. She went back to Mexico to visit my grandma. Car wreck."

"God, that's so sad."

"Yeah." She looked at me, shrugged, and gave me a sad, crooked smile. "Her name was Fabiola."

"What a cool name."

"I think so." She set down the book and tightened the laces of her knockoff Keds.

"My dad died in a car wreck, too."

"I'm sorry."

I pretended to read. Anita put back the book and pulled out *The Sneetches*. My Dr. Seuss collection was the closest thing to a family Bible that Cindy and I had. My best memory of childhood was of Cindy scrunched up on a little stool reading *Hop on Pop* while I sat in the bathtub and played with a yellow rubber porcupine.

Anita and I both had parents who died in car wrecks. It's like we were sisters somehow. Her mom and my dad were in car-crash heaven together. I was staring at pictures of "Dos and Don'ts" in the magazine when my phone vibrated. It was Kurt King. I let it go. A few minutes later, it vibrated again.

Anita stared at me over the top of the book. "Aren't you going to answer it?"

"Uh . . . it's just this guy who calls a lot."

"Is he good-looking?"

"Extremely good-looking."

She snatched the phone and flipped it open. "Hello," she said. "This is Tanya. . . . Tanya. . . . As matter of fact, I am Russian. . . . Oh, really? Ashley? No. . . ."

I grabbed the phone and turned to the wall. I said, "Hey, Kurt," in a slightly modified Kristy voice.

"How's it going?" he said.

"Pretty good." I ran my finger down a crack in the green wall.

"Who's your friend? Is she as beautiful as you?"

"Yeah. She has black hair, though." I picked paint off the wall, and it crumbled onto my blanket.

"Ashley, I have a question for you. What's your favorite color, sweetheart?"

"Blue."

"And how's your mama doing?"

"She's really sick. She's doing pretty bad."

"Sorry about that, sweetheart. You call me anytime. When can I see you?"

"Sometime. I've got to go now."

I shut the phone. Anita had closed the book. She looked at me carefully. She said, "Your voice sounds stupid when you talk like that, and that dude sounds like he's thirty."

69

Fourteen

Thursday night, after we shopped at Safeway, Cindy made me sit with her in the car. Things were worse at Kristy's house, and Cindy wanted to tell me about it. We sat in her white Grand Marquis with the smashed bumper as the orange-and-green sky faded behind the apartment building.

"I know you're having problems with Kristy." Cindy studied the backs of her hands and picked at her nails. "I've never really cared for that girl. She's been terribly, terribly spoiled. But her mother is a lovely woman. I just feel awful about what's happening to her. I feel like we should do something."

I wanted to scream. I wanted to throw open the car door and run as fast and far as I could. Everything about Cindy—the droning sound of her voice, the way she jammed her tongue under her upper lip, how she smelled like cherry fluoride treatment—made me feel like I had chemicals sizzling through my veins.

"What are we supposed to do? Make them a pot of macaroni and cheese? Bake them a cake? They don't eat that stuff! They eat spelt bread and organic vegetables. There's nothing we can do. They don't want anything from us. Don't you get it, Cindy? Kristy hates me."

"Leah!" Cindy crossed her arms and tightened her lips. "First of all, I am not Cindy to you. I am your mother. Be respectful! Second, you do not understand the situation. You're all wrapped up in your petty squabble. Connie Baker is dying. Do you know what that does to a family? Well, I do. I do! I've been there."

Of course! I had stepped on sacred ground, Cindy's tragedy, the dying of her husband, the great disaster. It was Cindy's trump card. Except Paul Lobermeir hadn't died of cancer; he'd died "instantly" in a car crash. Cindy's mom and dad had both died of cancer within two years of her graduating from high school. She thought she'd been saved by Paul, but then he croaked, too.

I had only been two years old. After the funeral and the four months she spent either in bed or in the bathtub while I sat in a playpen, Cindy went back to work and worked two or three jobs while I was at the babysitter's, and she didn't have a new coat for ten years because she was buying me shoes and paying for my six-month dental checkups. I could recite that

71

story as easily as *Hop on Pop*. The shabby peacoat with big plastic buttons still hung like a phantom in her closet.

"You have no idea how hard it's been for me to raise a child alone." Cindy's voice in the dark car was like an echo from another day, an echo from a thousand other days when she'd said the same words in exactly the same way. YOU have NO IDEA how HARD it's been for ME to raise a CHILD ALONE.

How many days had I been alive now? I started to do the math inside my head.

"Connie had another operation. There's nothing left they can take out." Cindy glared like she hated me as she described how horribly and slowly Kristy's mother was dying.

She finished with her death lecture and swallowed loudly. It was dark outside now. We sat in the glow from the streetlight. Something, maybe defrosting fish sticks, rustled in the grocery bag. There was no oxygen inside the Grand Marquis.

Cindy hung on to the steering wheel, stared out the windshield, and waited for me to hug her and tell her how much I loved her and how much I appreciated how hard she worked, though there was no way I could ever comprehend how difficult it had been . . . blah, blah, blah. Her mouth was bunched up like the end of a balloon.

And I did love her, but that was hidden beneath all the chaos and explosions going on inside. I blew a bubble and popped it with my tongue. I pulled down the visor so the little light came on, swabbed on lip gloss, and smiled at myself.

Cindy made a gurgling noise as if she were being strangled. She yanked at the seat belt until it finally unbuckled. She climbed out of the car, slammed the door, then limped to the building entrance—her bunion was killing her.

When I came in with the bags of groceries, Cindy was in her room with the door shut. I put the groceries away and turned on the oven. I boiled water for macaroni and cheese, put some fish sticks in the oven, and made an iceberg-lettuce salad.

Anita called. "I just had a breakthrough moment in my art."

"How so?"

"I'm finally getting the hang of chiaroscuro. I did this new drawing of a man's face half in shadow . . ."

When I got off the phone with Anita, I started to sing. I didn't mind making Cindy dinner. Someday soon, I'd leave her far, far behind, and she would be all alone and would have to bake her own fish sticks.

I knocked on Cindy's door to tell her that dinner was ready, as if she couldn't smell it. She didn't answer. I tried the knob, but she'd locked herself in.

I left her plate on the counter and sat down to eat by

myself. I inspected each soggy fish stick before putting it in my mouth, then washed my plate. Cindy had taped a magazine picture of a flowery meadow over the sink. The picture was faded and water-spotted, and the edge was torn.

I went into my room, closed my curtains, and sat on my bed with a stack of old magazines. I read advice columns and an article about a girl who'd lost her legs in a car accident but adjusted and had even more success in life. I read an article about a girl who had a giant tumor growing out of her forehead. The doctors were going to remove it when she finished her growth spurt. Other than the tumor, she was beautiful and happy. A picture showed her on a field surrounded by twenty-five preppy friends.

Cindy came out of her room.

She was wearing her quilted pink robe with the tiny bow at the throat. Her hair was rumpled as if she'd been sleeping. She didn't even glance at the dinner plate I'd left for her. She took the wedding wineglass out of the cupboard and filled it with ice and Chardonnay from the box in the refrigerator.

She took a long swallow, then toddled to the bathroom and returned with her plastic basket of manicure supplies. She backed up to the couch, dropped onto it, and turned on the TV. She flipped the channels until she found *Dancing with the Stars*. A week before, I tried to get her to watch a PBS special about an inner-city emergency room. She said, "Are you kidding me? It reminds me of work. I need escape!"

She picked up the glass, held it to her face, and gulped the wine. She set the empty glass down on the coffee table. She wet a cotton ball and rubbed polish remover onto her thumbnail. The smell of chemicals drifted into my room. Every night she did the same thing.

Cindy looked so small curled on the corner of the couch. She propped her foot on the pillow, looked up from her nails, and squinted at the TV screen. "It's the little luxuries that keep me going," she always said. "In my profession, I can't have long nails or wear bright polish, but I like to keep them pretty."

And Cindy wasn't an alcoholic if she just drank Chardonnay on ice, and she wasn't an alcoholic no matter how many times she refilled her wineglass because the wine came in a box, so there weren't empty bottles all over the apartment.

I dumped the textbooks out of my backpack onto my bed. The books felt like they weighed ten pounds each and had black numbers scrawled on their dirty edges. I tipped the chemistry book open to page 127. The corner of the page had dirty creases, and a dried yellow blot on page 126 looked like vomit. *Divide the mass . . . its molar mass . . . the number of moles of solute.* The words and formulas were gibberish; reading the text was like crawling through a thornbush. My brain already hurt from my life.

I put the books back in my backpack and crawled under

the blankets. I stuck in my earbuds and put Bruno Mars's "Just the Way You Are" on replay.

Bruno Mars. Sweetest man in the entire world. Five feet five inches tall, one inch taller than me. He'd been a chubby kid and didn't judge. He loved chunky girls. He had the most beautiful voice, and he could dance.

I listened to Bruno and read *The Lorax* for the thousandth time. An hour later, I cracked open my door, then stepped into the living room. Cindy was snoring, her chin trembling. I pulled on my hoodie and slipped out of the apartment.

Fifteen

I walked fast, hood pulled up, head down, hands in pockets. Just moving, invisible and nameless, dreaming through the chilly black night. I jumped over cracks in the sidewalk.

Two blocks from 7-Eleven, a black car slid up to the curb. I jogged to the corner and waited for a truck to pass so I could run across the street. The black car pulled up and blocked me. "Hey," he said. "Hey, girl."

My breathing tightened. The eyes, the cheekbones, the mouth, the hair in the dark car. Kurt King stared like he knew me, like he didn't know me. I was Ashley. I was Leah. I shyly tugged down my hood.

"I met you before, didn't I? Yeah! You—you're Ashley's friend." He smiled, real slow. His eyes and teeth shone in the streetlight.

The night with the soft wind, the lights, was like a huge room full of darkness and stars. I was Ashley and not Ashley.

"What are you doin' out here?"

"I don't know. Just walking."

"Uh-huh. Just walking." He nodded along with a song. He didn't recognize my normal voice.

"So," he said. "You just go out walking late at night, huh?" The engine hummed; the radio played low. He sat in his car and tapped his thumbs against the steering wheel in time to the music. He was wearing a black Metallica T-shirt, no jacket. A dragon with fangs, bat wings, and a snake tail wrapped around the curve of his muscle. I stood on the sidewalk and looked into his dark window. No rush, no hurry. Me and Kurt King.

"Come on. Let me give you a lift. It's no good for a girl to be out walking alone this time of night." He leaned across the seat and pushed open the door.

And there he was, waiting with his car door open for me. I got in and pulled the door closed. It wasn't real. I was dreaming. I hadn't even said a word. Had I said a word? Had I even spoken? I said, "OK."

Kurt King shifted into gear, and the car pulled away from the curb. The car's black interior was lit up in the green glow from the dash.

"So, how you been?" He turned the music up, then down

again. He rolled the steering wheel under the palm of his hand. "Let's just drive around for a while. It's a beautiful night."

The beautiful cool night blew in. I tipped my face into it. A song I loved came on the radio. Kid Cudi. This would end any minute. That's what my heart told me as it knocked in my chest: this wasn't real; it wouldn't last. Warm air from the vents blew against my knees.

He turned into Woodland Way, the neighborhood above the junior high. Spruce Street, Aspen Avenue, Scrub Oak Boulevard, Yucca Street. Kids lived either here or at Mountain View Estates or, if they were poor, down off of Tenth like me. I knew where almost everyone lived—people I hated, people I'd never spoken to. I wanted someone from school to see me pass by in the black car. They would think, *Was that Leah Lobermeir?*

Kurt King drove straight up Pine Avenue toward the mountain. He pulled to a stop in front of a ranch house. He turned off the engine and then the headlights.

The house was small, brick, with a big picture window. It was the ranch house where the junior high gym teacher Mr. Zimmerman used to live. Even though I wasn't on a team, Mr. Zimmerman would talk to me. He'd say, "Leah Lobermeir, you get prettier by the day and brainier by the hour. I can spot a smart girl a mile away." His house had been egged dozens of times, and kids threw baloney on his truck so that baloney-sized circles of paint peeled off. Halfway through eighth grade, Mr. Zimmerman quit and moved to Arizona.

We sat in the dark car in front of Mr. Zimmerman's old house. No lights were on. The big window looked gray and sad and empty. A loud commercial for a car dealership came on the radio. Kurt King turned it off.

He lit a cigarette in his cupped hand. The end of the cigarette sizzled. He shook the match, threw it out the window, and stretched his arm across the back of my seat. His hand dropped onto my shoulder and then began to work its way through the thick hair at the nape of my neck. I'd never had someone else's hand in my hair, ever. The roots of my hair felt electrified. I was rigid. "Jesus, girl, you got a lot of hair. Honey, where's Ashley tonight?"

His hand in my hair and the name Ashley tangled together. He twisted my hair around his fingers. I couldn't speak.

A police cruiser slowed as it passed. Kurt King watched it. He pulled his hand out of my hair and lifted his arm off me. He reached down and started the engine. "Let's head out." He moved slowly, delicately, as if trying not to wake someone. He held his cigarette between his teeth and steered with both hands. "We'll just go on a little drive. Shit. Cop's still watching. . . ." He slowed at a stop sign.

Beyond the stop sign, the houses ended and the hills were covered with scrub oak. Pine Avenue turned into a dirt road that wound up into the mountains. The summer before, I'd gone to a keg party up there with Kristy. She went off with a guy and ditched me, and I was stranded with people I didn't know. She finally came back, completely wasted and hanging on a different guy. I rode back with them even though they were really drunk, and it was terrifying because there are sharp turns on that mountain road where you can't see what's coming. . . .

I opened my car door and jumped out.

"What the fuck," he said.

"Bye. I'm sorry. I got to go. . . ." I waved like an idiot, pulled up my hood, and ran down the sidewalk toward Mr. Zimmerman's house.

He did a U-Turn and passed me, slowly, but I had my hood up and was Leah again. I didn't look. By the time the sound of his engine faded away, it was a dream.

The next afternoon, when he called, he said, "Guess what, Ashley? I seen your friend. The one, she's got thick dark hair."

"Oh, yeah? What do you think of her?" said the Kristy voice.

"She's all right. Big girl. Not as pretty as you, of course. . . ."

I started giggling, kind of hysterically. I laughed so hard, I was crying.

Cindy stuck her head into my room. "Who are you talking to?"

My phone had died.

Sixteen

It was Monday, the first of May. Anita and I had planned to meet early in front of my building and walk to school together. The craggy mountain stretched threateningly up through the smog into the pale-blue sky, but the air felt fresh. Little plants were growing out of the cracks in the sidewalk.

Anita and I had now been friends for two weeks. It was one of those cases where you and someone else are instantly friends — there's no doubt, no mistaking it. My phone was out of minutes, I had no money, and Cindy was keeping her purse in her room. For two days, I'd been just Leah, not Ashley. I spent the whole weekend in bed reading Roald Dahl.

Anita and I walked along Tenth Avenue and discussed our future careers. She was now pretty certain that she wanted to be an anime illustrator. Acting and screenwriting were both too risky. She kept having major breakthroughs in her art.

"I could totally see you as a doctor," she said. "Not a dermatologist, for sure. All those skin conditions are gross. Maybe a family doctor? You'd get to see a lot of different—"

Kristy's red Civic pulled to the curb ahead of us.

Anita and I stopped walking. Kristy's car whined back to where we stood in front of EZPAWN. The black metal grate was still locked over the glass door.

Kristy leaned over Corinne's lap and smiled at me, not at Anita. Her eyes were blank and blue as the morning sky. "Hey, Leah! Hop in. Leah, come on! I've got to tell you something."

Corinne, whose eyes had glazed over the day before when she passed me in the hallway, smiled sweetly and showed her dimples.

Fruity perfume poured out of the car. K103 was playing on the radio. Both Kristy and Corinne were wearing short-sleeved sweaters and tight jeans. Their hair looked shiny, and they had put on matching rose-colored blush and lip gloss.

I stood there stupidly. Anita stood beside me. Her face was locked into a weird frown. She pressed the giant guide to drawing manga against her chest.

I actually considered saying, "Can Anita come, too?" but one glance at her fringy leather jacket, the studs going up her ear, and her chewed, black-polished fingertips pinching the spine of her book killed that idea. Her black eyeliner curled up the outside corners of her eyes. *I'm sorry, Anita.* It was a silent little prayer.

"I've got to talk to Kristy. See you later, OK?" I said to her chin.

"You're going with Yertle?" she whispered. I pulled open the back door to Kristy's car and threw myself in. Kristy hit the gas and we sped away.

It was a sickening kind of relief to be back in Kristy's car. I didn't return her smile in the rearview mirror. She started whistling "Teenage Dream." I pictured Anita walking alone in her leather jacket, hanging on to her book like it was a life preserver, her face tight and serious.

Kristy continued to watch me in the rearview mirror. "Hey, Leah!"

I said nothing.

"Leah, come on. Talk!"

I stared out the window.

Kristy turned into the school lot and parked in her regular spot. She unbuckled and curled sideways in the seat with her back to the door.

"First of all, I am sick to death of Victoria Miller! She's an annoying, stupid cow. Leah, let's talk. I'm sorry about what happened over the past couple weeks. Corinne explained to me that you didn't mean to leave without asking how my mom was. Corinne says you didn't know my mom went to the hospital. For a long time, it was just hard for me to understand because my dad said he told you. But, anyways! I've just been in a really weird head space with my mom and all."

Kristy squeezed her eyes shut and shook her head. She picked out a curl and wound the hair around her finger.

"I'm sure it's really difficult for you to understand what it's like for me because your mom isn't sick. Your mom just comes home and says, 'Leah, what do you want for dinner?' or 'Leah, let's go to the mall.' For me, you know, it's a little different. Corinne, you understand because your mom had ovarian cancer. When was that, Corinne?" She squinted at Corinne.

"It was Derrick's aunt," said Corinne, crossing her legs. "It was, like, three years ago."

"Well, Leah, it's just really, really hard for me." Instantly, Kristy's face was streaming snot and tears. Her nose turned bright red. "My mom is very, very sick. I need you to be there for me."

I felt nothing but dull horror. "I'm sorry, Kristy. I didn't mean to leave without asking. I didn't know. I thought your mom was asleep when I left. Your dad said they were just making a quick trip to the emergency room."

"God, Leah, I forgive you. I forgive you. It's all right. Here, give me a hug." She reached between the seats, grabbed my head, and mashed it into her crinkly, green-apple-shampoo hair.

I started crying, too. "I'm sorry, Kristy."

"I'm sorry, too," said Kristy. "I treated you like shit, like shhhhhhheeeeeit."

Suddenly Kristy shoved off me and leaned back against the door. She closed her eyes, wiped her nose on her sleeve, and left a shiny streak. Corinne stared at the dash with a philosophical expression.

Kristy ran her fingertips under her eyes. "What are you doing hanging out with that weird chick? Anita Sotelo! She is so bizarre. Watch out! It might be catching."

"She's not that bad." How weak. "She's smart and she's pretty nice."

"She's OK," said Corinne. She flipped open the mirror on the visor and applied more liner. "But her clothes and hair and makeup suck."

Kristy widened her eyes. She shrieked. "Leah, check this out! Saturday, Corinne and I went down to Torrance Park for a few hours — sorry we didn't call you; it was in the middle of that weird head-space thing — and, anyways, guess who we saw on the way home? Mr. Corduroy! He drives a sweet black Mustang. We were driving back on Torrance Avenue, and suddenly he was right next to us. He yells, 'Pull over, girl! What's with your phone, sweetheart? Come on, let's party, girl! Let's do it! You are so beautiful, baby. . . .'"

"Really?" I said. My heart banged so hard it almost blocked out her voice. "Weird."

Kristy ran her tongue over her teeth and shook her head. "I'm just like, 'OK . . .' You know he's kind of intense, but he's so freaking good-looking."

"Kristy." Corinne pinched the bridge of her nose and leaned forward as if she had a sinus headache. "He is so gross. This is bizarre. He's old! Please don't."

Kristy snorted and rolled her eyes at Corinne. "Bullshit. The dude's hot. He got pulled over by a cop, so we didn't see him again. I'm still kind of in trouble and promised my dad I'd be home by ten. That's the only reason he let me go out."

Some lettered jackets appeared by Kristy's window. A lanky football player named Dwayne Lewis yanked her door open. Kristy screamed and fell laughing into his arms.

Seventeen

Tuesday. "OK, let's do this thing," said Carl Lancaster in his deep, manlike voice. Mrs. McCleary said no one could change lab partners again for the rest of the year. I was stuck with Carl Lancaster. "Where's your lab book?" he asked.

"What? This?" I waved my lab book around. I'd lent my first one to Kristy so she could copy my notes, but she never gave it back. I had to buy another from Mrs. McCleary. Cindy was incredibly pissy about it. A kid tripped over an extension cord and knocked over a five-foot-tall stack of old textbooks. I ignored Carl and observed the chaos.

"Leah. Leah! Look at me. Yes. That is your lab book. OK, let's open it up to a fresh page. Today is Tuesday, May second. We're measuring pH in acidic and basic solutions."

Kristy was watching Carl. She leaned over and jerked her body as if she were throwing up into her sink.

"Carl, back off."

"Come on, Leah." He leaned very, very close; I could see his excellent bones and all his distinct freckles. "We're lab partners. We have to do this together. Your work is going to affect my grade."

He was so close I could smell his tangerine breath and his neck. His neck smelled faintly like fresh bread. I could feel warmth rising off of him. I wondered if I stank like cigarettes.

He studied me with his calm green eyes. Half the people I knew had green eyes. Carl's were ocean-colored—at least what I imagined the ocean looked like in real life. I never got to see it when we lived in Florida. In my mind, the ocean was green, sparked with little flecks of blue. Carl didn't look mad, even though I'd blown him off in study hall the day before. He looked at me like he knew something. He looked like he was about to kiss me. Carl Lancaster! I was going to throw up.

But he didn't kiss me. He pulled back and looked down at his lab sheet. We put on our goggles. He said in his radio voice, "OK, first we have to label these test tubes. How about you write the labels? First tube: distilled water . . . Second tube: dilute sulfuric acid."

Something about his deep, steady voice and the long, slow way he said *sulfuric* made me relax. I leaned on the chipped lab counter. He put twenty drops of Solution A into the watch glass with a pipette. I moved a little closer to him.

Eighteen

I lay on my back, staring up at the picture of Damien Rogers and thinking that the muscle in his arm looked like an apple. He would be my boyfriend someday. I skipped lunch sometimes and did sit-ups in the tiny space at the end of my bed, because even if he thought I was beautiful just the way I was, like LaTeisha Morgan was beautiful, and our personalities were an excellent match, I wanted to be thin and look good for Damien. I wanted to look good next to him. It was the only way I could imagine myself with Damien—me being thin. I wanted to be ready.

I'd corralled Anita into a walled-off section of my mind. She was fine, I told myself. She had Iris and Maria to eat lunch with. I liked her, she was a great kid, but we were destined for different ways of life. I could not spend my high-school years with the members of the Anime Club. I still wanted to be a doctor but did not want to discuss that fact in public. I ignored her stares in the hallway, though sometimes the look on her face haunted me when I was trying to go to sleep. I constantly talked to myself, rationalizing and explaining so that it all made sense, because if I stopped and thought about it, it didn't make sense at all and it felt terrible, like I was letting something die.

I found a twenty in one of Cindy's old purses and bought some minutes. Ten minutes later, my phone vibrated. When I saw who was calling, the phone vibrated all the way through me. I flipped it open and held it to my cheek.

"Ashley. What happened with your phone? You got to keep in touch, girl."

I closed my eyes and became another person. I was like a girl drifting through space. It was like being pure me. Nothing holding me back, no Cindy, no Kristy, no thunder thighs, no puke-green walls or black bars. I could feel his hand in my hair. Had I dreamed that?

"I ran out of minutes. I can only talk a little while."

"Why didn't you stop the other night when I was trying to talk to you? I ran a red to catch up and got pulled over by the cops. That was a goddamn close call. Girl, you need to —"

"Sorry, my friend wouldn't let me stop."

"Girl, you keep that phone topped up."

"I'm sorry, but sometimes —"

"I want to be able to get ahold of you. Tonight I want to know how much you weigh."

"What? No way. That's creepy. I'm going now. . . ."

"Wait. Hold on, Ashley. Come on, little girl. Tell me how much you weigh."

"Why?"

"So I can imagine holding you."

I opened my eyes and looked at the clippings on the wall. Damien Rogers weighed 171 pounds in his socks. It said so in the newspaper.

"Ninety-three pounds."

"Ninety-three pounds? That kills my heart. You're so tiny. You're such a little girl. So delicate."

"I got to go now."

"OK, sweetheart. Sweet dreams. How's your mama?"

"Not good. Got to go." I hung up and lay on my back.

My heart pounded like someone was inside knocking, wanting to be let out. Kristy, Ashley, and I were locked in a tiny room together, and the room was getting smaller.

I turned off the lights, put in my earbuds, and turned up Kid Cudi. I floated on the darkness.

Nineteen

The next weekend we didn't go out. Kristy was grounded because she had a D in language arts, and Corinne had cramps. I didn't answer Kurt King's calls; I just listened to his messages. He left six voice mails and eleven texts. He said, "I need to see you, little girl." He texted: *thinkin bout u babe.*

Kristy was bored and kept calling. Saturday night, she rated the boys in our grade. "Carl Lancaster is gross. It's just weird to like piano that much. He's barely a two."

Sunday night, I was getting calls and texts from Kurt King and texts and calls from Kristy. It stressed me out—sometimes their texts came in at the same time. I was paranoid that somehow their texts or calls would cross in my phone, or I'd hit some kind of reply-all, and suddenly Kristy and Kurt King would be talking to each other. When I finally fell asleep, I had a dream about a phone vibrating and lighting up on a table. I couldn't answer, and I couldn't turn it off.

Monday, we had a lecture in chemistry. I pulled my chair to the farthest end of the table and didn't look at Carl. I was exhausted. I emptied my head of every thought and feeling and sat there as close to not existing as I could manage. Mrs. McCleary droned on for fifty minutes, but I didn't hear one word. I would never be a doctor. Every ten minutes or so, Carl turned his head and gazed at me.

Mrs. McCleary announced that there was a test on Friday. The bell rang. Carl stood up and waited for me to go first.

In study hall, I sat with my head down on my book, my cheek against the silky, dirty page. All the kids around me stared at their phones.

That morning, for some stupid reason, I'd said, "Mom, I think I might want to be a doctor." Cindy smirked at me over the top of her mug, then swigged down her coffee. "Pretty big for your britches, aren't you, Leah? Pardon me, but I need to go to work." She grabbed her red leather purse and slammed out the door.

I was stupid, I was fat, I was a loser. I lived in a hideous basement apartment that didn't even have Internet. Nothing I hoped for would come true. Becoming a doctor was a stupid idea, a ridiculous fantasy. That's what Cindy thought. That's what almost the whole world thought.

Across a landscape of heads and tables, I saw Carl sitting alone. He was bent over his textbook. I studied his hair, his neck, and his shoulders.

Dan Manke shoved his phone in my face. He was playing a video titled Four-Hundred-Pound Woman Pole Dances. "Fat-Ass, check it out—you might have a career after all!"

The woman looked over her shoulder at the crowd. She was smiling, but her face looked dead. I knocked Dan's hand away. "Get that shit away from me."

"Oooooh. Fat-Ass is feisty today!"

I stood and picked up my books. I walked across the library to the table where Carl Lancaster was sitting. I didn't even decide to do it. It was like taking a breath. You just breathe. He looked up, and we looked at each other for what felt like a long time, though it was probably just a few seconds. We just looked at each other. It was weird.

He waited for me to say something. "Can I sit here, Carl." It came out like a statement, kind of challenging, as if I was afraid he'd say no.

He shrugged and waved his hand at the empty chairs across from him. He got back to work.

"Carl."

He raised his face. There was something about the way he looked at me that was unnerving. He looked at me and saw me—he saw all of me, a person, with an inside and an outside, alive all the way through. Almost no one else did.

Most people looked and saw their idea of me: fat girl, Chubs, problematic overweight daughter.

"Carl, why aren't you in AP chemistry? All your other classes are AP."

Carl's cheeks flushed. He bit the inside of his cheek and squinted over his shoulder at the window. I'd never seen Carl lose his cool before, not even when paper footballs were pinging off the back of his head.

He sat back in his chair and chewed on the end of his finger. "Uh . . . it's not my best subject."

"You've got to be joking. You've got an A, for sure."

"Yeah, but I'm not certain I could get an A in AP, and my parents would shit bricks if I got anything less, and I don't want to deal with the fallout. My mother's always calling the counselor trying to get them to move me up, but I refuse."

"Wow. What's your GPA? What do you want to study in college?"

"I'm not going to college. My parents don't know that yet."

"Shhh!" said the librarian.

Carl Lancaster sat back in his chair in that cotton shirt and ran his hand through his hair. He looked at me so seriously and steadily, and his shirt was open at his neck. For a flash, he looked almost like a male model. Carl Lancaster.

"You've got such good grades," I whispered.

"Screw college," he mouthed. "Leah, you've got to figure things out for yourself."

"Carl?"

"Yeah?" He leaned across the table, and I leaned toward him so no one would hear, even though everyone else was fifteen feet away. Our noses were about four inches apart, and I could feel his tangerine breath. It smelled like someplace far from Hilton.

"Can we study together? I need to get a good grade in this class."

He sat back and regarded me again in that serious, smoky male-model way. He tapped his pen against the table. "What's giving you trouble?"

Twenty

I went with Kristy after school.

I got to ride shotgun in the afternoons because Corinne could never go with us. She had to babysit her little brothers every weekday until seven, when her parents got home. Kristy chewed with her mouth open and filled the car with the smell of grape gum. In the parking lot, she nearly backed up into some freshman girls. She lowered her window. "Sor-rrrreeeee. I really didn't mean to do that. Ha-ha-ha."

Kristy and I were like sisters now, half the same girl. I could see her so clearly, like I was looking at her through a magnifying glass: the tiny red bumps on her thin arms, how her knuckles whitened when she gripped the gear shift, the jewel-like gleam of her squinty eyes. She glanced at me and stopped chomping her gum. "What the hell are you staring at?"

Kristy stuffed more gum into her mouth, let the little white wrappers drift out the window, and threw a half-smoked cigarette after them. She chugged a Snapple, threw the bottle into the back, and changed the radio station in the middle of a song.

She kept her phone between her skinny thighs. "God, I'm bored! Want to go to the mall? Or want to go downtown?"

"No. Kristy, no one will be there. Want to go to Animal Kingdom?" We used to take the bus there when we were thirteen; it was dark and smelled like mice. We'd stand in front of the aquariums and watch the angelfish and the schools of bulgy-eyed goldfish. The parakeets squeaked and the aquariums bubbled peacefully.

"Are you kidding? No. Gross. Boring."

"Let's just go to Corinne's."

"Fine," she said. She did a U-turn, the tires skidding on the gravel.

We passed Anita walking home alone. Kristy blasted her horn. I ducked. "Kristy, damn it . . ." That morning, I'd passed Anita, who was sitting on the floor in the hallway before first period. She was drawing in her sketchbook. I walked over and said, "How's it going?" She slowly lifted her face and stared at me like I'd farted, then closed the sketchbook, hopped to her feet, and sauntered away.

I sat up. A black car was coming toward us.

I adjusted the side-view mirror and looked behind us. It wasn't the Mustang. But one day it would be, because it was not just possible: it was going to happen. Kurt King and his black Mustang would suddenly pull up behind Kristy's Civic, and he'd flash his lights, and Kristy would laugh maniacally and turn into a parking lot. It was just a matter of time.

"Why are you so quiet? It's weird," said Kristy as she turned into Mountain View Estates. She pulled into Corinne's driveway, turned off the engine, climbed out, and slammed her door. She trotted to the house without waiting for me. She'd started trotting on her toes like a pony—it was a way to stick out her boobs and her skinny little butt at the same time.

As usual, the inside of Corinne's house was a catastrophe. The counters, table, and chairs were piled with wrappers, dirty plates, half-eaten waffles, black banana peels, school papers, junk mail, bills, catalogs, coupons, and empty milk jugs. Plastic action figures in weird contortions lay scattered around the floor. A jumbo box of maxi pads sat in the middle of the kitchen table. Cases of juice boxes, fruit roll-ups, and Aldi pop were pushed up against the wall. The sink was piled to the faucet with plastic cups and ketchup-smeared plates. Corinne babysat while her mom and stepdad ran a house-cleaning business.

Corinne stood watching a cooking show on the kitchen TV while the microwave whirred. She held Jimmy on her hip. His yellow diaper bulged around his fat legs.

"Hey," Corinne said over her shoulder. The microwave dinged.

She took out the plastic bottle, shook it hard, then squirted formula onto her wrist. Jimmy snatched the bottle and sucked it.

"What's new?" said Corinne wistfully, as if something amazing might have happened in the hour since school let out. She pulled open the back of Jimmy's diaper and sniffed.

"Nothing!" said Kristy. "I'm bored as hell. Jesus, that kid stinks. Can I light a cigarette to cut the smell?"

"Let's go on the patio." Corinne grabbed a bag of candy and lugged Jimmy through the sliding glass door.

Corinne's patio was a slab of concrete on the edge of a yard worn to bare dirt. Pieces of broken plastic toys stuck like arrowheads out of the ground. A wimpy aspen tree, held up by wires, grew in the corner of the yard. At Mountain View, you could do anything you wanted behind your cedar fence, but the front yard had to be either thick green grass or a gravel garden. There were three shades of beige paint you could choose from.

Corinne threw a pack of cigarettes and the lighter down

next to the Folgers can that we used as an ashtray. "Derrick was being a total dickwad last night. Just screaming at everyone. God, I wish I was playing softball."

Even Kristy allowed a short, respectful silence at the mention of softball. Corinne's inability to be on the team was one of the tragedies of our grade. Corinne was talented, a natural, an incredible pitcher without ever attending any of the expensive softball camps Kelsey Parker and her friends had gone to every summer since elementary school.

My dream was so far away and almost impossible, but Corinne's was right there in front of her, and the only reason she wasn't living it was because of her stepdad and stupid little brothers. Corinne didn't look tragic, though; she just looked tired.

Kristy sat down on the concrete, scooted back against the green siding, and lit up. She closed her eyes. "I can't believe your mom allows you to smoke."

"Can't you say anything original?" I asked.

"What?" Her eyes snapped open. She stared at me with her lip hiked up over her teeth. She got out her phone.

"Sorry," I said, "but you've said that exact sentence about a hundred times before."

I took a drag and gagged. I decided right then that I was going to quit smoking. Not that minute, but soon. Cigarettes made me stink, and my teeth were turning yellow. I couldn't breathe, and my lungs hurt when I ran. I couldn't afford it. Plus, it was ironic for a doctor to smoke, though lots of them did. I saw them in their blue scrubs shivering outside the hospital. But a doctor who's fat and smokes is a little too much. Anita had told me that cigarettes were a conspiracy of rich white men to make a fortune while slowly killing off the underclass. I'd started smoking with Kristy when I was thirteen.

Kristy tried to hawk up some spit. "Go to hell, Chubs. Whatever." She shook her head like I was an idiot and stared cross-eyed at her phone's screen.

"Quit fighting, you two." Corinne held Jimmy between her knees and forlornly blew smoke away from his big head. "You wouldn't believe the woman they had on *Top Chef.* I just caught the end of it. She was awesome."

Carl Lancaster floated up into my mind and looked at me. "Corinne, what do you think of Carl Lancaster?"

"Total geek," said Kristy.

"Pretty awkward," said Corinne. "But he's an OK guy."

Jimmy sat in his wadded-up yellow diaper and flapped a plastic bag against the concrete. His pink stomach hung over the top of his diaper. He had black threads of toe jam between his little toes. A breeze blew through, and goose bumps popped up on his squashy legs. He curled his toes and smiled. He had eight teeth.

Corinne picked a blue M&M out of the bag with the tips of her nails. She had shadows under her eyes and sad smudges around her mouth. "Last night, I made chicken Kiev, and Mom said it was better than the Olive Garden's. But the boys wouldn't eat it, so Derrick said I couldn't make it again."

I said, "That sucks. Pass me the candy."

Corinne tossed me the bag. I dumped out a handful, then remembered I was transforming myself for Damien Rogers; I poured the candy back in. I wasn't sure who I liked more, Kurt King or Damien Rogers. At this point, it was kind of a toss-up. I'd never really talked to Damien Rogers, but Kurt King was a little intense.

"I'm going to get a drink of water." I'd recently read that drinking a gallon of water a day was one of the top ten diet tricks.

Kristy gritted her teeth as if she was about to vomit from the smell of Jimmy's diaper. I got up and scooted through the glass door into the kitchen.

I filled a giant plastic cup with water and walked into the living room. A mound of clean underwear and towels had been dumped onto the carpet. On the other side of the laundry, Corinne's three other brothers huddled around the computer.

"What are you guys playing?"

Ryan rubbed his ear against his shoulder, but none of

them answered. They were skinny boys with wild khaki-colored eyes and blotchy freckles on their cheeks and square noses. They leaned closer to the computer screen.

My phone vibrated. It was a text from Kurt King. *Meet me tonight 7-11 @ 10:45.* The room tilted and I was standing in a different place, though I hadn't moved.

I closed the phone, drank the entire cup of water, and walked over to the boys. They were looking at a picture of a woman whose naked breasts lay in her lap like watermelons. It was a really sad picture. Her smile was tight and forced, like she thought the guy taking the picture was the ickiest man she'd ever met. Ryan giggled and rolled his forehead against the desktop.

Alex clutched his throat. "I'm going to throw up."

"Gross, you guys. Turn it off!"

Alex didn't even turn his head. "Shut up, Leah. You're not the boss of us."

I grabbed a handful of toffee nuts and headed back to the patio. "Your brothers are looking at porn."

"Damn them!" Corinne stubbed out her cigarette and got to her feet. "Here, take him." She jammed Jimmy into my arms and charged into the house. Jimmy wrapped his legs around my waist and grabbed a handful of hair with his sticky hand.

He stared at me with his tiny, clear eyes. There were creases in the fat around his wrists. Drool poured off his lip. I rubbed my cheek against his warm velvety head. He smelled like pee and candy. The screaming moved to the kitchen.

Kristy was on her feet. "I'm stressing. Let's get out of here. I can't stand this place."

The three boys surrounded Corinne. They jammed their fists into their eyes and screamed, "Don't tell!" The six-year-old, Kelvin, threw himself on the floor, hit his head against a chair leg, and shrieked. Corinne squeezed her eyes shut and stretched her face with her hands. She looked like an alien.

Kristy shoved her phone in her bag, put on her sunglasses, and jiggled her keys. "I cannot be here one more minute. This is so depressing and stressful. I'm heading out." Something crashed inside.

"Kristy, wait! I've got to give Jimmy back." At the sound of his name, Jimmy tightened his grip on my hair and wound some around the crease in his wrist. I leaned over to keep my hair from pulling and squeezed back in through the glass door.

Corinne had Alex by the shoulders. "Calm down, Alex. Breathe, breathe . . ."

"Corinne, sorry, here's Jimmy. We're gonna go. Kristy already went out the back gate."

I untangled Jimmy's hand from my hair and handed him over. His fat legs bicycled through the air. Corinne took him without looking at me. She turned tiredly back to Alex.

Sometimes the exhausted expression on Corinne's face

spooked me. She looked as stressed and harassed as a middle-aged woman, as though that woman was already there inside the fifteen-year-old girl, biding her time, just waiting to shed Corinne's young skin and hair and clothes.

Kristy's car was waiting in the street with the engine running. "What took you so damn long?" Her little fingers tapped an impatient rhythm on the dashboard.

"I was saying good-bye to Corinne, OK? I feel sorry for her. She's always stuck there. It's not her fault."

Kristy raked her fingers through her hair and checked her nostrils in the mirror. "I know it's not her fault. I just couldn't stand her life." She drove down the street and ran through the stop sign. "I couldn't stand to live her life for even one hour, unless, of course, it was Saturday night and Corinne was out with Jason Coulter. Then I could stand it."

Jason Coulter, a tall guy with glossy black hair and high cheekbones, was considered to be one of the best-looking senior boys. Kristy was baffled to a religious depth by his lack of interest in her. He'd taken Corinne out twice.

"Have you seen Corinne talking to Kelsey Parker lately?" Kristy struggled to pull out a cigarette.

"I'm not sure."

"I don't get that friendship at all. I don't think they're actually very close. Oh, I'm so bored. . . . I'm dying, I'm so bored. Let's just drive around."

I said, "OK, but not downtown."

She turned onto Tenth and headed toward downtown. My phone vibrated.

"Who's texting you?" Kristy said.

"I don't know. I don't want to go downtown."

"Maybe it's Anita Sotelo. We thought of a new name for her: Anita Slutella," said Kristy. We drove across a bridge over a riverbed full of rocks and mud. We passed the freeway entrance and then drove through the outskirts of downtown past warehouses, run-down brick buildings, and auto-body shops surrounded by weeds.

"Don't call her that. It's stupid."

"Anita Sucktella."

"Kristy, just shut up." My phone vibrated again. I reached into my backpack and turned it off. "Let's go. No one's here."

In the afternoon light, the downtown's brick buildings and sidewalks looked bleached out and faded. The street was full of potholes. Weeds grew out of the cracked sidewalks. A third of the store windows had SPACE FOR LEASE signs. A few Chevy trucks, SUVs, and little rusty Dodges were parked along the crumbling curbs, but there were no black Mustangs.

There were a few old people wandering around, but otherwise nobody at the First Colorado Bank, the Seventh-Day Adventist Church, Charlie C.'s, the Gold Dust Saloon, ABC Plumbing, Jorge's Casa, the New Life Church, the New Beginnings Church, the Bucking Bronco Bar, the Computer

Outlet—$99 COMPUTERS—where Cindy bought my laptop, Kenny's Paint and Wallpaper/Linoleum, or the Pregnancy Help Center. I had to get out of Hilton. Maybe I'd move to New Jersey.

Alamo Park—with its peeling benches, scabrous little trees, and thorny grass where Hilton's tweakers hung out on Saturday nights—was deserted except for a squirrel with a bald tail. Old men in seed caps sat holding paper cups of coffee in the sun in front of the Burger King. A vinyl sign loose on two corners flapped over the entrance to the new Jade Garden Restaurant. There was an empty storefront with dirty windows where the Starbucks was supposed to have been.

The wind picked up. A tumbleweed bounced down the street until it caught in a bus shelter with a shattered glass wall. Little dirt and leaf tornados whirled on the sidewalks. Everything was lit up in the dull yellow light that shot from the sun, balanced like a ball on top of the mountain. The little downtown was the color of Chardonnay. "I can't believe we left Florida to come here. I'm so depressed."

"Oh God, give me a break. I don't need it," said Kristy. She suddenly sat up straight. "Shit. I need to run home for a minute. I just need to check on my mom, then we'll split." She turned off the radio, fumbled around trying to plug in her iPod, and almost crashed into a truck that was turning left. At a stoplight, she called home and left a message.

"Mommy, we're almost there. Be there in a second." She didn't talk again the whole ride home.

"There's this gap," said Kristy as she pulled into her driveway. "Daddy works Monday nights, and there's a gap between the day nurse and the Monday-night nurse. Usually, the neighbor—" She drove the car into the garage door and cracked the wood. "Crap!"

"Wait here." Kristy climbed out and yanked her purse onto her shoulder. She headed to the house without stopping to look at the splintered door.

I turned on the phone. First message: *Meet me tonight 7-11 @ 10:45.* Second message: *R u coming?* Then three more: *Ashley come tonite, Ashley come tonite, Ashley come tonite.*

Kristy dumped her stuff on the ground and tried to unlock the door of her house. I texted back: *OK CU @ 10:45,* and climbed out of the car.

Kristy was still trying to unlock the door. She stamped her foot and dropped the keys. Her front door had a fancy gold handle and a narrow frosted window. The doormat had a picture of a smiling scarecrow. I'd stood outside that door a thousand times. She shook the keys, jammed one in, and the lock turned. She kicked the door open.

"Mom?" Kristy called. "Mommy!" She looked around the kitchen and the living room, then jogged down the hallway toward the bedrooms.

I hadn't been in Kristy's house since before she and

Corinne had ditched me. The curtains were pulled open to let the afternoon sun shine on the rumpled tan carpet. The air was full of dust and a heavy sad smell. A stack of blue hospital pads, a box of Kleenex, and lotions and medicine bottles were arranged on the coffee table. I could hear Kristy and her mom talking.

"Leah . . . She's fine . . . Mommy, she doesn't need . . ."

Mrs. Baker teetered down the hallway toward us. It seemed impossible, but she looked worse.

Her gray skin was stretched like plastic wrap over her skull. A few hairs waved on top of her head. Her pink pajamas pouched all over with emptiness. She'd put on a crooked line of pink lipstick.

"Leah, where have you been, sweetheart? . . . We've missed you. . . . Kristy said you were rehearsing for the school play? . . . I never hear anything. I'll make sure Brian attends."

Kristy's mom tipped toward the chair. Kristy took her arms and lowered her onto the recliner. She leaned forward, and Kristy stuffed pillows behind her back. Kristy laid the orange-and-brown pom-pom blanket across her mother's lap, but her mom said, "No, Kristy. It's too heavy."

Kristy pulled off the blanket and threw it on the couch. She hovered over her mother and clawed at her own skinny arm. "Mommy, we've got to get you back to your room. The nurse will be here any minute."

Kristy's mom smiled brightly. "Kristy, I want to talk

to Leah. Sit down, Leah." She patted the edge of the coffee table. Her bones seemed as fragile as little twigs. Veins floated beneath her watery skin. I sat down.

Kristy rocked back on her heels and snapped her gum. "Mommy, Leah doesn't . . ."

"Leah, how are you doing? Are you doing OK, honey? . . . Keeping up your grades? . . . I'm counting on you, Leah, to keep Kristy on the straight and narrow. . . . She doesn't like to read. You get her to read, sweetheart. Tell her some good books. . . . How's your mom doing? She works so hard. It's so hard, Leah, for your mother. . . . She's done such a good job. . . . I'm so lucky with Brian."

She started and stopped as if she were pulling down words and sentences that drifted around inside her head. I nodded and smiled and whispered answers to her questions. Her pupils were huge and inky. I could see myself in the shiny black curves. Her eyes throbbed as if from too much feeling or medication.

Kristy scratched her neck and dragged her fingers through her curls. "OK, Mommy, back to bed." She lifted her mom up by the armpits.

Kristy's mom stood swaying in her tennis socks. She had a funny, crooked smile. "Leah, do you want to see something crazy?"

I stood up to get out of their way. "Sure, Mrs. Baker."

Kristy's mom's hands trembled as she unzipped her pajamas and pulled them apart. From the bottom of her neck all the way down to the top of her baggy panties, she had a ropey scar as if she'd been sewn up with purple yarn. Her chest was as flat as an eight-year-old's. She was skinny and gray like a little starved doll.

"Have you ever seen anything like that?" she said. She fumbled with the zipper.

"No, Mrs. Baker, never." I was afraid she'd see my heart beating through my shirt.

I'd never be a surgeon. I couldn't cut Mrs. Baker open.

With a pale, blank face, Kristy zipped up her mom's pajamas. She still had her big purse with gold buckles jammed under her arm as if she was about to fly out the door.

"It's just life. . . . I just want you girls to know, it's just life . . . nothing to be afraid of," said Mrs. Baker as Kristy led her toward the bedroom.

Ten minutes later, Kristy came back down the hallway with her big round sunglasses shoved crookedly into her hair. She stopped halfway down the hall and stared at the Disneyland picture for a long time.

"Let's go," she said without looking at me. "We're going to wait in the driveway until the nurse comes."

We sat in her car and listened to the radio. Kristy tipped back her head, lowered her sunglasses, and turned the music up. A tear dripped out from beneath her sunglasses, ran down her cheek, and hung from her jaw like a raindrop. It finally fell onto her shirt and left a dark spot.

She had her fists clenched on her knees. I put my hand over her hand. She grabbed my fingers and crushed them for five minutes, like she was dying and I was the only thing keeping her alive.

Twenty-One

A car turned into the driveway. Kristy gunned the engine and backed out without even waving at the nurse. We drove out of Mountain View Estates and down to Tenth.

"I should go home," I said after a minute. "I have a lot of homework to do."

"You'll go home soon enough," she said. Her mascara had dried in little streaks under her eyes. Her nose was still red and dripping.

Kristy turned onto Las Vegas Avenue, a strip of gas stations, auto-glass stores, and gun shops. We passed Loco Liquors and the UnBank, where Cindy had gone at least twice, even though they took 25 percent of her paycheck, because she needed wine. The dialysis center—now, that was depressing. Diabetes destroys your kidneys, then you have to have your blood cleaned three times a week, and you could still go blind and lose your toes. The ancient motels with neon signs: CIRCLE K MOTEL: FREE HBO; CHIEFTAIN MOTEL: VACANCY/ICE; 4-U MOTEL/APARTMENTS. A huge red banner stretched across the Howard Johnson: FREE HIGH-SPEED INTERNET.

Kristy's hand was a little ball of white knuckles on the gearshift. I felt strange and stirred up after seeing Mrs. Baker. I was going to be a doctor, for sure—just not a surgeon.

"Kristy, do you ever think about what you want to be? For a career. When you're older?"

"I have no flipping idea."

Kristy pulled into the parking lot of Paradise Liquors and drove around behind the building. A skanky guy stood next to the Dumpster.

"Kristy, what are you doing?"

Kristy didn't answer. She pulled up next to the guy, who lurched around as he jammed a little bundle into his pocket. The guy was wearing a dingy jacket and grimy jeans. He had surfer hair with long bleached bangs, but his face was creased and he had sores around his mouth. He was like a young man in an old man's body.

Kristy waved a folded bill between two fingers like she'd done this a thousand times. "Dude, buy me a six-pack of hard lemonade and you can keep the change."

He shifted his jaw back and forth, then snatched the

twenty. "Go park across the street under those trees. They got cameras here."

"If you don't come back," Kristy yelled after him, "you better watch out! My dad's a cop." Humming and looking around like she was at a shopping mall, Kristy pulled the car across the street and parked along the curb under the trees. The branches were covered with shiny pale leaves.

"Kristy, what are you doing? That guy's going to steal your money. Anyway, what are we going to do? Get drunk and go home? I'm sorry, but I have homework to do."

"Leah, don't be a douche."

She pressed her index finger against her mouth and watched in the rearview mirror. Five minutes later, the guy came around the side of the building. He pulled up his hood and jogged with a limp across the street, looking over his shoulder like a criminal on a cop show.

He leaned on the car roof with one hand, wheezed, and coughed up gunk. He wiped his mouth on his wrist, then held out the lemonade. "Look what I got."

"Thanks, dude," said Kristy, sighing, bored. The guy handed over the six-pack, then stuck his head in Kristy's window. "Hey, babe, let's party." His teeth were brown and broken like pieces of dirty dishes.

"In your dreams." Kristy hit the gas and the car screeched forward.

"You ran over my foot, bitch!" he yelled after her.

Kristy gunned the car down the street. A woman yanked a stroller out of the intersection.

I pressed back against my seat. "Watch out! Kristy, slow down. My God."

"Open me one," she said. "They're twist-off. That guy's breath smelled like shit."

"I'm not opening you one."

At a stoplight, she grabbed a bottle out of the cardboard carrier and opened it with her teeth. She drank half of it down. "OK!" she said, wiping her mouth. "Where to? God, I think I chipped my tooth."

"I don't know where you're going," I said, "but I'm going home. I'm sorry, but . . ."

Kristy ignored me. She turned onto the freeway, and we zoomed past downtown with its one ten-story skyscraper surrounded by little brick buildings.

She finished her lemonade, threw the bottle under my feet, and grabbed another one. I stuck the rest of the six-pack behind her on the floor of the backseat. She held the second bottle between her legs and wiggled her front tooth. "I think I actually chipped it!" she said.

Steering with her elbows, she opened the second bottle and stuck it in my face. "Cheers. Drink this. Don't be a pain in the ass."

I glared at her and took the bottle. It was sweet and syrupy. I was drinking hard lemonade, while Cindy got drunk on Chardonnay. Kristy stretched into the back and grabbed another bottle.

Her phone went off. "It's my mom."

She put the lemonade between her legs and took the first exit. "Hey, Mommy. . . . We're at Leah's. She's helping me with geometry. I'm having dinner over here. . . . Yes, very healthy. I think it's like pasta and salad . . . . Yeah, Mrs. Lobermeir knows I can't eat wheat. Yes, I'll thank her. Hi, Leah. That's from my mom. . . . OK, Mommy, I'll be home before nine, give Daddy a kiss, K. Bye."

She looked at me. "We're going to Damien Rogers's house."

"You don't even know where he lives."

"Victoria Miller figured it out. Relax. We didn't go in."

"Victoria Miller likes Damien Rogers?" Who was this girl slowly turning the wheel of her car while she chewed her gob of gum like a goat? I wanted to hit her. She and Corinne had always sworn: only I could like Damien Rogers.

"Not anymore. She's going out with Dwayne Lewis."

We passed Arapahoe High School. The mascot painted on their banner was supposed to be an Arapahoe man with a large crooked nose and a feather sticking off his head. Next to the school was a nail salon with a broken plastic sign.

Kristy swayed her shoulders to a song on the radio. She waved her bottle in time to the music and turned the wheel with the tips of her fingers. She chugged the second

121

lemonade and tossed the bottle onto the backseat. "Did you know Brian isn't my real dad?" she said.

"What are you talking about? Are you serious?"

She wasn't smiling. She squinted into the distance and felt around in her purse with one hand. "Damn it, are we out of cigarettes? Yeah, I'm serious."

"Are you sure?" I tried to remember if I'd seen any pictures of baby Kristy and her dad. Nope. A bittersweet pain like a beam from a flashlight shone around inside of me. Kristy didn't have a father, either? Mr. Baker was no more Kristy's dad than mine?

"Yes, I'm sure! I was at the wedding. I was like three. He adopted me. That's why I call him Daddy."

"You never told me that." We pulled up to a stoplight. I waited for the red light to blink off and the green to flash on, and drank half my lemonade. The sugar and the alcohol hit my bloodstream, and softness spread through my arms and legs. Mr. Baker was not Kristy's real dad. . . .

Kristy hummed along to the radio and drummed her fist against the steering wheel. She suddenly waved her little finger in my face. "Want to know what I want to be? When I grow up?"

"What?"

"I want to be . . . a fashion designer."

"What? You don't even know how to sew."

"It's the only thing I want to do. I found a school for

fashion in Florida. Mom says it's a great fit for me, and she says I can go."

"OK. Well, you better learn how to sew. And that is so weird about your dad. I can't believe you never told me before. Does Corinne know?"

Kristy looked over at me and bit her lip, trying not to smile.

"Were you kidding? You're messing with me. I don't want to go to Damien's." I didn't want to go anywhere. There was nowhere to go. "I want to go home."

"Yeah, I'm kidding!" Kristy fell giggling against her door. "I'm sorry!" She sat up and wiped her nose. "I just wanted to know if you ever wondered what your dad was like."

"You're a freak. No, I actually don't." Because he wasn't even a person to me. He was just Paul, a loser who died in a car crash and ruined our lives. He left me alone with an incompetent parent.

We drove through a neighborhood I'd never been in. Some kids ran through the yards and rode their bikes down the middle of the street. The sky behind the mountain turned orange. All the shadows were blue. We passed a house with a rusty swing set in the front yard and a big work truck in the driveway. Dandelions exploded in the yard.

"I want to go home," I said again. To the home inside my head.

"I don't know what I'd do without my dad. He's just

everything to me," Kristy said. She gnawed one of her knuckles. "I think I chipped my tooth. It feels funny. We just go three more blocks, turn left, and we're at Damien's."

"When were you there? Did you talk to him?" My vision blurred. There was a hammering somewhere in my body. "I don't want to go to his house."

"Tough!" She drove past a huge apartment building covered with chunky wood shingles and turned onto a street of small houses with big garages and driveways full of trikes, motorcycles, and old cars covered with tarps.

She stopped in front of a split-level with faded blue siding. An old van and a truck were parked out front beneath a crooked basketball hoop. On the main floor, in a yellow-lit kitchen, a family sat around a table.

A mob of little boys pulled up on their bikes and surrounded Kristy's car.

"What are you doing?" I said.

She hit the horn.

"Kristy! What are you doing? Stop it! Go! Go! Go!" I grabbed her wrist, but she wrestled away from me and pressed on the horn with both hands.

A dark-haired woman with bangs and a braid came to the window, shook her head, and lowered the blinds. I covered my face with my hands. My lungs were not working. I willed myself to lose consciousness, and everything got gray and fuzzy.

"There he is," said Kristy. "Leah, there's Damien."

I unpeeled my hands from my face. Damien Rogers filled the doorway of his house. He shook the dark hair out of his eyes and yelled, "What do you want? You're pissing off my mom."

Kristy looked over at me with a shy smile—she hadn't chipped her tooth—then she turned back to Damien and screamed, "Leah Lobermeir wants your body, Damien!"

She put the car into first, it jerked forward, then the engine died. She started it up again, and the little boys scattered. We shot down the street. She laughed so hard that tears streaked across her face.

Twenty-Two

Cindy was on the couch bundled in her terry-cloth sick robe. The TV was on, but the sound was off. She slowly turned and looked at me. Her eyes were puffy, and the tip of her nose was red. She had the blue-and-white shoe box of old pictures open on her knees. The wine box was on the coffee table.

She dropped the photos back into the shoe box. "Where were you?" She wiped her nose with a crumpled Kleenex and stared at a framed poster with cracked glass that she'd bought for a buck at a garage sale. Monet at the Denver Art Museum.

"Kristy's. I had dinner over there. We were doing homework."

"Why didn't you call?" Cindy dropped her head back against the couch and closed her eyes. Without lip gloss, her lips looked so thin.

"Sorry, we were really busy. And Kristy's mom talked to me for a long time. She said to tell you that she's thinking of you. She really likes you."

"That poor woman. It's so tragic." Water began to seep out the corners of Cindy's eyes. The tears rolled into her ears. She sopped the tears up with a tissue, then twisted the tissue and smiled. Her nose and eyes were swollen.

"Honey, maybe we should start going to church again. I'm a little down, Leah. Come play Yahtzee with me. We used to have so much fun! Just one game. Come on!"

"Mom, I can't play Yahtzee. I was helping Kristy with her homework. Now I need to do my own homework. I don't have time."

"Oh, Leah, come on. One game. I bet you can't beat me!" She tipped her head back and smiled at the ceiling.

"Maybe some other night." I shut my door.

I had a headache from the hard lemonade but decided that I was going to do my homework. I was going to do all of it. I needed to pull up my grades or I'd never get in to med school, and I'd end up drunk on a couch playing Yahtzee. I sat cross-legged facing the door and pulled out my notebooks and textbooks. I built a little fortress out of algebra and chemistry and Spanish and language arts. It was a red wall. All the textbooks were taped up in shiny Coke book covers.

"What are you doing in there?" Cindy's voice sounded fake and high-pitched. "Do you want me to wax your lip tonight?"

"No! I have to do my homework, OK?"

"That's fine," she said faintly. I heard the bottom of her glass scrape against the coffee table. "I'll just play a game of Yahtzee solitaire!" She rattled the dice in the plastic cup and threw them onto the table. "Damn!" she said. She shook the dice again.

I wrote five paragraphs about how literature contributes to society. I wrote that literature made people see things they couldn't see before, invisible stuff that was right in front of them. Mr. Calvino would like that. It drove him nuts that we only read excerpts. Only AP language arts got to read entire books and write whole papers.

I took out a probability test for algebra. The two-page stapled worksheet calmed me. I sharpened a pencil and read the first question: "*We know that there are six ways to get a total of seven with a pair of standard six-sided dice, and since . . .* " I read the problem three times and finally understood, and then it was like I disappeared.

While I was working on a problem about a village of 130 people where 60 percent of the people own cars and 55 percent of the car owners are male, Cindy quit shaking the dice. At first I thought she was hiccuping.

The sound of crying always made the hair stand up on my arms. She went, "Uh-huh-uh-huh-uh-huh," squeaked, then "Uh-huh-uh-huh-huh-huh-huh," then she kind of screamed. I opened my door a crack. She was curled up in a ball, rocking with her arms wrapped around her knees, the wineglass dangling from two fingers.

I quietly shut my door, sat back on my bed, and willed myself to figure out what percentage of women owned cars. My forehead was covered with sweat, and I could feel huge pit stains spreading accross my shirt. I read through "Brønsted Acids and Bases" twice. The chapter made me sweat even more, and my brain hurt. I went over it again. I'd talk to Carl about it. I read the first three books of *The Odyssey,* all about Penelope and her suitors and Telemachus's journey to find out if his father had died. I studied irregular Spanish verbs— *niego, niegas, niega, negamos, negáis, niegan.* The whole time I had to force myself to keep breathing. After forty-five minutes, Cindy stopped crying. I tipped over backward.

My face was numb with exhaustion. My heart felt hard. I had closed it against her. I couldn't play Yahtzee. I had to do my homework or I'd never have a plan or any kind of life and I'd never be a doctor.

At 9:30, I finished my homework. The apartment was

silent. I closed my Spanish textbook and looked at the cracked green walls a few feet on either side of me. I was as flattened as someone who'd just run a marathon.

Bruno Mars rippled shinily over me. When I had insomnia, his voice was the only thing that could get me to sleep. He sounded so calm, so cool . . . so sweet.

After a thirty-six-hour shift, I walked down a New York street. I was exhausted but still looked gorgeous in my blue scrubs. The wet sidewalk glittered with lights. I stepped into a café with low lights and candles lit in round red candleholders. I sat at a table in the back, where it was dark and private, so I could rest, get a salad, and go online. I'd just ordered a drink and opened my laptop when someone touched my shoulder. Startled, I spun around. It was Bruno Mars. He was wearing a black jacket and a red shirt. He looked stunned, as if he'd been searching for the girl he'd always dreamed of and finally . . . "Excuse me," he said. "Could I join you?"

"I'm thrilled to meet you, seriously," I said, "but I'm an intern and just got off a thirty-six-hour shift. Can I call you?"

"Of course, but please . . . tell me your name."

"Leah. And you're Bruno."

"God, that's a beautiful name. It's perfect for you. And, yeah, I'm Bruno." He laughed and wrote his number on a napkin that he tucked into the breast pocket of my scrubs while staring into my eyes. . . .

I got off my bed and stepped quietly into the living room. People laughed silently on the TV.

Cindy's head was thrown back as if she were exposing her neck for a vampire. Her mouth was open in a little O as though she'd been taken by surprise. She was wearing pink socks. I lifted her feet back onto the couch. I was careful about her bunion. I covered her with the blanket, picked up the wineglass, and turned off the TV. The carpet in front of the couch was soaked with wine. I threw a kitchen towel over it.

I washed and dried the wineglass and put it back in the cupboard. When the last wedding wineglass finally broke, Cindy would probably use it as an excuse to drink an entire box of wine in one sitting. I could just see her crying while I tried to study for finals.

A tiny spider struggled to keep its footing in the drain. This was not my stained sink with gray bits of meat stuck in the strainer. This was not my faded, water-spotted magazine picture of a meadow. This was not my wedding wineglass. I did not play Yahtzee. This was not me. This was not my life.

I opened the refrigerator and took out a package of cheese slices, a jar of mayonnaise, and bread. I made a cheese sandwich, swallowed it in two bites, then made another. I decided to eat until I was sick, and then the only thing I'd have to think about was how fat I was. That was simple. I could eat carrots and lettuce and cottage cheese. I could do Zumba with a DVD in the living room. I could spend my whole life trying to lose fifteen pounds.

I was halfway through the second sandwich when I remembered that I, or Ashley, was supposed to meet Kurt King at 10:45. I checked my phone; it blinked with messages.

I threw the rest of the sandwich in the garbage and went into the bathroom. I stared at the girl in the mirror. I saw my mouth, my eyes, my hair. I was a girl, just a girl, like any girl. I could have been named Ashley. I washed my face and armpits, put on my gold hoops and my double teardrop necklace, then went back into my room and shut the door. I put in my earbuds and blasted "Treasure" on my iPod. I whirled around. I went crazy in that tiny space.

When I stepped out of the apartment into the hallway, I had the fantastic feeling that I was leaving behind my crappy life. I could be anyone I wanted to be.

Twenty-Three

I jogged down the orange carpet through laugh tracks and the smell of burnt toast, then up the stairs. In the entry, Mrs. Martin was unlocking her mailbox.

She turned and looked me up and down. Her hazel eyes clicked to a stop at the sight of the neckline on the tank I was wearing under my hoodie. She was old, but her brown freckled face was smooth and unwrinkled. She wore orange lipstick and her white hair in a tight bun, and got a manicure once a week. She was a retired principal.

"Where do you think you're going this time of night?"

I stuffed my hands in the pockets of my hoodie and smiled the empty polite smile I gave adults when I wanted to be invisible. "Hi, Mrs. Martin. My mom's really sick. I'm going to Safeway for cold medicine."

Her huge eyes blinked. She did not smile back. "Watch yourself. It's after curfew."

"Oh, I will. Thanks, Mrs. Martin. See you later." I pushed through the door and headed out into the night. Mrs. Martin watched me walk down Vargas.

I had ten minutes to kill and actually did go into the Safeway. They were about to close. I had no money and wandered around the store like a shoplifter. I stopped at the baby-food display. The little jars looked so colorful and enticing but contained substances like mashed green beans and liquefied bananas. Sometimes I got to feed Jimmy. I loved scooping up stuff like sweet potatoes and bringing the rubberized spoon to his tiny open mouth. His breath smelled like icing.

A woman stepped in front me, grabbed five jars of pureed beef, and tossed them into her cart beneath a car seat. A scrawny little girl, clutching a Barbie, straggled after her. The kid was probably a little tired since it was ten thirty on a school night.

In Florida, the grocery store was called Piggly Wiggly. I'd hang on to the side of the metal cart so I wouldn't lose Cindy in one of the long, narrow aisles packed with people in shorts and flip-flops. Sometimes in the parking lot, while she loaded me into the car, she'd accidentally burn me with her cigarette. She'd scream at me for crying. She was always lost in thought, her eyes shiny and blind, her teeth buried in her lip. I wanted to fix whatever was wrong. I wanted to make her happy. I liked school back then. It was peaceful to sit in rows with other kids, scratching in workbooks with a pencil. The cafeteria was warm and smelled like sour milk. Everyone got reduced-price lunches. It was hot in Florida, and the air was swampy. I never saw the ocean. I turned ten, Cindy quit smoking and we moved to Colorado.

At the end of the aisle, I saw a flash of blue uniforms. Cops with little plastic baskets were shopping for their midnight snack. When they turned down the cereal aisle, I headed for the door. If the cops were bored, they'd bust me for curfew.

At ten thirty on a weeknight, Tenth Avenue was bleak lights and empty parking lots, all lonely and end-of-the-worldish. The sky was dark blue, a mess of stars. Black mountains, dotted with lights, bulged into the sky on the edge of the town.

The 7-Eleven sign lit up the end of the block. It suddenly occurred to me that I wasn't Ashley. I stopped, feeling the darkness all around me, and tried to feel who I was. Cars honked; the light turned green. The lights in the Safeway went off.

Twenty-Four

The black Mustang, parked at a slant, took up three spaces in the 7-Eleven parking lot.

Kurt King leaned against the brick wall. He was wearing a black T-shirt, black jeans. I felt for the tube of lip gloss in my pocket and smeared some on. I held in my stomach and walked closer. I stopped and looked up at him from the potholed parking lot. White light flooded from the store, but the edges of the parking lot were black.

He pinched his cigarette, took a long drag, then flicked the butt so that it arced like a tiny firebomb over the Mustang; we both watched it. He turned without a smile and looked me up and down. He was chewing something tiny. "You again."

I ran my fingertips across my forehead. "Ashley couldn't come tonight. She told me to tell you."

"Where's Ashley at? She's supposed to be here."

"She couldn't come." I tried not to blush or smile. We knew each other. I'd ridden in his car. We talked almost every night. I talked with my regular voice, my Leah voice, the one he didn't recognize.

"So you could come, but Ashley couldn't. How come?"

"She got grounded."

He shook his bangs out of his eyes and tipped his head back against the bricks.

I was sweating and my mind began to blur. I yawned uncontrollably, got something in my eye, turned away, and tried to rub my eye without smearing my mascara. "Sorry . . ." My phone buzzed in my hoodie pocket; I turned it off.

Kurt King squinted at me with his mouth open, his arms folded across his chest. His fingers played piano on his arm. One side of his mouth tilted up in a kind of smile. I couldn't tell if he was laughing at me. He picked a piece of tobacco off his tongue. He slid the bottom of his boot back and forth over the concrete.

"Well, you just keep poppin' up. So, what's going on tonight?" He ran a finger across his upper lip and smiled real slowly. He knew that he looked like a movie star. He watched me watch him.

"Nothing's going on. I just came to tell you . . ."

"Want to hang out?" He stepped down off the curb into the parking lot.

It was bizarre talking to him in real life after talking to him so many times on the phone. I could only look at him for a few seconds at a time before I had to look down at the gravel clotted in tar. I felt the cold air on my neck and chest, turned away, and zipped up my hoodie. He laughed.

"Let's move out of this light. It's too bright." He touched the small of my back with his hand. I felt electricity shoot in all directions. We moved toward the Mustang.

With the lights behind him, I couldn't see his face, just the outline of his shaggy hair, the slant of his cheekbones. But I could feel him. "Let's go for another ride. That was a good time." The Mustang gleamed in the light from the store. It had just been washed.

"I have to go."

"Where you got to go? You don't want to go for a ride? Well, then, come out back with me for a minute. There's a nice place I like to sit and have a smoke. They got lilacs blooming. Don't be shy. Come on, have a smoke with me."

He strolled across the parking lot and called over his shoulder, "Don't you disappear on me. You took off like a little scared rabbit last time." His boots clicked on the asphalt. He headed into the darkness beyond the lights of the store.

I felt completely alone with the sound of my own

breathing. Not a thought in my head. And then Anita flashed through my mind with her chin out and her arms crossed. "Don't be an idiot." But Kristy would go. Corinne wouldn't, but Kristy would run back, laughing and flinging her hair over her shoulders. *I know him,* I thought. *I talk to him almost every night. I rode in his car and nothing happened. He's just a guy.*

A car full of junior girls pulled into the parking lot, did a slow U-turn, and left. Kurt King stepped out of sight. I followed him. A chain-link fence rang alongside the alley. Security lights blazed by the store's back door.

A scraggly lilac bush hung over a low cement wall that ran behind the Dumpster. Kristy, Corinne, and I had waited here when he bought us beer. Kurt King sat down on the wall, leaned back, stretched out his legs. He shook the hair out of his eyes. "Sit down. What'd I tell you? We got lilacs."

He offered his pack of cigarettes. I tried to pull one out but couldn't, so he shook one into my hand. He held out his lighter. I leaned forward, and the flame lit up my face. I felt like a woman, a movie star. I remembered how he'd held my cheek and said, "Thanks, sweetheart." I wondered if he'd kiss me. I saw myself sitting in a café with Bruno Mars. He reached out to touch my hair. . . .

My body tingled like every cell had lit up. I wasn't exactly happy, but I was alive. It was different. I was somewhere else.

No Cindy, no crappy little apartment, no Kristy. There was me. Leah. I was dreaming, wide awake and dreaming, the best place to be.

A delivery truck pulled around. The truck backed up, beeping, blowing out clouds of exhaust. A man dropped down from the cab, threw open the back, and started unloading crates. The man was bald with big ears and a belly that hung over his belt. He looked like somebody's dad. He carried the crates across a crooked rectangle of light that fell from the store's open door.

"So." Kurt King softly punched my arm. "Talk to me. Tell me about Ashley."

A familiar sadness snaked through my excitement. I crossed my arms, blew smoke away from him. "Oh, Ashley? Ashley's fine."

"Me and her talk every day. I saw her. I talked to her downtown last weekend," said Kurt King. He lifted his arms and stretched back his shoulders. "I want to get something going with that girl."

The delivery man grabbed a crate, stopped for a minute outside the light, and squinted at us, a teenage girl and a man smoking in the dark by the Dumpster. He snorted, bit down hard on his gum, and hauled the crate into the store.

Kurt King moved closer so that his thigh pressed against my thigh. "Listen . . . you know that Ashley. I'm not in love with her or anything. I'm just curious. The girl sends out certain signals. I just want to check in and clarify the situation. You know, you send out different signals. You strike me as a girl with a steady boyfriend, a guy I wouldn't want to mess with. Am I right?"

"Maybe."

His arm came to rest around my shoulders, and his fingertips stroked the top of my arm through the hoodie. The toe of his cowboy boot slowly tapped against the asphalt. The leather of his boot was worn almost white.

I was struck silent by the heat and hardness of a grown male body pressed against mine. The weight and warmth of his arm lay across my shoulders. I could feel him breathing, could feel his ribs through his shirt, his bony hip, his leather belt. I breathed in the smell of cigarettes, beer from his breath, a whiff of BO when he moved. His fingers were still stroking my arm. He made little circles on my arm like he was daydreaming. Even Kurt King could see Damien Rogers's mark on me. I wondered how long it would be before Damien Rogers held me like this.

"You know that Ashley," he said again. "She's not so special. She's no more special than you are." He ran his thumb across my cheek. Nerve endings from every part of my body followed that rough thumb.

I looked up into his face. My eyes had adjusted to the

darkness. A stranger with a bristly chin stared down the front of my hoodie. He had wrinkles around his eyes, and his breath smelled like onions.

"I got to go."

His hand slid down my arm onto my wrist. He pulled my arm behind my back. "You're not going anywhere."

Then: "Just kidding," he said. He let go.

I jumped up and turned around to face him, my arms crossed over my chest. I walked backward, glancing over my shoulder for potholes so I didn't trip and fall. "How old are you? Why don't you date people your own age? Ashley's too young for you."

He spit, shook his head, laughed at the ground between his knees. He got up, stepped into the light, smiled. "Don't be like this. Why you being like this? I'm not too old for Ashley. Man, I'm, like . . . I'm twenty-two."

"Yeah, right. Ciao, Mr. Corduroy."

"Ciao? Mr. Corduroy? What kind of jackass name is that? You tell Ashley that Kurt King wants to see her and he's a real gentleman."

"Gotcha, Mr. Corduroy. I'll tell Ashley straightaway."

The truck door slammed shut. Its engine roared, and the truck backed up and drove down the alley. Except for a buzzing electrical box, it was quiet. The back door of the store closed. I kept walking backward down the alley toward the street.

"What's with the jackass name? Hey, hey, hey . . . stop."
He shook his head and rubbed his thumb against his chin. "I
offended you, but I don't know what I did. Come on, come
sit with me. Man, I'm having a hard night. Come here, come
on back."

"I got to go." But I stopped.

He held his hands up like an outlaw giving himself up.
He took two steps toward me. "Honey, I don't know how I
blew it here. What did I do wrong? Listen, how about this?
Come here for a sec." He tipped up his chin. "I'll tell you a
secret. But you got to tell me one. Come on."

I stood where I was, but felt it. It was like being pulled by
an invisible rope. "What's the secret?" Maybe the secret was
that Kristy wasn't so gorgeous after all. She was blond but
kind of scrawny. You, on the other hand . . .

"Don't be mad at me." He walked toward me and slowly
reached out, his hand all veins and fingers and smooth brown
skin. He ran a finger along my throat. I felt myself loosen at
his touch, and it made me feel crazy because I didn't know
what it meant—like was it fate? Was this what fate felt like?
My head ached and my skin tingled and my brain felt sleepy
and I didn't know.

"OK. Tell me the secret."

"My secret is . . ." Kurt King grinned and shook his head.
"My secret is that I'm not really twenty-two. I'm twenty-six.
OK, I'm fessing up. And the other secret is—I'll tell you

two secrets—I just broke up with my girl. She's pregnant by another dude. Man, it was ugly. Broke my heart."

"Sorry to hear it. I have to go." His face was in shadow. We were between the brick wall and the chain-link fence, and it was late and dark, and it had gotten cold. The darkness felt thick and heavy, like something I'd have to fight to get through.

He stepped toward me. He breathed on my forehead, and his hands touched my hair. No one in my whole life had ever touched me that gently. My nose brushed his chest, and I could smell him. It was like life had snatched me up and thrown me into a boiling river.

"You got to tell me a secret," he said into my hair. "Fair is fair."

I had so many secrets. My mother got drunk on wine every night. I lived in a crappy little apartment. My dad was dead. I weighed 182 pounds. I was in love with Damien Rogers. I both loved and hated Kristy. I disliked lots of people but I hardly ever showed it. I usually smiled. I didn't have Internet access. I missed Anita Sotelo. I loved Dr. Seuss. I wanted to be a doctor.

I closed my eyes. Kurt King was rocking me back and forth like we were dancing.

"I want to know where she lives."

Kristy, Kristy, Kristy. It always came back to Kristy. She

was like a radioactive substance that had contaminated the entire world.

I pulled away. "Why don't you ask her?"

"Why don't you just tell me? I know you know." A chunk of streaked bangs hung between his eyes and made him look crazy and cross-eyed. "Man, don't take offense that I'm into her. She's a beautiful girl. I even got her on my phone."

He pulled a cell phone out of his front pocket. He had a cheap flip phone just like mine. He opened it, the screen lit up, and there was Kristy, one inch tall, standing under a streetlight in the parking lot at Torrance Park. She was wearing her pink spaghetti-strap tank. Her hair swirled in a crazy white cloud around her.

I touched the screen. There was tiny Kristy lit up with electricity. "You have her picture."

He snapped the phone shut. "The girl just does something for me." He ran his hand over my side and pinched my stomach. "Just like your boyfriend's into fat girls."

My face felt icy, then boiling hot.

"You're a creep."

He spit over his shoulder and wiped his mouth with the back of his hand. "Whatever you say, fat girl." He shook back his bangs and reached for my arm. "Come on. I'll give you a ride."

I jerked away. I ran with my arms tight across my chest.

After two blocks, I had to quit—my lungs burned and I couldn't breathe. Every block, I stopped and turned back to see if he was following, but there were just lights, parked cars, empty streets, and shadows. He never even asked me my name.

Twenty-Five

The only sound in the building was the sizzle from the fluorescent tube lights. The door to #3 was ajar.

The lights were blazing. Mrs. Martin and Cindy sat together on the couch with their knees touching. They looked up at me.

Mrs. Martin got to her feet. "I'll go and let you two work this out."

"Thank you for your concern, Frances." Cindy blew her nose.

Mrs. Martin walked out of the apartment without giving me another glance.

Cindy had a long red crease on her left cheek, and her makeup was smudged in grainy streaks under her bloodshot eyes. Her hair bunched on one side. The living room reeked like wine. "Close the door. Lock it," she said through her teeth.

I mechanically turned around, pushed the door shut, and rotated the dead bolt. The lines in the fake wood were too even, too regular. It looked so phony.

"Turn around! Look at me!" She stumbled to her feet, her hands in fists, and screamed in a whisper, "Where were you?"

"I was on a walk."

The crazier she acted, the more numb I felt. When my face got vacant and expressionless, she became even more psychotic.

"I am so embarrassed." She cupped both hands over her face and swayed. Her robe came open. She was wearing a black T-shirt and purple underwear. She had such skinny legs, such pointy, bony knees. "You left the door unlocked! Mrs. Martin came in and woke me up. I have never been so humiliated! Where were you?"

"Nowhere. I went on a walk."

"You went on a walk? Bullshit! Were you drinking? Were you smoking pot? I want to smell your breath!" She tried to tie her robe, but her hands were shaking too badly.

"Mom, I was walking! I wanted to clear my head, so I went on a walk."

"A walk at eleven thirty at night? I never heard such crap!" She staggered and hiccuped a sob like Jimmy did when he was exhausted. "I called three times and you didn't pick up! Who were you with? Are you slutting around? Were you meeting a boy?"

"No!"

"You could be killed! You could be raped or murdered. Give me your phone! You are under house arrest!" The people in the apartment above ours banged on their floor.

"No way."

"You are grounded for two weeks! Two weeks! And I promise that I will be calling on the hour to make sure that you are here. Now give me your phone! It's confiscated!" She lunged at me, her eyes blazing and insane, and snatched at my phone. "Give me your phone! I am the parent! I am in charge here!"

She was not in charge, and there was no way in hell that I was going to let her see the texts from Kurt King. And find out about Ashley. I jumped over the coffee table, ran into my room, slammed the door shut, and locked it. She hammered on the door. "Leah, open this door! Open this door!" The door wobbled against its loose hinges. It was hollow and already splintered at the bottom from a kick. She was gone for a minute, then hit the door with what sounded like a saucepan.

"Don't you defy me!" she shrieked. *Bang, bang, bang* went the ceiling.

She whapped the door a few more times, then leaned against it and cried. I sat against the bottom of the door and listened to her. After a few minutes, she moaned, "Oh . . . the hell with it." She shuffled across the hall. Her door shut.

My phone blinked with messages. I turned it off and sat on the end of my bed like I was waiting for a bus, listening for the total silence that meant Cindy was passed out. It took forty-five minutes, during which I barely moved. My head crackled with static.

I snuck out of my room and then out of the apartment, up the stairs, and back down the orange carpet under the fluorescent lights, past Mrs. Martin's door, and out through the entryway, where someone had dumped a hundred flyers for a pizza company.

In the dark parking lot, I wedged the phone under the rear tire of a red truck. I knew the owner left for work at six. He'd run over my phone and destroy it. The calls and texts from Kurt King would stop, and no one would ever find out what I'd done.

I opened Cindy's door. She was asleep on her back with her legs bare, but I didn't go and cover her. I fell asleep in my clothes with my head buried under pillows.

Twenty-Six

It was all over. My phone was mashed into black plastic shards and wires in the Belmont Manor parking lot on Tuesday morning. That night I'd tell Cindy, "Mom, I accidentally dropped my phone in the parking lot and it got run over." She'd be pissy about it, but she wouldn't be able to read my texts, and I would never have to talk to Mr. Corduroy again.

In second period, Carl Lancaster was waiting for me. I brushed past him, dumped my books on the lab table. "Carl, I don't get this lab at all and I'm tired. Can you just do it?" He stood quietly, waiting for me to look at him, but I stared at the floor.

"It's really easy, Leah. It's just a titration."

"I'm sorry. I'm just really tired."

"Sure," he said finally. He did the lab and explained what he was doing, and I wrote down what he told me to. I didn't learn a thing, but it was restful—it was very peaceful, sitting nearby while Carl Lancaster worked. "Done," he said.

"Thanks, Carl." I dropped my lab report, we both bent down to pick it up, and our hands and heads touched. We stood up and didn't look at each other. Kristy made a noise and wiggled her tongue at us.

At the end of class, Kristy skipped out, cackling with Victoria Miller. Carl said, "I'm going this way, anyway," and began walking with to me to language arts. I knew his next class was in the opposite direction. I didn't look at him but felt him beside me. It felt like pressure building up, a chemical reaction, something about to explode.

I stopped in the middle of the hallway. "What are you doing, Carl? No." I stared straight ahead until I felt him disappear.

I walked the rest of the way alone, pushed, jostled, my insides burning and hollow, and whispered to Carl inside my head. *I'm sorry, Carl. I'm sorry. I'm sorry. I'm sorry. I just can't do this.*

I sat down in language arts. Dan Manke breathed into my hair with his chewing-tobacco breath. "Saw you in the hallway with Lancaster. Ooooh, Fat-Ass has a boyfriend."

Mr. Calvino read an excerpt of *The Odyssey* out loud. He read slowly, pausing and stretching out words, like he'd fallen into the story and we weren't even there. He looked up and found thirty kids staring at him like he was insane. Only LaTeisha and I didn't stare. I fiddled with my pencil.

"Oh, my apologies," he said. "I got a little carried away by the language. Let me check my pacing guide and see what my instructional best practice should be."

Mr. Calvino jumped off his desk, and his striped oxford shirt came untucked from his orange pants. He popped open a Diet Coke. He guzzled the entire can, and his huge New Jersey Adam's apple bobbed up and down on his unshaven neck.

He swung around and raised his fist. "That was a literacy event, kids. An act of literacy, as the Colorado Board of Education likes to phrase it!"

"You're so cute, Mr. Calvino," said LaTeisha. "Can I read the class my favorite passage? It's from Book Twenty-Three, when Penelope and Odysseus reunite after twenty years, but she doesn't recognize him at first because he looks so nasty." Mr. Calvino was giving us thirty extra-credit points for reading the whole book.

"Yes, LaTeisha! Bless you, LaTeisha. Yes, please read."

LaTeisha serenely smiled as she paged through her text. She had dozens of Post-it notes stuck between the pages and an emerald chip on a gold band on her ring finger.

*   *   *

Before lunch, I stood with Kristy at her locker. It felt like a hundred years since I last saw her, but it was only Tuesday and yesterday had been Monday, and that was the day Kristy's mom unzipped her PJs and showed me her scar, and that was the day that Kristy drove to Damien Rogers's house and screamed that I wanted his body, and the same day I met Kurt King in the parking lot of 7-Eleven at 10:45, but that was like a dream.

It was like a dream, except that he had her picture on his phone. It was a picture from the night she wore her tank top and no jacket, even though it was cold. Every time he turned on his phone, he saw Kristy.

I lifted a tangled curl of Kristy's hair. "You're getting a rat's nest."

"God, don't touch me." Kristy jerked away and smoothed her hair. It was flat and snarled. Since I'd seen her the day before, she'd painted her fingernails a bright metallic blue and put on thick blue eyeliner that made her eyes look even smaller. She had purple rings under her eyes. Her face looked skinny and her nose even bigger than usual. Her camisole was inside out.

"My God, just look at them." Kristy squinted across the hall. "He's using her. If he really liked her, he'd ask her to be his girlfriend."

Corinne stood with her head tipped back as she smiled up into Jason Coulter's sunburned face. He had a long scrape on his arm from the last baseball game. The video shot of him sliding into home plate had played on the school's daily news show in a repeating loop both mornings that week.

The crowd in the hallway suddenly opened up. Kelsey Parker and her friends made their way through the mob.

Kristy stiffened. Her chest and neck got splotchy. "Hey, Kelsey," she said, waving her little hand.

Kelsey glanced at Kristy. "Skank," she said, and continued with her friends down the hall.

"Wow, I wonder what's up with her. Hope everything's OK. She's usually so sweet." Kristy tore at the lacy neckline of her camisole and stared after Kelsey and her friends.

"Are you kidding? She's always like that."

"Not to me, bitch. She and I are actually pretty close." Kristy yanked open her locker door and all her stuff slid onto the floor. She crouched down and picked up a folder. "Damn it! Could you help?"

"Sure," I said. "But I don't want to be late for lunch. They ran out of pizza yesterday." I set down my books, tugged up the back of my jeans, knelt, and started packing the stuff back in. Kristy stood up.

"Kristy, I'm not doing this all by myself." I picked up purple pens, broken pencils, notebooks with glittery covers, the backs scribbled on in purple pen in her huge, messy handwriting. She dotted her *i*'s with circles, sometimes hearts. Candy wrappers, candy-flavored lip gloss, a pink comb, hair bands, a bottle of dried-up green nail polish. It was all little-kid junk.

"Quit looking through my shit!" said Kristy. She glared at Corinne and Jason Coulter. Jason bent over Corinne, who was pressed against the lockers. "Jesus, get a room!"

"Come on, Kristy, leave them alone. I closed her locker door and stood up with my books. "You're welcome."

Corinne pulled herself out from under Jason and trotted over with her hands folded under her chin. She joyfully clicked her nails together. "He wants me to go to his game a week from tomorrow and then we'll hang out afterward. I'll probably be able to go!"

"Great. Fantastic. Wonderful for you, Corinne." Kristy turned, unsmiling.

Corinne immediately adopted a serious expression, though her face was still rosy with happiness. "Kristy, is everything OK? You look really tired. How's your mom?"

Kristy coughed, opened her locker door, then kicked it shut. "Not great, Corinne. Not great. They put her on more pain meds, and now she's doing really inappropriate behavior. I'm like, Mom, I know you're really sick and everything, but could you please try to keep it together when my friends are around?"

I dropped my head down. "Yeah, yesterday when I was over, Kristy's mom unzipped her pajamas and showed me her surgery scar. It goes from here to here." I put one hand on my neck and the other on my stomach. "It looks really painful. . . ."

"Why are you lying, you dumb fat bitch?" Kristy stared at me.

Keeping her eyes on me, she said, "Don't listen to Chubs, Corinne. For whatever reason, maybe because she has such a boring life, Leah loves making up stories. But she doesn't bother to stick around and see if my mom is OK when she goes to the emergency room. That shit is sick, Leah."

There was a tile missing next to my foot. Gravel, hair, and the shreds from the edges of notebook paper were stuck to the dirty adhesive. Heat spread over my body. My face felt like it was boiling. But what could I say? The scrawny little bitch's mom was dying, and this was my punishment for pretending to be a skinny girl with long blond hair. Kristy shoved her face into mine. She obviously hadn't brushed her teeth because her breath was terrible. "Keep away from my mom," she said. She took off at a jog down the hall.

Corinne covered her face with both hands. "God, she's so crazy! Can't we have one day of peace? Leah, she's losing her mind. I just feel so sorry for her. . . ." She gave me a hug and trotted after Kristy.

"I'll talk to her!" she called over her shoulder.

Kristy was just turning the corner with her hair flying.

She yelled, "We'll save you lots of pizza, Fatty!" Corinne caught up with her, and they disappeared.

I stood as if paralyzed and studied the cover of my notebook until everyone in the hallway was gone. A fluorescent tube sizzled and popped over my head, and the light went out.

The assistant principal came winging around the corner and blew his whistle. "What are you doing in the hall? You're either supposed to be in class or at lunch." He stared up at the ceiling. "When did that damn thing go?"

The assistant principal had a beefy face with a thin topping of carefully combed brown hair. It was only eleven o'clock in the morning and he already had a five o'clock shadow. His white polyester shirt had yellow sweat stains in the armpits. The shirt stretched so tightly over his chest and belly, you could see his nipples through his sleeveless undershirt. He had one thing going for him—dark-blue eyes with black lashes. The story was that he'd once been a track star and prom king at our high school.

"I have lunch now, but I feel sick."

There was a ripple in the blue of his eyes; possibly it was sympathy. "Grab your stuff. Let's go to the office. We can try to get ahold of a parent."

"My mom can't be reached except in an emergency. Maybe I could just lie down for a while."

I followed him down the dingy pathways of hell and

became mesmerized by the jingle of his keys and by the jaunty movement of his butt in his black polyester pants. He walked like a jock.

He led me into the office. The office lady looked at me over her bifocals. "What's wrong with this one?"

"I found her in the hall. She said she's too sick to eat lunch. She looks a little off to me."

It was the office lady with the drawn-on eyebrows, orange hair teased in a fluffy cloud, and armloads of silver jewelry.

"Follow me, sweetheart," she said. She led me to the nurse's room and frowned at her tiny turquoise-studded watch. "The nurse will be back from lunch in twenty minutes. Lie down until she comes."

I set my backpack on the floor and lay on the cot. I closed my eyes. Faint noises came through the half-open door—the phone ringing, the whir of the copy machine, a blur of voices. Maybe if the nurse documented what an incompetent mother I had, the authorities would let me live in this room, at least temporarily.

I'd put up Bruno Mars posters. I could eat breakfast and lunch here and just skip dinner and get skinny. The toilet always worked in the teachers' bathroom, and they brought in lotion and antibacterial soap. There was junk food stashed in the teachers' lounge. After all the sports and clubs and community ed meetings had ended, I'd run up and down the halls and sing Bruno Mars songs at the top of my lungs.

When there was a home game against Arapahoe, I'd watch from the center of the stands. I'd sit there just like the senior girl Stacy Ross, who always wore tight baby-blue turtlenecks. She sat on the bleachers perfumed by Obsession and her own perfection like she was the queen and the whole world and everything in it honeycombed off her.

During a time-out, Damien Rogers would look up at the crowd and spot me. He'd stare and think, *Where do I know that girl from?* After the game, he'd push past Kristy to get to me. Because everyone had finally realized that Kristy wasn't really beautiful. She was just an ordinary kid and way too skinny.

I was woken by someone shaking my shoulder. "Come on, sweetheart. Sit up."

It was the school nurse, who did double duty as the school counselor. She told the kids to call her Shannon. She had freckles, brown eyes, and red hair cut in a seventies shag. She sometimes wore purple mascara. "Open up. Sorry about that, the ear thermometer is broken."

Shannon had black circles under her eyes. She was old, at least forty, but everyone said she stayed up late smoking pot. She knew the words to every song in the musical *Rent* and sang them as she walked through the hallways.

"OK, open up. . . . Let's see. . . . You've got a slight, a very slight, temp. We can't get ahold of your mom? Most places allow parents to pick up sick kids. It's kind of the law."

I pushed my hair behind my ears. "My mom works for an asshole."

"Oh, that's too bad! We'll just skip it, then. I'll write a note that you should probably stay home tomorrow so you can rest and your body can fight this off. Probably a virus."

I sighed and shrugged as if I were disappointed. "I'll give it to my mom."

"Just go back to sleep," said Shannon. She patted my forehead and left her hand there for twenty blissful seconds. Then she briskly stood up, turned off the lights, and stopped in the doorway. "I'll wake you when school's over."

A dream catcher slowly turned over the cot. A little gray-and-white feather ruffled in blowing air I couldn't feel.

Shannon would be an OK mom, though probably annoying. We'd have hummus and carrot sticks for dinner too many nights, and she'd read my texts when I was asleep, for sure. Cindy could have been a cool mom, but she was too busy drinking wine and painting her nails.

There was a commotion outside the door. Shannon stuck her head in. "Leah, sorry to bug you, but we need to store some boxes for Mrs. McCleary until the end of school. OK, sir, right in here. Sorry, it's our sickroom!" A skinny man in blue pants wheeled in some boxes and stacked them in the corner of the room. The boxes appeared to contain slides, test tubes, a couple of new microscopes. Mrs. McCleary was going to be thrilled.

He paused on his way out and looked down at me. "Got anything catching?"

"Yep." I coughed hard so he'd leave. The door shut. I was alone.

Twenty-Seven

Shannon woke me at 1:50. I hunched on the edge of the cot for a few minutes, then stuck my feet into my shoes and picked up my backpack.

Anita stood in front of the office counter. She was wearing a Black Veil Brides T-shirt and was balancing a stack of graphic novels against her stomach. When she saw me, she blinked real slowly. She opened her mouth and moved her jaw around like she had a jaw ache. She looked away from me and stared at the giant district calendar that hung behind the secretary's desk.

For a second, I couldn't move or speak. I started to count. If I got to a hundred and twenty and she didn't look over and say something, I'd leave and never try to talk to her again.

One, two, three—I counted silently in my head like I was doing sit-ups. At ninety-three, she turned back to me.

She looked me over like she was trying to assess whether or not I was human. She'd gotten her nose pierced and had a tiny blue stone in her left nostril. "What are you doing here? You sick?" she said.

I sniffed, swallowed, tried to think of words to say. Yes. I was sick. My backpack sagged in my arms. I was so sick of myself and life in general that I was about to tip over. "You got your nose pierced."

She tossed back her bangs. "Yeah, so? I saved up. My dad said he didn't care as long as I paid for it. He finally took me down to Dragon's Lair. He had to sign. They say you won't feel anything, but it hurt like a son of a bitch. The dude did it really slow. . . ."

"Doesn't it cost like fifty bucks?" Anita and I seemed to be having a conversation. I walked out from behind the counter. "Where'd you get the money?"

"I babysit for two hours every morning before school. My neighbor has to leave for work at five, so I wait in her apartment until the grandma gets there. I just sit there, wake the kids, get them dressed, make them breakfast."

"You do?"

"Yes, I do," she said in a singsong. She looked hard at me for a minute, then ran her fingers through her bangs and squeezed her hair into a ponytail. She looked briskly around the room. "Where the hell are all the office ladies?"

She turned and headed out, then stopped in the doorway. She said over her shoulder, "You riding the bus?"

I nodded. We pushed through the steel doors and walked down the cracked sidewalk through the crowd of kids. Neither of us said anything. I followed her up the steps of the bus. Anita sat down in the back and moved over by the window. I sat next to her.

Anita folded her hands on top of the books, stared out the window, and took a quick breath through her nose. The bus jerked forward. She talked slowly so I would catch every word.

"You have been acting like a shit. Are we friends or not? Do you consider me a weirdo you don't want to be seen with? Decide." She turned and looked at me.

I slid down in the seat. I was close to throwing up. Something pulsed like neon in my forehead—I could feel it with my hand. I squeezed my eyes shut. "I've been a total bitch and a complete asshole. . . ."

"I'm not going to argue with you," she said, "but could you lay off the melodrama? Just don't treat me like garbage."

I opened my eyes. "OK. I'm sorry." I forced myself to turn and look at her. "I am so, so sorry, Anita. You are a really good friend and I've just—"

Mikey Peterson hung over the seat back and stuck his bristly head and wire-covered teeth between us. "Whas up, Anita? Whas up, Fat-Ass?"

Anita rapped him on the head with her knuckles. "Go back to your kennel, Mikey."

"Ow, dang it, Anita, you didn't have to do that!" He fell back into his seat.

She slid down. "Oh my God, I think he's crying," she whispered. "I'm so tired." Anita's eyes were huge; her face was papery. Even her hair looked exhausted.

"Are you sure you're not anemic from being vegan? Your nose looks a little red around the stud. You might have . . ."

"God, quit with the doctor stuff. I'm fine." She closed her eyes.

"You are such a good friend." And she was. The kindest, most interesting, most encouraging friend I'd ever had, and I barely knew her. And I'd ditched her. It made me feel hollow to know what I was capable of.

"Nah . . ." she said. "Now chill. Just chill, Leah. As long as you don't start pulling that crap again, we're cool."

Anita opened her eyes and traced the outline of the person on the cover of her book with the tip of her finger. The bus pulled into the street. There were a couple minutes of somewhat uncomfortable silence. She shrugged, as if uninterested. "So, what's been going on?"

The bus went over a pothole and I fell into the aisle. Anita pulled me back onto the seat.

My chemistry textbook in its red book cover poked out the broken zipper of my backpack. On the edge of the cover, in little tiny print, I'd written *Carl Lancaster.* "Let me think. . . ."

The bus stopped at a red light. A black Mustang turned in front of the bus toward the school.

I looked out the back window, but there was another bus behind us.

"Leah?"

Anita was real, with her black bangs scattered across her forehead, her crooked bottom teeth, and her brown eyes that glowed — there was a person inside, and she saw the person in me. She glittered she was so real. The whole world glittered. Before it had been liquid and dreamy like a movie, and I could slip in and out of it, but the world had crystallized, and everything had become hard and sharp and solid.

"Leah, what's wrong?"

I breathed with difficulty and could barely keep my eyes open. "I'm kind of having a panic attack. This guy just drove past. He keeps calling. . . ."

"What guy?" she said. "Is it that thirty-year-old?"

"Yeah."

She straightened her shoulders against the back of the

seat. "Tell him to piss off. If he tries anything, sock him in the balls."

I had a pounding headache in my forehead where the neon had been. I dropped my face into my hands and breathed in the smell of salt and erasers. "Good idea."

She shook my shoulder. "Hey, hey, look at me. Listen. Stay away from the dude. Block his calls."

"I put my phone in the parking lot where a truck would run over it. I did it so I wouldn't have to talk to him anymore."

Anita winced. "OK. You know, you could have just blocked him."

I pulled my backpack onto my knees and hugged it. I pressed my forehead against the seat back in front of us. The seats were covered with vinyl stamped with swirls like fingerprints you could barely see. My throat ached like someone had died. But Anita was alive and humming an old Weezer song next to me.

I lifted my face. "I love that song."

Twenty-Eight

Cindy poked her head into my room. She had green rings under her eyes. "You sure don't look sick," she said. She got stressed when I was sick because her health insurance had a high deductible.

"The nurse said I had a temperature. I'm just going by what the nurse said."

"Let me feel!" She scooted between the dresser and the bed in her purple uniform. Her hand was cold and sticky with lotion. "You don't feel hot to me!" She ran her finger over my upper lip. "Leah, we probably need to wax tonight."

"God, don't touch me!"

"Oh, pardon me, missy! Well, you are not allowed to snack and watch TV here all day. Get your homework done.

If you're up to it, get out my Zumba DVD. If you do it every day, it does amazing things."

I looked up at her bloodshot eyes and the web of tiny veins on her cheeks. "Sure, Mom."

She crouched in front of the dresser mirror and touched the top of her hair. "My God, I really need to color my hair. I meant to last night but didn't get around to it. Is the gray very noticeable?" She watched me in the mirror. I carefully did not look at the inch of gray next to her scalp.

"You look fine. I don't even know what you're talking about. I can hardly see it."

She smiled and squeezed my toes through the blankets. "I gotta run, sweetie. Say, I'm missing some money from my wallet. I don't know what I did with it. Let me know if you . . ."

"You gave me ten dollars last night, Mom."

"Of course! That's right. Keep it, keep it. Fun money! Love you. Get better, munchkin. Maybe we could play a game of Yahtzee when I get home." She backed out of the room with a smile that looked like it would break her face.

I lay back in my nest of blankets and slept until a slab of sunlight from between the curtains reached my face. I pulled on my robe and stumbled down the hallway to the kitchenette. I felt like someone had tied weights to my ankles and wrists.

Cindy had left the paper folded on the kitchen table. She

subscribed to the newspaper no matter how broke we were and acted like reading the paper was a sacred middle-class custom.

I made a cup of instant coffee and turned to the obituary page just to make sure Kristy's mother hadn't died. She hadn't. The obituary page was in the back of the sports section. On the front page of the sports section was a large color photograph of a high-school baseball game. In the corner of the field, in a green-and-white Arapahoe uniform, Damien Rogers stood holding a mitt. I was almost sure it was him, though the face was blurred and the number on the uniform wasn't visible.

I cut out the picture and taped it to my wall. The other two pictures had already yellowed, so I pulled them off. Then I tore down the kitten poster and the picture of the puppies tumbling out of a basket. I crushed both posters into balls.

"In Vietnam they eat puppies," I said to the room. Mr. Shlukebier told us that in geometry freshman year. Exhausted, I lay back on the bed. I'd just slept twelve hours.

I put on Bruno Mars, lay down again, and stared up at him. He sang "When I Was Your Man," and it's a very sad song, but I couldn't feel it. The poster was rumpled. It wasn't Bruno Mars on my cracked green wall—it was just a cheap poster from the store at the Rocky Mountain Mall.

I squeezed my eyes shut against the light and pulled a pillow over my face.

It was the fourth inning. The bases were loaded, and Damien Rogers was up to bat. I had a gorgeous tan from sitting in the stands all summer. I was dressed all in white—white tank top, white sunglasses, white jeans, size four—I'd lost a ton of weight from living off of watermelon smoothies. Damien stepped up to the plate, lifted the bat, and . . . I sat there, perfect, sexy, and beautiful . . . a little bored because I'd sat through games all summer. Trying not to get anything on my white pants, kind of difficult because there was bird shit on the bench and I'd already gotten a splotch of watermelon smoothie on one knee. I felt like I might be getting my period. . . .

I threw off the pillow and rummaged under my bed until I found a half-empty notebook from freshman year. I grabbed a pen, sat up against the green wall, and stared at the white page with its faint blue lines. I thought if I could write it down, it would make sense.

I stared at the paper and began to see his face. No matter where I hid, Mr. Corduroy was waiting for me.

Twenty-Nine

I fell asleep for a few more hours, then got up, went into the kitchenette, and opened up a new box of frozen French toast. But what was I doing? I needed to change my life. I needed to have a plan. I needed the motivation to change my life and become the girl Damien Rogers would choose to be his girlfriend. Because even if we had problems in our relationship—for one thing, he would have to accept that I was going to be a doctor—I still thought we could make it work. I put Mr. Corduroy out of my mind—I would figure that out later. Right now, I just needed to lose weight. I had to concentrate.

Today would be a day for discipline and new habits that would transform my life. I shoved the box back into the freezer with the crumb-covered frost and ate the breakfast printed in a little black box on the back of the diet cereal: a cup of black coffee, ¾ cup of cereal, ½ cup of skim milk, ½ small banana, 1 teaspoon sugar (optional).

After breakfast, I went out in front of the building and searched the ground for butts with lip-gloss prints that looked like mine. The air was chilly, as if it had blown off the top of the mountain. Orange slabs of sunlight lay on the scrawny grass. I found three bent, half-smoked butts. I lit one, inhaled, and wondered whether you could catch herpes from a cigarette butt. I tried to think of a scientific explanation for why butts tasted so horrible when you relit them.

The coffee, which I didn't usually drink, made me jittery. I went back to the apartment, put in Cindy's Zumba DVD, and pushed the table away from the couch. I swung my arms, marched in place, and swiveled my hips to Latin music.

"You are beautiful!" the lady on the DVD shouted. Her eyes bulged. She had a ferocious smile. My head crackled and went black. I closed my eyes and lay on the couch until my heart stopped pounding. I was starving.

I went to the kitchenette for some cheese and crackers and turned the television on to a talk show.

Running between commercials, I got more cheese and crackers because cheese is protein, and protein is very important. I tried to fill up on fruit and ate all the bananas. I found a can of ravioli, ate it cold right out of the can, and then had two peanut-butter sandwiches, a whole box of single-serving cookies, and, finally, the French toast soaked in Karo syrup that I'd wanted all along.

The topic of the second half of the show was "frenemies." A woman talked shit about her friend, whom she pretty much hated, for twenty minutes, then after the commercial, the host brought the woman's frenemy out from behind the curtain. *Zing. Surprise!*

Cindy burst through the door four hours early. She slammed the door, dropped her purse, squeezed her eyes shut, and pressed her fingertips against her temples.

"I've had a horrible headache. I must have caught your virus. They had to call Renée in. She was so ticked off. . . ." Cindy opened her eyes.

I felt like a cockroach caught on the kitchen floor when the light is turned on. I had a frozen angel food cake on my stomach and had just torn off a handful. The coffee table was covered with plates, cups, and wrappers. The laughter from the TV suddenly sounded stupid, tinny, and prerecorded.

"Leah, my God! What am I going to do with you? You've been eating all day! You're going to end up big as a house. You eat a week's worth of groceries in one day! I can't afford it! Sweetheart, you're breaking my heart. I don't want you to be obese. . . ."

"Don't use that word!"

"It's a medical term, Leah."

A medical term like *halitosis* and *hirsute* and *flatulence*.

Ugly scientific words that made people feel like cockroaches. I would never use those medical terms when I was a doctor.

I swung my legs off the couch and put the cake on a plate. "I'll clean this up after I shower. Please leave me alone. I'm sorry, but I'm really stressed."

"Stressed?" She put her little hand on her forehead and shook her head in wonderment. "Honey, most of your problems are just normal adolescence. The problems you need to think about are the ones you create for yourself! And they are aplenty!"

I shuffled toward the bathroom. She said, "Please don't slam the door. And don't leave your towel on the floor. Did you remember to take out the trash?"

I locked the door and showered until the bathroom was fluffy with steam. She hammered on the door. "Let's give a little thought to the environment!"

I wrapped up in a towel and rushed from the bathroom to my bedroom so she wouldn't have to see my obesity. I crammed my fat, scalded body into my baggiest sweats.

When I came out, Cindy was wound up in the afghan like a mummy. She clutched the wineglass beneath her chin and scrabbled around in a saucer of pretzels with her other hand. She stared through me while I cleared the dishes and picked wrappers off the table.

I threw away the trash and wiped down the counter and stove. As I washed the plastic plates and cups, I stared at the picture of the meadow. A Screamo song I didn't even like went through my head. I dropped a plate and looked over at Cindy. She glared at the TV.

Cindy stared feverishly at the TV like she wished she could live in TV-land forever and never have to come back to our ratty little apartment and her teacup collection and especially me.

I got the orange juice concentrate from the back of the freezer. I scraped off the ice crystals, scooped a spoonful into a teacup of water and carried it to her.

"Here, Mom. You've got to eat something more than pretzels. They don't have any nutrition."

She craned her neck so she could see the TV around my legs. "I can't see, sweetheart."

The landline rang and Cindy snatched it up. "Hey, Corinne! How you doing, honey? Yes, she's here. Yes, she made an amazing recovery. She'll definitely be back at school tomorrow."

I took the phone to my room. Corinne said, "Did you run out of minutes again? I texted you, but you never answered. I was going to call yesterday, but Jimmy threw up."

"I lost my phone." It felt like hundreds of years since I'd last talked to Corinne.

"Sorry about yesterday. When Kristy gets like that, there's no talking to her. But I think she's already feeling bad."

I shut my door. The sound of Corinne's voice made me

feel stiff, injured, and pathetic. "What makes you think that?"

"Well, she talked about you. After lunch, she said, 'Where's Leah?' And I said, 'I heard she's sick. She went to the nurse's office. She has the flu or some such shit. She had to go home.' And Kristy had this look in her eyes, and she just looked kind of worried."

"Oh, really. Wow." With one hand, I opened my notebook and wrote *Yertle is a psycho bitch.*

"Leah, I feel so bad for her. Her mom is doing really horrible. She's really, actually dying. I talked to my mom about this, and she said there's no way I can abandon Kristy, not with her mom dying and everything. My mom said she's lashing out at you because she's stricken with grief." Corinne's words began to echo, as if she was calling from Mars, from ten million miles away.

Like a sudden memory of a dream, I heard Kurt King's voice in the dark parking lot. His Mustang turning toward the school. Over and over and over. "Do you know if Kristy's talked to Mr. Corduroy?"

"Leah, I can hardly hear you. What are you talking about?" said Corinne. "Leah, I'm sorry, but I can't abandon Kristy. My mom won't even let me. So, it may look like I'm taking Kristy's side, but I'm not. I'm still your friend. I'm just trying to help her."

"OK, gotcha, Corinne. You know what? I've got so much

homework to do and my mom's sick. . . . Yeah, sure. See you tomorrow."

I put down the phone. I wanted to fall into the blackness of sleep—that was my escape hatch—but I'd slept all morning. I had to lie there and be alive with my obese self. A faker. Frenemy to all.

I stared at a white page in my notebook. And then I closed it. And then I opened it—and closed it.

Thirty

I finished my homework at 10:45 and opened my door a crack. Cindy was asleep on the couch with her face squashed into the couch cushion. I turned off the TV. She usually curled her toes like something was biting them. She'd just given herself a pedicure, and her toenails were painted with sparkly purple polish. Her bunion looked sore. I pulled the blanket over her feet.

She let out a little snort and drooled onto the cushion. Cindy didn't have a boyfriend or a husband. She was just Cindy with her double-pierced ears and auburn hair that was gray at the roots, her nail polish and boxes of wine, and her lonely nights in front of the TV. She was the old broken Barbie with her head on backward.

Every time she breathed out, Cindy let out a little moan—*wooooo*. Music, laugh tracks, and garbled voices from TVs seeped through the walls and ceiling. The shiny beige lunatic walls of #3 crept closer.

I put on some mascara and a hoodie, scooted into the hall, and locked the door. Ever since Kristy had driven us by Damien Rogers's house, I'd been thinking about the shortest way to get there on foot. He only lived about four miles from my apartment building. I could walk there and back, and burn four hundred calories each way.

Outside the Belmont Manor, wind shook the tops of the trees. I walked through an ocean of swaying shadows. I pulled up the hood of my jacket and headed down Vargas toward Tenth.

When I got to Tenth, my heart thumped my ribs as if I were walking toward my execution. But I deserved it. If I saw Kurt King, I would tell him: *It was me. She never talked to you. Leave her alone. Take her picture off your phone.*

No one was at the 7-Eleven, except the guy behind the counter who swayed as he stared at the bags of chips. I kept walking, cutting through the dark cool air with my head down. I ran across the empty highway and crossed a bridge onto Costilla Street.

A creek ran alongside Costilla. All the buildings had flat roofs. There were old craggy trees, yards full of rusted junk, dogs tied on chains. Aladdin's House of Treasures, a tiny white building with bars over the windows, was closed. The lights were on at Dragon's Lair, where Anita had gotten her nose stud. Three bikers with fat pink arms sat reading magazines in the lobby. Water rushed over the rocks in the creek.

When a dog leaped, barking, against the fence of a black yard or a car door creaked open behind me, I bolted to the next shadow. If I'd thought about what I was doing—walking alone through a bad neighborhood at eleven at night—I would have been paralyzed with fear. So I didn't think. Instead I imagined Dr. Seuss books in my head, like I was turning the pages, the pair of pale green pants with nobody inside them, and all of *Oh, the Places You'll Go!* I'd come to a place where everything was dark.

I passed the empty fields and dark parking lot of Arapahoe High School. The nail salon's broken sign squeaked in the wind. I turned down El Paso Boulevard. A car slowed. Its engine hummed in the darkness. I hid behind a Dumpster that reeked like rancid cooking oil until the car drove off.

From then on, I ducked behind bushes whenever headlights approached. I finally reached the end of Damien's street. The driveways were cluttered with tricycles and broken cars. Everything was silent and motionless.

I stopped at the end of his driveway. The security light over the front door flashed on. I stepped back into the street and looked up at the split-level house with faded blue siding.

The basketball hoop's net was torn. The light went off. The dark windows shone like metal.

Damien Rogers lived in this house with paint peeling off the fake shutters and oil stains on the driveway. I dropped onto the ground at the end of his driveway, hugged my knees, and sang "Grenade." I closed my eyes and suddenly knew, knew for certain, that Damien Rogers would be my boyfriend. He and I would double-date to prom with Corinne and Jason Coulter.

I crawled across the cold grass to what might have been Damien Rogers's basement bedroom window. He was sleeping ten feet from me.

A truck door slammed. The air was smudgy gray, and there was spiky grass next to my eyes. My clothes were clammy. For a second, I didn't know who I was, or where. I was stiff and cold, curled in a ball.

The sky was orange over the roof. A man fumbled around in the lit cab of the truck. He wore a gray sweatshirt with the hood pulled up over his head. He twisted around and rummaged behind the seat. His mustache was black and brushy.

He held a wrench up to the light for a second, turned off the light, and backed the truck out of the driveway. Damien Rogers's dad did not notice me lying on his lawn.

Once the sound of his truck engine faded, I crawled

across the grass toward the street. I got to my feet, then tripped and fell onto a yucca plant that stabbed my stomach through my shirt.

I stood up again and took off at a stiff jog, praying the whole time: *Please, Jesus. Please, God. Please let me get home before anyone finds out I slept in Damien Rogers's yard. Please don't let anyone know that I was stalking Damien Rogers.*

The soles of my Vans were thin, and I felt extremely heavy, like I'd gained a hundred pounds and had rocks in my pockets. I thudded along, running, then walking, then running again. I could hardly get any air, and my lungs felt like they were tearing apart. Halfway home, yellow light exploded on the east side of town. The air turned orange-pink. It was like running through apricot jam. By the time I got back to my building, I was wheezing and coughing up cigarette gunk.

A middle-aged man with bags under his eyes and comb tracks through his greasy hair held the entryway door open for me. "Good run?" he asked.

Cindy was in the shower. My door was shut. I went into my room, pulled off my sweats, and tugged on my robe. When the bathroom door opened and Cindy's door banged shut, I headed for the bathroom. I said, "I need a note," through Cindy's closed door.

She made a noise that sounded like a cat coughing up a hairball. "I'm not in the mood for this kind of last-minute demand!" she said in a high-pitched voice. Two minutes later, I heard the door slam.

I sat at the kitchen table, drank a cup of instant coffee, and read Cindy's note:

> *Per the school nurse's instructions, Leah Lobermeir*
> *stayed home sick yesterday. She has made a quick*
> *and full recovery.*
>
> *Kind regards,*
> *Cynthia Lobermeir*

Life preservers of cereal floated in the milk in my bowl. I swiped a couple of bucks from Cindy's hope jar and headed out.

Thirty-One

In chemistry, I was so tired that my eyes wouldn't focus. The cabinets and tables and chairs and people blurred into a bad fluorescent-lit dream. Kristy stared at me from the back row, and Carl Lancaster swiveled on his stool and pretended not to look at me. I couldn't cope with either of them. I pretended Carl Lancaster was not there and Kristy had never been born. Mrs. McCleary was giving a lecture on oxidation numbers. "The last quiz showed me that you guys really do not get this!" she said.

I stuck a magazine inside the chemistry book and read.

"Leah . . ."

"Leave me alone, Carl. I cannot deal with anything today." *You don't exist. I don't exist. Kurt King doesn't exist. I will never be a doctor.*

We had a new instructional unit in language arts. In the next two weeks, each of us would have to present a piece of original writing to an authentic and intended audience, and then be judged as to whether our writing had the effect we'd intended it to have.

"In other words, you have to write a commentary on our society and make a presentation to our class," said Mr. Calvino. "You can write about anything you want as long as it's not racist, violent, threatening, homophobic, obscene, or bigoted."

Everyone groaned. "That's not fair!" someone said.

"Write about something you care about! Write about something you feel strongly about!" Mr. Calvino paced back and forth in front of his desk and waved his hairy hands around. "There are so many fantastic, amazing things to write about. Obscenity and violence aren't actually very interesting." He stopped walking and looked us. He really, really looked at us.

Dan Manke farted, his on-demand specialty, and said, "Bullllsheeeeeet."

LaTeisha whipped around in her desk. "Please, Dan! That is so disgusting."

Mr. Calvino gazed sadly at Dan Manke. His shoulders slumped as if he'd lost all his wind. He picked up a Diet Coke can and shook it.

He'd lost weight since he started at West. He was picking

up weird mannerisms. When he graded our five-paragraph essays, he held his fingers against his mouth as if to keep from screaming, and his head ticked like a woodpecker's.

The bell rang. Mr. Calvino stood near the door and watched our faces as we crowded out. He caught me by the shoulder. "Stop by after school. I'd like to talk to you, Leah."

After Mr. Calvino's class was fourth-period lunch.

I turned away from my locker. Kristy stared at me with her glassy blue eyes. Corinne stood behind her. They both smiled. Kristy's earlobes sparkled in the fluorescent lights — she was wearing the diamond studs she'd gotten for her thirteenth birthday.

I did not allow any expression to form on my face. I waited silently, prepared for an insult, possibly a physical attack. I protected my chest with my books.

Kristy and Corinne looked at each other, then turned back to me. "Hey," they said in unison.

"What do you want?"

"What do we want?" Kristy raised one of her white eyebrows. "Come on, Leah, let's let it go. I can't even remember why we're not talking."

I allowed my mouth to fall open and stared at this girl with white curls sprouting out of her little skull. She squinted back at me. She was there, behind the blue, hiding from me.

"You've got to be kidding me," I said. But it was too

dangerous to get into again. Kristy had the ace in the hole—her mom was dying.

She stretched her arms over her head and scrunched up her face. "Come on, Leah!" She swung her arms down and opened those eyes again. "Let it go! Come have lunch with us. We're going down to the park Saturday night. . . ."

"I probably can't go. I'm grounded." Anita and I had planned to eat lunch together.

"You're grounded? How come?" said Kristy. We began to walk down the hall. It was disgustingly comfortable to fall back in step slightly behind Kristy and Corinne, sort of like lighting up a smoke after you'd quit for a week. Something massive pounded in the back of my head. Every wall we passed was decorated with a Coke poster or banner, but I had no money for a Coke. "God, I'm thirsty."

Kristy stopped walking, grabbed my arm, and held me. "Why. Are. You. Grounded?"

"Uh . . . the other night I was out late and got busted. I'm dying of thirst." We began walking again. The water fountain was covered with a black garbage bag and a hand-printed sign: DO NOT USE.

"What the hell were you doing out late?"

"Sometimes I go for walks at night." I was so tired. I just wanted to topple over and disappear.

"How weird. OK."

Kelsey Parker and her friends approached, heading straight toward us. An army of five, the girls wore tiny crosses on gold necklaces, string friendship bracelets, fleece jackets unzipped to the same point on their chests. All five girls stared at their phones.

Suddenly, Kelsey stopped and grabbed Corinne's arm. "Corinne, I need to talk for a sec. Meet you at our table," she said to her friends, who'd stopped in a pack and swiveled their heads.

Kelsey pulled Corinne over by the lockers. Kristy and I trailed behind.

"Corinne, did you hear about the game yesterday? It was horrible."

"Yeah. Sorry, Kelsey."

"Hey, Kelsey." Kristy stood at Kelsey's elbow. She was practically trembling.

Kelsey squinched up her face like she had a bad headache. "Can I just talk to Corinne for a second, Kristy? We had a really horrible, shitty game yesterday. There's something else that's totally stressing me out."

Corinne wore her zoned-out look of concern. "What's wrong, Kelsey?"

"I heard"—Kelsey lowered her voice—"that Dean and LaTeisha sat together on the band field trip yesterday and were talking the entire time. I'm like, what the fuck? I heard LaTeisha and Ray Ramirez are breaking up 'cause he's going to college. Dean hasn't asked me to prom yet. Corinne, have you heard if Dean likes LaTeisha?"

Corinne started to yawn and quickly hid it behind her hand. "Um, no . . . not at all," she said.

"There's no way. No way, Kelsey!" Kristy was standing on tiptoes, jiggling up and down. "First of all, he acts like he really, really likes you. Plus, I heard LaTeisha and Ray aren't breaking up. They're going to try it long-distance. LaTeisha was probably trying to turn Dean into a Christian. Everyone thinks that Dean's practically in love with you."

Corinne started to hum and stared down the hallway. I leaned against her and put my head on her shoulder.

"Seriously, Kristy?" Kelsey finally looked at Kristy.

"Yeah, and, Kelsey"—Kristy cautiously took Kelsey's arm—"I'm pretty sure you and Dean were voted cutest couple in the yearbook. First or second place, for sure."

"That would be cool. We should go to Tea Garden sometime. . . ."

"I'd love to. Anytime. Text me," said Kristy.

"Sure. I'll text you. Gotta go."

I stood by, taking up space but invisible, while Kelsey, Corinne, and Kristy all shoulder-hugged. Kelsey plunged into the crowd, her blond head bobbing as a path to the cafeteria opened up for her.

"Oh my God," said Kristy. Her nose turned pink. "Cool. I always knew Kelsey and I would start hanging out." She pulled out her phone and maniacally tapped with her thumbs. "Maybe Kelsey and I can go to Tea Garden today after her practice."

The next water fountain was full of lumpy black liquid, as if a squid had been massacred in the bowl. The pounding in my head was getting louder and louder. I could hardly hear anything but the pounding. "I saw Mr. Corduroy. I talked to him at 7-Eleven."

"What!" Kristy screeched. She stopped in the middle of the hallway and put her hands on her knees as if to keep herself from falling over. She flung her hair around like she was onstage at a club. The other kids shoved past us and stared at her just the way she wanted them to. Corinne crossed her arms, snapped her gum, and looked down the hall.

Kristy stood up, hooked my arm, and pulled me close to her bony little body. "How long did you talk to him?"

"I don't know, half an hour, forty-five minutes. He's old, Kristy. He's weird."

"You talked to him for forty-five minutes?" she said. Out of the smear of faces, one came into focus. Anita stood against a locker. She watched me walk down the hall with Kristy. I lifted my free hand and waved. She didn't move.

"Kristy, you're not listening. He's old. He's a creeper."

We came to the cafeteria. Kristy said, "Corinne, go save us a table." Corinne blew out a breath and walked toward the tables.

Kristy said to me, "I'm gonna just get a Coke. Hurry up, before the line gets long, and then I want to hear every word. Oh my God, there's Kelsey." Kelsey Parker looked quickly at Kristy, then scooted her chair around so her back was to us.

On the way back with my tray, I stopped at the Anita's table. "Hey."

Iris and Maria glared. Jamie Lopez sat reading at the end of the table. He was wearing a Bullet for My Valentine T-shirt and reading a book about Zen Buddhism. He used his thumb as a bookmark and calmly looked up at me. I sat down on the edge of a chair. "Anita, I really, really want to talk to you, but there's something going on with Kristy. . . . I have a test after school, but maybe I'll see you tomorrow morning on the bus?"

"Fabulous. See you later. Oh, and I couldn't do anything today anyway." She looked up from the drawing that she was shading and gave me a big fake smile. I stiffly got up and walked over to Kristy's table. It felt like an ocean crossing.

Lunch was sloppy joes with canned green beans. The green beans were gray. I touched one with my fork, and bean mush squirted between the tines. Kristy pulled me down into a seat. "I want to know every detail. First off, what's his name?"

"I don't know."

"Well, shit," she said, "what did you talk about?"

"I don't remember."

"What's he like? Did he ask about me?"

"Yeah, he asked about you, Kristy. He's a creeper." I picked up the sandwich and took a bite. Red grease dripped down my hand.

Across the table, Corinne shook her head and mouthed, "He's so gross." She was watching a cooking show on Kristy's phone.

Kristy yanked my arm while I tried to wipe off the grease with a shredding napkin. "He asked about me? Hey, tell him anything he wants to know. Dude is gorgeous."

"You're not listening to me. He's old. He's creepy. Kristy . . ."

She chewed on her lip, trying not to smile. She pulled out her strawberry lip gloss and smeared some on, then rubbed gloss off her thumb onto her jeans. She laughed into her Coke can, then chugged it.

The pounding drowned out all the voices and crashes in the cafeteria. I heard myself say from deep inside my hollow head. "Kristy, he's been talking on the phone with a girl named Ashley. He thought he was talking to you. He thinks you like him."

It sounded ridiculous. It didn't even make sense. But it made sense to Kristy.

"He thinks I like him? Ha-ha-ha. Uh . . . that's cool! God, I hate the name Ashley. I'm so glad my parents didn't name me Ashley. That name sucks. Corinne, don't you detest the name Ashley?" Kristy lunged across the table and grabbed Corinne's arm. Corinne shook Kristy off and kept watching the show.

Kristy closed her eyes and ran her fingertips over her eyebrows. She patted her cheeks and squawked. "My mom is going to shit if I start dating a guy in his twenties!"

I was still extremely thirsty and tore open the carton of milk. I drank half of it before I remembered that Mrs. McCleary had said that milk glands were modified sweat glands, so milk was in a way a kind of cow sweat.

Kristy opened up her lunch bag and took out a hummus-spelt wrap that her dad had made. Her mom was too sick to make lunch anymore. I had pushed Mrs. Baker out of my mind because all the feelings I had for her took up too much space. Now she came back in, sat down in her pink fuzzy pajamas, and looked at me with her sad eyes.

Kristy put her earbuds in. She picked the carrots and cucumbers out of her hummus wrap and threw them on the table.

"Kristy!" I said. "Kristy, you're not listening to me."

She squinched her eyes shut. "Today is such a great day," she said really loudly. "Corinne, give me my phone back! I want to see if Kelsey texted yet."

"He's got your picture," I whispered. She threw a piece of cucumber at me and laughed.

Thirty-Two

In study hall, Carl and I sat on opposite sides of the library and didn't look at each other. The entire hour I was aware of him—it felt like he was sitting right next to me—but when I turned around, he'd already left.

After school, Kristy wanted me to skip a makeup algebra test.

"No way." I walked down the hallway and sat in Mr. Bauer's empty classroom and attempted to do eighteen math problems while he graded papers and scratched his head and snorted and sneezed and looked at what was in his tissue. My head felt funny, like a balloon that was trying to float away. I laid my head on the test and slept for a couple of minutes until Mr. Bauer let out a huge snort and a *kak-kak-kak* like an angry goose. I sat up.

After the test, I remembered Mr. Calvino.

I walked down the dim, empty hall toward language arts. Notebook papers, wrappers, pen caps, and broken pencils lay scattered on the floor. Way down the hall, a custodian pushed a broom past the lockers.

I looked in Mr. Calvino's door. The fluorescent lights were off. He liked natural light. He was sitting with his feet crossed on the desk and staring out the window at the mountain.

He noticed me, swung his feet onto the floor, and straightened the papers on his desk. "Hey, Leah. Didn't think you were coming."

"Sorry, I had a makeup test." I stepped into the room. I felt a weight dragging behind me, a filthy torn parachute, all the stupid things I'd done.

"Come on over here and have a seat."

I wandered in and sat on the top of a desk in the front row. "Yeah?"

"Can you sit in the seat? It will feel more like a conversation. So, how's it going?"

I dropped my backpack and sat. "All right."

"OK! Great. So, I would like to move you up to AP language arts next year. It'll look good on college applications, and you can get college credit. But I need some metrics. Your test scores are good, but I need some demonstrated proof that you can do the work that I can put in your file. I need you to write me a couple of extra-credit papers, Leah. Eight to ten pages. What do you say?"

A warm blossoming inside me immediately turned black, a poisoned flower. "I don't think so. You don't want me in that class."

"I think I do! You're an excellent writer. You've got great ideas. You could easily do the work. I'd love to have you in the class."

"I don't like the kids in that class." How could I tell him: *My mom won't let me. She thinks I'm too dumb.*

"Ah." He sighed and started shaking the Diet Coke cans on his desk. "Leah, you've got to think beyond your immediate present and imagine a future that you want."

I looked out at the mountain. What did he see when he stared out at it? Or when he looked at me?

"Leah? Leah." He leaned forward. His shirt was all crumpled, the sleeves shoved up his hairy arms. He was so skinny, and with his five o'clock shadow, messy hair, and haunted eyes, he looked like a disaster survivor. "Leah, may I ask you a stupid adult question?"

I was sitting in natural light with Mr. Calvino. In those New Jersey eyes, I could see gray oceans, Coney Island, enormous cities looped with train tracks, huge apartment buildings, sidewalks rumbling with subways, a street of colored lights, tightly packed brick buildings, fruit sellers, people of every kind talking, riding by in the sad light of a bus, walking at night.

He looked at me like he saw me there.

"Nope." I shook my head once and leaned over to pick up my backpack. "I got to go." Without looking at him, I stood and walked toward the door.

"See you tomorrow, Leah," he said softly.

Why did he have to say that? He'd be looking for me, paying attention, not allowing me to be invisible. It hurt being seen. Because then I was real, and everything that had happened to me was real. Being who I was usually felt like it would kill me.

In the doorway, I stopped and looked back. Because he was still watching me; I could feel it. He refused to allow me to disappear. "What did you want to ask, Mr. Calvino?"

He put his feet back up and rested his cheek on his fist. "You still interested in medicine?"

"Yes."

It felt like the first word I'd ever said. Or a door swinging open. And all the other words were pressed up against the door, waiting to rush out.

Thirty-Three

I sat on the school's concrete steps and waited for Kristy. I lit my last cigarette. It was spring, really spring, green grass and endless cloudless skies. All that blue exhausted me.

Fifteen minutes later, Kristy pulled up in front of the school. She was playing hip-hop so loud, I could feel the bass through the concrete. She blasted the horn when I was two feet away. I got into the car and turned down the music. "I have a headache."

She finished her juice and threw the bottle into the backseat. "Want to go down to Torrance?"

"No. I just want to go home."

"Want to see if Mr. Corduroy is at 7-Eleven?"

"God, Kristy, no! If we have to go somewhere, let's go see Corinne."

"How boring! Fine." She pulled out into the street as she texted Corinne. A motorcycle blasted its horn and swerved out of her way.

She steered with her knees and dug a pack of gum out of her purse. She unwrapped five pieces and stuffed them into her mouth. She chewed with her mouth open and made horrible wet noises. Her big teeth were shiny with sugary spit. "God, I wish I'd been there the other night when you talked to Mr. Corduroy...."

I closed my eyes.

I opened my eyes and grabbed her skinny little arm.

"Kristy. Listen to me. OK? Listen. Mr. Corduroy is a creep. Stay away from him. He's twenty-six years old."

"Um, could you let go? You're breaking my arm. And you're spraying spit all over the side of my face."

She pulled her arm away, and tugged down the front of her shirt. At a stoplight, she stretched, looked in the rearview mirror, and ran her tongue over her teeth. She flopped back in her seat. "Sorry. Dude's gorgeous."

I stared at her. "He's old. He's disgusting. He's probably a rapist." I almost choked on the last word.

"Jealous . . ." she sang under her breath. She turned into Mountain View Estates. "And what's up with your phone? I texted you last night."

Kristy jerked the car to a stop in front of Corinne's house, grabbed her purse and her cigarettes, slammed her door, and ran inside. On the walkway to Corinne's front door, I tripped on a silver toy pistol and landed hard on my knee. I hobbled to the door with my bloody jeans sticking to my leg.

Corinne and Kristy sat on stools at the kitchen island with a bowl of trail mix between them. A wad of purple gum was stuck to the top of a pop can. Corinne stared at a cooking show on the kitchen TV. Her hair was pulled back with metal clips, and her face was so pale she looked anemic. She'd taken out her contacts and put on her glasses from junior high — peach plastic frames with scratched lenses.

The three older boys ran in a circle through the kitchen, living room, and dining room. One of the boys yanked Kristy's hair as he darted past.

"Brat!" Kristy screamed.

Corinne yelled, "Quit running around, you little monsters." She buried her hand in the trail mix. "Do you see that knife she's using? I'm getting one of those for Christmas."

I nearly fell on top of Jimmy. He banged into my leg with his plastic walker. He rammed my knee again, and I lifted him out. He was wearing a white fuzzy one-piece with yellow stains down the front. He wriggled, kicking his legs. He was like a warm, smelly loaf of bread. He stared into my eyes, pulled my finger into his mouth, and chewed it with his hard wet gums.

A commercial came on, and the boys ran through five

more times. Corinne stared into the trail mix and scooped out a blue M&M with the tip of her nail.

"Oh, I forgot to show you!" Corinne pulled a brochure out of the stack of junk mail. A man in a white chef hat stood on a lawn stirring a pot in front of a brick bell tower. "I got this about Western University's cooking institute. Only problem is that it's super expensive."

Kristy looked at the brochure for half a second and tossed it onto the counter.

"Kristy's going to fashion school," I said. "Her mom said it's OK."

Kristy stared at me like I was an imbecile. "What the hell are you talking about?"

"You said the other day! Like in Florida or something."

"No!" She made a noise of disgust in her throat and swiveled on the stool. "I'm thinking Boulder. . . ."

"That would be fun," said Corinne. She tossed an M&M into the air and caught it in her mouth. "Party school."

I said, "Isn't it kinda hard to get in? What would you major in?"

Kristy stared at me like I was a dissected worm, closed her eyes, and slowly shook her head. "Leah, you're so boring. . . . You sound like a mom."

Jimmy let go of my finger. He gripped my wrist with both hands, grunted, and blew raspberries. His face turned deep red and his tiny eyes bulged. A terrible hot smell rose from his diaper. I was going to avoid any kind of medicine that had to do with poop or intestines.

Kristy abruptly stood up and covered her mouth like she was about to puke. "Let's go have a smoke."

"Put him in the playpen," said Corinne, sliding off the stool.

When I tried to set Jimmy down in the playpen, he hung on to my arms and huffed. I pried off his hands and shook him loose. He wailed, clung to the webbing of the playpen, then fell backward on the toys and shrieked.

I stuck my head out the door. "What do I do?"

"Just leave him. He's fine." Corinne waved the smoke away from her face. "Leave the door cracked so I can hear." I squeezed out the door and sat down next to her. "Guess what? Jason Coulter gave me a lift home."

Kristy scraped the Folgers can across the concrete. "I can still smell the kid's shit pants. Could you maybe, possibly, change him?"

Corinne shook her head and silently laughed. She pulled the coffee can back next to her leg and looked at the sky.

For a while, we were quiet. The concrete slab was cold. Our backs curled against the rough wood siding. Jimmy's screams slowed down to sobs, then to hiccups. The spring afternoon shone bluely over the cedar privacy fence. It was almost possible to believe that everything was normal, nothing had changed. My little world with Kristy and Corinne was just the same as it had been, and it always would be the same. My heart beat in my chest; vague thoughts floated like clouds through my mind. Mr. Calvino wanted to move me up to AP language arts. The spring wind blew through and washed everything clean.

Kristy disturbed the peace. She tossed her pack into my lap. "Why aren't you smoking?"

I decided it that second. "I quit."

"You quit? Why?" said Kristy. She tapped her ash into the grass. "Did Slutella talk you into it?"

"I can't afford it." My knee ached. I started to roll up the leg of my jeans, but my calf looked enormous and bristled with hairs. "Plus, I hate stinking like smoke."

Kristy wiggled around as if she had ants crawling up her back. "Whatever, Chubs. Let's go down to the park Saturday night? Corinne? Hello?"

"Sure. Why not?" said Corinne.

There was a crash in the kitchen, and Jimmy screamed. Corinne's head dropped between her knees. The TV volume went up in the living room. The boys started shouting. The phone rang.

"I'm telling Mom that you're not helping Jimmy," Alex yelled.

Kristy raked her fingers through her hair. She jumped to her feet and poked out her hip. She shook her keys and fluttered her fingers like a stressed-out movie star.

"Get that kid to shut up," she said, "or I'm leaving."

Corinne raised her face. She had a stony expression behind her peach glasses. "Don't let the door hit you in the ass."

Kristy's face went white. She swayed on the heels of her little cowboy boots. "OK! That's nice, Corinne. See you later! I don't know how you can stand spending time in this shit hole. Come on, Leah!"

The sun went behind a cloud; it was suddenly shadowy and cool. Corinne's eyes were tired behind her glasses, but her jaw was tight. "Kristy, I'm not sure I can go to the park Saturday. I might be hanging out with Kelsey."

"Bitch," said Kristy.

Alex stuck his head out the door. "Mom wants to talk to you immediately!"

Corinne stabbed out her cigarette and pushed up off the concrete.

"I'm staying," I said.

"You want to stay? Fine. Have fun, Chubs! I'm out of here." Kristy picked her way across the yard, texting the entire way, and slammed the gate shut behind her. It bounced back open.

I went into the kitchen, lifted Jimmy out of the pen, and

held him against my chest. His face was red and swollen and streaked with snot and tears. He arched his back and tried to scratch my face. The smell from his diaper made me gag, but I held him and swayed. His crying gradually slowed and his body relaxed. He leaned his head against my shoulder, stared out the glass door, and blinked his spiky wet lashes.

Corinne hung up the phone. She walked over and stared at Jimmy. "God, he reeks." She looked pale and empty, like someone had taken a vacuum and sucked out all her Corinne-ness.

"Maybe you should change him before he falls asleep."

"In a minute." She turned on the kitchen TV and leaned on the counter. The talk show was interrupted by a news bulletin. A blond man wearing a navy blazer stared from the TV screen.

"Police say that a twenty-two-year-old woman was abducted as she walked to her apartment on Costilla Street at approximately one a.m. last night. Police say the woman was raped, beaten, and left . . ."

Corinne flipped through the channels with the remote. "*Top Chef*'s coming on in five minutes. Have you been watching?"

My head rang like someone was pressing a doorbell and wouldn't let off. Jimmy felt like he weighed three hundred pounds and would pull me over onto the kitchen floor that was covered with hair and splotches of dried spaghetti sauce.

"Corinne, take him! I feel like I'm about to pass out. I didn't sleep much last night."

Corinne sighed and pushed away from the counter. She pried Jimmy from me. "Come on, Fatso. Let's go change you before Mom gets home."

I said, "I shouldn't have let Kristy go alone."

"She's fine," Corinne said over her shoulder as she carried Jimmy to the bathroom. "She'll get over it."

I called Kristy from Cindy's landline at ten and eleven thirty, just to see if she'd answer. It went to voice mail both times.

Thirty-Four

The next day I walked into chemistry, suddenly barely breathing, numb, not sure at all what I was thinking or feeling, but Carl's stool was empty. The whole room seemed emptier and bleaker. An announcement came over the intercom: "Musicians who will be performing at the end-of-school assembly should meet for the duration of second period in the cafeteria." I had to do the lab alone.

In language arts, Dan Manke stood in front of the class and struggled through his five-paragraph essay: "Why Guns Are Great for Society." Everyone — except me, LaTeisha, and Mr. Calvino, but including all of Dan's friends — hooted when he mispronounced words. But at the end, Dan said, "Are guns great for society?" and everyone but me, LaTeisha, and Mr. Calvino roared, "Yes!" Mr. Calvino, looking haggard, checked off boxes on the assessment sheet and totaled up the score. Dan succeeded in his competency.

At the end of class, on my way out the door, Mr. Calvino tried to nab me. "Leah Lobermeir. A word."

I pretended that I hadn't heard him and pushed out with the others.

I went to lunch and carried my tray to the Anita's table. "Can I sit here?"

Iris and Maria huddled together and cackled over a video Iris was playing on her phone. Iris had dyed her hair bright blue and looked remarkably like a cartoon character. Jamie Lopez sat next to Anita. He wore thick black eyeliner and black nail polish, and still had his Zen Buddhism book.

Anita looked up from her drawing pad. "Have a seat, if you're willing to lower yourself." She tipped her head to the side and bit her pencil.

She narrowed her eyes and watched Kristy for a minute. Kristy hunched at her table with her hands buried in her hair. She was talking in a rapid-fire monologue to Corinne, who looked patiently irritated. A football player in a letter jacket wrapped his arms around Kristy from behind and said something in her ear. She punched him.

I stared down at my tray. Lunch was cheese bread with a puddle of grease on top, watery tomato sauce, and a black banana. I threw the banana onto the middle of the table. I hadn't smoked a cigarette in twenty-one hours. I had the chills and felt twitchy. I hid my face in my hands.

I uncovered my face. "Anita," I said, "can you come over today? Please? I quit smoking and feel like I'm having a nervous breakdown and I'm going to throw up." I slid my tray across the table. "Do you guys want this?" Iris and Maria looked with disdain at the tray, then Maria picked up the cheese bread. Iris dipped a baby carrot in the tomato sauce and licked it.

Anita paused in her drawing and watched them for a minute. She erased a hand, then blew away the little pink bits of eraser. "I'm a bit fatigued today and I've got a lot going on. But I can come over for a while."

I felt a shadow and smelled a familiar perfume, strawberry-kiwi. Kristy stood behind Anita with her fists on her hips. She leaned over, pushed her hair behind her ears, and studied Anita's drawing. "How's it going, Anita Sotelo? Am I saying that right? Slutella? Wow. That is such a good drawing. I could never do that. Hey, Leah, what are you doing over here? We missed you. So, tomorrow night, right? It will be the bomb. OK, see you after school, Leah?" Kristy gave me a stern look as she turned.

Kristy stopped and looked back. "Slutella. The po' bitch!"

"God, Kristy! Just go," I said.

She winked at me.

The skin over Anita's cheekbones tightened. She leaned back in her chair, folded her hands together, and pressed them against her mouth as if considering one of the mysteries of the universe.

"Sorry, Anita."

"That girl is your friend." She squinted at her drawing.

Kristy wove between the tables toward the door where Corinne waited. Kristy was wearing knee-high boots with three-inch heels and tried to swagger, but stumbled and wobbled a little with each step.

"Not exactly." Whatever it was between me and Kristy felt like a weight, like a huge heavy duffel bag slung over my neck and shoulders. I'd borrowed a picture of her and stuck her in a dream. The dream had come to life, but it wasn't Kristy in it, and it wasn't me. "I've known her a long time and feel kind of obligated. . . ."

Jamie leaned toward me with his velvety eyes and shaggy black hair. He tapped his finger against his nose. "Leah, listen to me. It's OK for you to be friends with Kristy even if she's a total ass wipe. Because Kristy is just reacting to pain inside of herself, but Anita doesn't let Kristy get to her, so the shit, the chain of suffering, stops with Anita."

"Oh, I might punch her one of these days." Anita rested her face on her fist and closed her eyes.

"Leah, do you understand what I'm saying?" Jamie stroked the back of my hand.

"Kind of." What I did understand was that high school was a giant science experiment. Question to be tested: How much misery can your average kid inflict, and how much can they take? Hypothesis: There is unlimited capacity.

Anita licked the corner of her mouth and hunkered down over her drawing. Jamie leaned over her shoulder and watched her work. "Do you mind?" he said. Jamie and Anita were real. They were real and solid in a horrible simulated high school where everyone else was a hologram.

Someone opened the door, and Kristy disappeared in the bright-white light that flooded in from the hallway.

Thirty-Five

Half a block from the school, the bus stopped. I couldn't see his face, just the dashboard, the steering wheel, part of his lap, the shiny black hood of the Mustang. He had a six-pack jammed next to the gearshift. His hands ran up and down his thighs, then came to rest on the steering wheel.

Kristy's red Civic was third in line to leave the parking lot. She turned and drove the opposite way down Navajo Avenue. The line of school buses blocked Kurt King's view; he didn't see in his rearview mirror as she drove away. He sat there and tapped the steering wheel with his dirty thumbs.

The bus jerked and started to move forward. Anita looked at me with her tea-colored eyes. "You look like you're going to puke."

"I have to get off." The world had gotten shiny and slippery like glass. My head felt huge and empty.

"What?"

"I have to get off the bus. Wait for me in front of my building. I'll be there soon."

I stood up and staggered like a drunk to the front of the bus. Everything was reeling. The bus driver's round grizzled head sunk into his collar. "Get back in your seat!"

"I need to get off."

"Not allowed. This ain't a stop." He had chubby hairy hands, and a dirty Band-Aid around his thumb.

"I'm gonna to throw up. I'm going to throw up all over." I hung on to his seat with both hands. "Swear to God. Please."

"For Chrissake." The driver pulled the bus to the side of the street and yanked open the door.

I ran, coughing. My backpack banged against my shoulder. The thudding of my feet and my breaths rang through the air as though there were no other sounds. The black Mustang was still there, half a block from the school. A trail of exhaust rose from the back.

I slowed to a walk. Sunlight glared off his windshield, and I couldn't see his face over the steering wheel. I walked up to his car. I stopped two feet back from his passenger-side window. The window was open. Kurt King didn't turn his head. He twisted the knob on the radio: static, classic rock, news, hip-hop, country, laughter, a man's loud, fast voice . . .

"What do you want?" Tired, bored.

I wanted to take it all back, and undo it, and never have done it. Roll back time as if it were a huge cloth wound over a cardboard tube. I wanted Ashley to disappear.

"I need to tell you something. But first . . . can I borrow your phone? Just for a second?"

He looked at me. I had no idea what he saw and I wasn't sure what I was seeing. He was all hands and eyes and mouth and streaky bangs.

"Nah." He shifted. The car shuddered and jerked forward. The engine popped like a gunshot as he took off toward the downtown.

Thirty-Six

Anita sat hugging her knees on the steps of the Belmont Manor. "What the hell was that about? I have approximately ten minutes."

She followed me into the building, through the entryway, down the stairs, and into our apartment. I grabbed a box of protein bars, and we went into my room. I tossed her one.

I closed my eyes, leaned back against the wall, and chewed. We sat in silence for five minutes. When I finally opened my eyes, Anita's head hung down and her hair hid her face. She looked up at me through the strands. "You don't want to tell me?"

"No." I tore open another one of Cindy's protein bars—I could just hear her screaming, *Don't eat my food! Now I have to go to the store again! You eat as much as a family of five!* I didn't care.

Anita pushed her bangs out of her eyes, studied the wrapper, then took a tiny bite. "Why don't you have fire egress?" she said.

"What are you talking about?"

"The bars?" She pointed to the window. "How are you supposed to get out of here? If there was a fire, you'd roast."

I looked back at the black-barred window. "This was a one-bedroom apartment, so this is just a closet or a storage room. Listen, Anita, I need to buy a phone. I only have three dollars."

"Man, you can't get away with that in public housing. . . . So, you need money. You want to buy a phone. So you can fix the problem you won't tell me about."

"Yeah. I need to use the same number. I had a phone, but . . ."

"I remember what you did with your phone." Anita propped her feet up on the cracked green wall. "You can't tell me anything more?"

What could I tell her? That guy, in the car, that was him. I dreamed about him, the smell of him, and it yanked me out of sleep. I heard him whisper when I was alone. I could tell her how raspy and monotonous his voice was. He called me Ashley. He could already see her in his hands, in his bed. The me in the dream. But he saw Kristy.

I pressed my head back against the wall and breathed in. "It has to do with Kristy Baker."

"Kris-ty Baker." Anita twirled her hair and stared at the ceiling.

"Yeah . . . Kristy Baker. She's in danger. I'm not joking."

Anita tipped back her head. "What'd you do? Pay someone to kill her? Having second thoughts?"

"No! God, Anita." Everything that I'd done and said and pretended and faked walled me in. I looked out at Anita through an icy little window. "Anita, this is serious. That guy . . . I can't explain."

"OK, sorry. This is stupidly mysterious." She reached up and ran her thumb along the bottom of her left boot where it was tearing from the sole. "Cheap-ass fake leather boots . . . OK, sure, I'll lend you some money. I have to leave anyway. Come on."

"We're going to your house? I'll pay you back."

"Apartment. And, yeah, pay me back sometime. That would be super." She marched out of my room and left the rest of the bar uneaten on the bed.

I picked it up and followed her.

We walked without talking down Vargas Avenue. It was dreamlike walking through the beautiful afternoon when I felt so sick. I was glad I was sick. I deserved to be sick. What I did was sick.

The light glittered as if it were shining through crystals.

A jet whined miles overhead. A kitten staggered through the grass in front of a little house with a sagging porch. Anita dropped to her knees and pulled off her messenger bag. She lay in the grass and rubbed the kitten's tiny throat with her thumb.

She got to her feet and tossed the kitten toward the porch. "Go home, dummy."

Anita lived ten blocks from me in a five-story building made of rose-colored bricks. There was a playground next to the building. Chains without seats dangled from the swing set.

Anita waved her arm toward the swings. "The most disgusting playground in the city," she said. "Used condoms, broken glass, human feces, and needles."

Her building was called the Briarwood. In the entry was a wall of locked metal mailboxes. She had a key to get in and a key to use on the elevator, which was tagged with graffiti inside and out. We rode up in silence, facing the scratched silver doors.

The fourth floor had a narrow dim hallway with a shiny green floor and door after door after door. One of the doors creaked open, and someone peeked out from a dark apartment. Except for some hip-hop thumping in one apartment and TVs blaring from a couple more, it was quiet. Cooking smells oozed out from beneath doors.

Anita commented on each door in her hallway. "Nice

family . . . Real quiet guy . . . Old lady . . . Sweet kids . . . Drug dealer . . . Old lady . . . Old lady . . . Mentally ill guy who goes through everyone's garbage . . . Really sweet old lady, super-duper tiny . . . The mom here weighs six hundred pounds, but super-cute kids . . ." She tapped on #417. "I like to bug him. Hoarder, big-time, you wouldn't believe."

We walked farther down the hall, and Anita unlocked her door, #428. As she pushed it open, she said, "Home, sweet home."

It was completely dark in the apartment except for the TV and a light over the stove. A man sat on the couch in the glow from the TV. He was watching *Jeopardy!* A contestant gave the correct answer, and the people in the audience applauded.

Anita threw her keys on the counter, walked over, and leaned over the back of the couch. She combed her fingers through the man's hair. "Hey, Dad," she said. "How was your day?"

He whispered to her in Spanish. She nodded and continued to pet his head. TV light flickered across his face. In the kitchenette, a black frying pan coated with white grease and a little sink stuffed with crusty plates and a haystack of forks and knives waited for Anita. The refrigerator was duct-taped shut.

Anita took my wrist and pulled me down the hall. "You stay in my room while I go get Evelyn. I'll be right back."

I grabbed her sleeve. "Let me come. Who's Evelyn?"

"My little sister. Her bus is coming in two minutes. It'll be faster if I go alone. Wait in my room." She opened a door. "I'll be back in four and a half minutes."

There was a white pencil of daylight beneath the shade. I felt around for the switch and the room exploded with color.

The walls and the ceiling and even the floor were covered with art. Van Gogh's *The Starry Night*, kid artwork, manga drawings on every size of paper, concert posters, a bookstore poster for *The Melancholy of Haruhi Suzumiya*, pictures torn from magazines, a huge blue print of an old man curled up and playing guitar, paintings in unpainted wood frames. A heart-shaped frame decorated with sequins and paper flowers hung over the bed. The frame held a photograph of a dark-haired woman hugging a tiny girl.

Pierce the Veil and Escape the Fate posters were taped up sideways. Her bedspread was bright blue and woven through with little metallic threads. She had TEST TUBES, NOT BUNNIES and FUR IS DEAD bumper stickers stuck to her headboard. Orange and purple spirals of construction paper hung from the ceiling. Postcards were taped in a crazy mosaic over the whole floor.

Charcoal, pencils, and pens were lined up on the top of an old-fashioned yellow wooden school desk. A sketchbook waited in the center of the desktop.

I heard a cough from the couch and stepped back into

the hallway. Anita's dad's eyes were black and shiny. He had long fluffy bangs over a skinny, wrinkled face. He stared and said nothing.

"Hi, Mr. Sotelo." I waved, stepped into Anita's room, and shut the door.

One thought pounded my brain: *If I could just have one cigarette, every problem in my life would be solved.*

Five minutes later, the door opened and Anita came in holding a large child. She set the child on the bed. The little girl was about seven years old, with long stringy brown hair, huge teeth, and glasses with brown frames propped crookedly on her nose. She had little blue studs in her pierced ears. She squinted up at me.

Anita sat down next to the kid, put her arm around her, and pulled her so close they looked like a two-headed person. "This is Evelyn."

"Hey, Evelyn."

The little girl snorted and looked away as if I were the most boring person she'd ever seen. She was wearing lavender stretch pants and had a round stomach. She swung her little leg.

"Let's get that patch off," said Anita. She pulled down the waist of Evelyn's stretch pants and the top of her polka-dot underwear, and peeled a white patch off Evelyn's hip.

Anita dropped the patch into the black-and-white garbage can. "I hate this stuff. It makes her dopey, but her social worker says she has to wear it to school and the nurse checks. I'll go get us a snack." Before I could say anything, she left me alone with Evelyn.

Evelyn put her hands between her knees and stared at me with her mouth open in what appeared to be disgust. There was nowhere to sit but at the desk or on the bed next to Evelyn. I felt like a giant in the tiny room. I sat on the postcard-carpeted floor. The tape was yellowing and crackly and had dust and little hairs caught on the sticky part.

"Evelyn, where do you go to school?"

She stared at me like I was a beast at the zoo and put her fingers in her mouth.

"OK," I said, "we'll just wait for your sister." I dropped my head between my knees and listened to Evelyn breathing through her stuffed-up nose.

Anita pushed the door open with her hip. "I made some popcorn," she said. "Sorry it took so long. I had to wash the bowl." She set the bowl of popcorn on the floor and sat cross-legged across from me. Evelyn scooted off the bed and rooted through the popcorn with her spitty fingers.

"Go ahead," said Anita, holding out the bowl. She looked anxious, so I took some.

Anita looked at her little sister and slowly brushed the hair off her forehead. "How was your day, Evie?"

"Stupid." Evelyn crouched like a monkey. She lifted out handfuls of popcorn, then dribbled them back into the bowl.

We watched Evelyn play with the popcorn. Anita said, "Welcome to the family."

I ran my finger over the postcards underneath me: *Buenos Días from Cancun, Aloha from Maui,* palm trees, the Eiffel Tower, an obese cat, and mountains topped with white ice and snow. "Where'd you get the postcards?"

"Evie and I hit a lot of garage sales. An old lady sold me a shoe box full of them for twenty-five cents. Then a tenant left a gigantic roll of packing tape when he moved out. I was up late one night, feeling kind of manic." Anita combed Evelyn's hair with her fingers. Evelyn got bored with the popcorn. She tipped over backward. She lay on her back and puffed out her stomach.

"What's up with your dad?" I ran my finger around and around the wheel of a bicycle on a postcard.

"Clinically depressed and alcoholic," Anita said in a blasé voice as if she were saying, *My dad is the manager at RadioShack and plays golf.* She looked down at Evelyn's sweaty spaced-out little face. "He's got bad liver problems. He's a mechanic and used to run a garage, but he's on disability now. He's had a really rough time since my mom died."

"Sorry."

"Yeah, it sucks." She shrugged and started braiding Evelyn's hair. The room's colors exploded around her.

"I like your room," I said. "It's incredible."

Her face broke into a huge grin. "Really?" She looked

down at Evelyn and tried to stop smiling, but she couldn't. "I think of it as my first art installation."

I stood up to look at the picture over her bed. "This is your mom? She's so pretty."

"Yep," said Anita.

Tacked next to the picture of Anita's mom was a photo of a band playing in a garage. A girl with dark hair like Anita's hunched behind the drum kit. "Is that you? You play drums?"

"Just a little. Me and Evelyn stayed with my aunt for two weeks. My uncle has a set. So we were playing one Saturday morning."

In another picture, a skinny redheaded boy was bent over a microphone. "Is that Carl Lancaster? You play in a band with Carl Lancaster?" Carl Lancaster appeared to be gyrating his skinny body.

"Nah, we just messed around a couple times. Have you ever heard him sing? My God. He's fabulous. He's moving to Austin as soon as he graduates." She scooted back against the wall, crossed her legs, and twirled a piece of hair between her fingers. "You guys going out?"

"What? No." I sat back down and pressed my fingers against my temples. Evelyn lay across Anita's legs and looked at me sideways. She drooled on Anita's jeans.

"I like Carl," Evelyn said. She stuck her index finger into her nostril and dug.

"OK, we are here for money." Anita lifted Evelyn's head off her knee. She stood up and stepped over me to get to the dresser. "Evelyn, close your eyes. Close your eyes. Now!" Evelyn scrunched her eyes shut, then covered her glasses with her sticky hands.

Anita lifted up the dresser scarf and ran her hand underneath it. She moved her hand around and knocked over bottles of nail polish. She gathered the ends of the scarf and picked up all the jewelry and makeup in a clinking bundle and looked underneath. She set the bundle back down. She stood motionless with her back to us for a minute. Evelyn opened her eyes, and we stared at each other.

Anita turned around. Her face was stiff. "Let's go," she said. "Let's get the hell out of here. Let's go, let's go, let's go!"

Evelyn rolled onto her back. "I don't want to go."

Anita hauled her up by her arm. "Get your butt up. I've got to get out of here, or I am going to have a panic attack." Anita threw her messenger bag over her shoulder, grabbed Evelyn's hand, turned off the lights, and charged out of the room.

"Shut my door," she said over her shoulder. She ripped Evelyn's jacket off the kitchen table as we walked through.

Anita's father had scooted to the edge of the couch and was yawning in the TV light. "Anita," he said. "Anita . . ."

"Bye, Dad. Be back soon," she sang through the door as she locked it.

She jogged down the hallway, dragging Evelyn behind her. "If I don't get out of here, I'm going to explode." She rode down the elevator with her eyes closed.

Once we were out in the parking lot, she screamed, *"Aaaaaaaaaack!"* She covered Evelyn's ears with her hands. "I love him but I hate him so much! He took my money! Thirty bucks. That's two days in the Johnsons' apartment at five in the morning, and it reeks like cat pee. I was saving up for another piercing. I already gave him twenty. He'll say he had to get groceries. . . . I know he needs to buy stuff, but it's not fair. God, it's not fair! I hate my life! I got to run. . . ." She ran down the street, pulling Evelyn along.

I jogged after them. I managed to run for two blocks, then had to stop and put my hands on my knees. Anita circled back and waited, shifting from foot to foot.

"Where are we going?" I was wheezing and coughing up gunk that tasted like old cigarettes.

"Carl's. Carl is loaded."

"Carl's her boyfriend," said Evelyn. Her little baseball jacket was open over her chubby stomach. She was panting.

"He's not my boyfriend, Evelyn."

"We're going to Carl's?" The ground was littered with crushed cigarette butts. My nose was running and my head felt hollow, and it was all because I didn't have a cigarette.

"Carl plays at weddings and funerals a couple times a

month. He's rich. He's saving up so he can move to Austin, but he'll help us." Anita turned, ready to take off again.

I grabbed her arm. "Anita, stop. Why are we doing this? You hate Kristy."

Anita ran her fingers through her hair. She closed her eyes, took a breath, and opened them. "We have to save Yertle."

The expression on my face must have made her feel like she had to explain.

"It's excellent karma to help someone you hate. It's a law of the universe."

Evelyn squinted up at Anita; her tiny nostrils were almost completely plugged with yellow crusts. Anita kissed Evelyn's forehead. She pulled Evelyn against her stomach and cradled her until Evelyn wiggled away.

"OK, I feel a little calmer. We can walk now," said Anita. She straightened her messenger bag, snapped her jacket up, and took Evelyn's hand. She took a few steps, stopped, reached back, and pulled me after her with her other hand. "Come on, come on, come on. . . ." The afternoon sun soaked the trees and rocky cliffs on the mountain in orange light.

Thirty-Seven

Carl Lancaster lived in Mountain View Estates in a two-story house with skylights. He lived only four blocks from Kristy and two houses down from Ray Ramirez. Anita marched straight up the walk. I said, "Are you sure Carl Lancaster lives here?"

The house had a big green lawn, flower beds, and pots of pansies that had just been planted in black dirt. There was an old-fashioned lamppost in the yard. A flag decorated with a pink rabbit hung from a flagpole. A big straw mat painted with the word WELCOME in green ivy leaves lay in front of the door.

Anita pushed the doorbell button, the door opened, and a

lady smiled at us. She had Easter-egg-blue eyes and streaked hair that swung in a shiny curtain. She had large white teeth. She looked like a mom in an ad for dishwasher detergent.

"Hello, Anita!" she said. "Carl will be so happy to see you. Good heavens, what have you done to your nose? And, my goodness, who is this? Is this the Evelyn I've heard so much about?"

Anita pulled Evelyn around to face Carl's mother. "Hello, Mrs. Lancaster. This is the famous Evelyn. And this is Leah, another friend of Carl's."

"Hello, Leah!" She smiled joyfully, like I'd just presented her with a golden trophy. She crouched down and tilted her head. "Evelyn, would you like a cookie?" She took Evelyn's hand. "Girls, would you mind taking off your shoes?"

Evelyn kicked off her shoes and was led away.

"Thank you, Mrs. Lancaster!" Anita and I left our shoes on a flowered mat and walked through the cleanest living room I had ever been in.

Everything was beige or white. The carpet was thick and white. The couch had tight fat cushions and was piled with so many white pillows there was nowhere to sit. A big glass vase held two dried white flowers. A gold-framed painting of two swans floating in a bright-blue pond hung over the fireplace. There were coasters on the coffee table and a stack of large books with shiny covers—the book on top was *Flowers of the World*. A black piano with a raised lid stood in the corner.

I had walked past this house hundreds of times, stared into its windows, heard the piano playing, and never once considered that Carl Lancaster might live here.

"PTA mom. Carl's an only child. She always wanted another. She's lonely—Bob travels," Anita said over her shoulder as we headed down a hallway. "I love Patty."

We passed a blue bathroom—there were folded towels and a shell-shaped blue soap in a little dish next to a blue sink. We went up some stairs. "I've been here a couple times before," Anita said over her shoulder, and rapped on a door.

"Come in."

Carl Lancaster sat at his computer. As we walked in, he rolled his chair around so that he faced us. "Good afternoon. Greetings and salutations," he said in his deep voice. He played it cool. No surprise at all at finding Anita Sotelo and his lab partner in his bedroom.

Anita sat on the end of his bed, crossed her legs, and said, "Shut the door." I did and sat next to her.

"Carl," she said. "I'm not going to bother with small-talk shit. Leah has a problem she can't tell us about, but she needs help to fix it." She looked at me.

"Yes. That's the situation."

"Can I ask a question?" he said.

"Sure." said Anita, throwing out her hands.

"Leah, what's going on? Why do you treat me like that?"

"Carl, we don't have time to work out your relationship problems right now. . . ."

"No, I need to know. Leah, you know what I'm talking about."

Anita covered her face with her hands. "OK! I'm going to the bathroom." She scooted off the bed, banged out of the room, and left me alone with Carl Lancaster.

I knew what he was talking about.

I was sitting in Carl Lancaster's bedroom. And Carl was sitting there with me, two feet away. There wasn't even the possibility of invisibility. It was so weird to be in his bedroom. I felt scared and alive. I felt my aliveness in every cell.

I lifted my face and looked at him. "I'm sorry."

He held my gaze. "Apology accepted."

"Thanks, Carl." I let out a huge breath and my shoulders sank a little. My throat ached.

"Now what?" he said.

"Now what?"

"Yeah, Leah. Now what?" He slowly swiveled in his chair and watched me. He was wearing a blue cotton shirt, open at the throat, the sleeves rolled halfway to his elbows. His eyes never left me.

"What do you mean, Carl?" But I knew.

"God, Leah!" He rolled around and stared at his screen saver and swallowed. He pushed himself back around to face

233

me. He squinted and winced like it hurt to say it. "Do you like me? Or not? I would just like to clarify this. Because, Leah, I really, really . . ."

"Yes, Carl," I said. Anita rapped on the door and opened it.

She sat back on the bed and bounced. Her eyes were bright. "Everything cool here? God, Carl, what a nice bathroom! I got the soap wet. It's lavender scented. Smell." She stuck her hand under my nose. "I used the lotion, too. And there's super-soft toilet paper."

"Cool." My face was hot. I could feel Carl watching me.

Anita clapped. "OK, guys! Do you mind if we get back to the business at hand? I kind of love a crisis. Even though I don't actually know what this crisis is . . . So, Carl, Leah has this problem. It involves Kristy Baker and potential harm that could come to her." Anita raised her eyebrows and tilted her head.

"Kristy Baker," said Carl. "Kristy Baker?" The way he said her name suggested a long, ugly history.

"Yes. Kristy Baker." Anita pulled her hair over her shoulder and started braiding it.

"And why does Kristy Baker," he said, as if it tasted bad to say the sounds that made up the name Kristy Baker, "and her problem involve me or you or Leah?"

"Well." Anita crossed her legs. "Leah will explain, but she can't really tell us much."

There was a rhythmic knock, the door swung open, and Carl's mom poked her blond head in. "Sorry to interrupt, kids! Can I get you anything?" We all shook our heads. She gave Carl a strained smile and backed out, leaving the door open six inches.

When we heard Mrs. Lancaster talking to Evelyn downstairs, Anita said, "Go ahead, Leah. Tell him. Explain a little."

Explain. Explain? How could I explain? I closed my eyes and caged my face in my fingers. "I quit smoking yesterday. I feel extremely sick."

"You quit yesterday? That's terrific, Leah," said Carl. "This is the worst part. You are at the most acute phase of withdrawal. In a few days, your body will have eliminated many of the toxins, and your cells will have become accustomed to the lack of nicotine. I did a science-fair project. . . ."

"OK, Carl!" said Anita. The chair squeaked as Carl slowly swiveled back and forth. "Go ahead, Leah. Just give him a little clue about why you feel responsible."

Responsible. Responsible, responsible, responsible. I'd heard that word so many times in my life. If you say a word enough times, it loses its meaning, it just sounds like a strange noise. Was I responsible? How could I explain?

Maybe I could explain that one night Kristy and Corinne and I were at 7-Eleven, but then I'd have to explain why I was there with them, and why I was friends with them, when Kristy and I actually sort of hated each other. That was too hard to explain. We were in the store and as we came out, there was a gorgeous guy standing there. He told Kristy that she was the sexiest woman he'd ever seen. How could I explain that? She's tiny, she weighs ninety-three pounds, and she looks like she's twelve. Kristy laughed and got in her car. I ran back to the store because we forgot to buy Flamin' Hot Cheetos, and I'm always the one who goes back—that's easily explained. As I went in the store, he touched my arm and gave me a matchbook. He said, "Give this to the blond girl. Tell her to call me." But I didn't give it to Kristy. I kept it. And I couldn't explain why I did that. A week later, I called him. I couldn't explain why I did that. Then he called and he started talking to a girl named Ashley. It was me. I was Ashley, but he saw Kristy in his head. Ashley was like a third girl who sort of existed and sort of didn't. Ashley only existed when she talked to Mr. Corduroy. She was a girl with my feelings and thoughts, but she had a tiny skinny body and long blond hair, and a mother who was sick and a father, and they both loved her. She lived in a big house and had a room full of roses.

I opened my eyes. I was in Carl Lancaster's bedroom. Everything was boyish and classy. He had a big wooden desk with a stack of drawers on either side. I looked up at a poster of the galaxy, then down at the brown carpet.

I began to feel numb. When things got really hard, I wanted to stop existing. "I need to talk to someone. . . . I need to use the same number as my old phone ... so I can prevent something from happening. ... Oh God, this is so humiliating." I closed my eyes.

"I'm conversant with the feeling," said Carl. He drew his knees up and sat cross-legged in his desk chair. Anita rubbed my back for a few seconds, then put her hands between her knees and stared at the bedspread.

"Who does this involve?" said Carl. He bit the end of a pen.

"Kristy. This guy. Me." And Ashley. But there was no Ashley. "There's a misunderstanding. ..."

"OK, gotcha," said Carl. He looked so serious and sad. "And when exactly did this incident take place?"

Anita's hands flew out. "Just let her talk!"

"It's not one incident. ... It's kind of been ongoing for a month or so. ... OK, I'm done."

Carl rapped a pencil against his desk. I kept my eyes on the carpet. It had been just voices and dreams that ended when I snapped my phone shut. It hadn't seemed real. I had pretended to be a girl who didn't exist, who had never been born. And if Carl found out what I had done, he probably would not like me anymore. And that possibility, suddenly, almost killed me.

Jeans stretched tight over a girl's legs, one small hand held the other, a bent thumb, half-moon at the bottom of a pink nail, restlessly rubbed against the other thumb, and feet pressed together, obedient and ladylike, in navy-blue Vans. Was this me? Was I real? Was I sitting in Carl Lancaster's bedroom? He squeaked back and forth, swiveling in his chair, and watched me with his steady eyes. Anita leaned her hard little head against mine.

Carl's mother burst into the room with a plate full of oatmeal-raisin cookies and Evelyn in tow. "Why so serious, kids?" She'd cleaned out Evelyn's nostrils. Mrs. Lancaster set the cookies on Carl's desk and handed each of us a paper napkin. I looked away from her; Mrs. Lancaster would not give me cookies and a napkin if she knew the things I had done. Carl and Anita woke themselves from their thoughts and sat up.

Carl's mother said, "Carl, this is a special treat. I don't mean to set a precedent. Try not to get crumbs on the carpet."

"Sure, Mom." He pulled on the middle finger of his right hand and cracked the knuckle.

"Carl! Do you remember what Miss Lindsey told you about that? It's an insidious habit. Come on, honey, can we cooperate?" She put her arm around Carl's shoulders and squeezed—even his freckles whitened—and turned to Anita. "Is Evelyn allowed to watch television? I thought I'd put on a Disney movie for her, if you think it would be all right with your parents."

Anita sat up straight and folded her hands on her knee. "I'm sure it would be fine."

"Well, then, I will leave you kids to whatever you are doing! Schoolwork?" Mrs. Lancaster sniffed, as if checking for pot smoke, and took Evelyn's hand. Evelyn, looking drugged with infatuation, followed her out of the room.

"Cookie?" said Carl, holding out the plate. "She's a nice lady. I'm trying to hang on until I turn eighteen. Please shut the damn door!"

"Carl, watch the language." Anita took two cookies and kicked the door shut. "Now, back to the business at hand. Leah destroyed her phone and she needs to buy a new one, but she only has a couple of bucks, and my dad took all my money."

Carl made a church out of his fingers. He turned his head and stared longingly at his screen saver. "Money," he said. "You came here for money. Gee, that's nice, Anita."

"Carl, I've only borrowed money from you twice. And I paid you back." Anita shoved her hair behind her ears, leaned toward him, and put her hand on his knee. "Carl, yes, we need money, twenty bucks, maybe another fifteen for a phone card, nothing huge. We came here mostly for your support."

"Hmmm," said Carl. He turned back to the computer and ran his fingers over the keyboard. "Ho-hum. Carl the ATM."

"We trust you, Carl. Plus, we don't have anyone else to go to," said Anita. She took a tiny bite of her cookie and thoughtfully chewed it. "Are these cookies vegan? Probably not."

Carl swiveled around and faced me. "Leah, give me a straight answer. Is this really important?"

"Oh God, Carl. Yeah, but . . ."

"You're smart. And I trust you." He tipped up his chin. "If you say it's important, I believe you."

I started to sweat just like in chemistry. Carl had that effect on me. I had to close my eyes and block out Carl and his room and Anita and her weird little sister and Carl's house and his Mary Poppins–like mother. I felt dizzy from lack of nicotine. It felt like my head was about to float away.

I sat very still for a minute and then opened my eyes. "Yeah, Carl, it's important. I need another phone. I can't think of any other way."

Carl opened a desk drawer, pulled out a cash box, and unlocked it with a key. He pulled out two twenties and put the box back in the drawer just as the door swung open.

"Carl, why is the door—?"

"Let's go," said Carl. We all stood up. He grabbed a military jacket I'd never seen him wear before. "We're going, Mom."

"Where are you going?"

"We're just going for a walk, Mom. We need a breath of fresh air."

Anita and I slid out the door past Mrs. Lancaster. Her

head swiveled as each of us went through. Up close, she was a little wrinkled and smelled like lemons.

I said, "Nice to meet you, Mrs. Lancaster."

Anita jumped down the stairs two at a time and marched into the living room. "Evelyn, it's time to go."

Evelyn didn't move. She didn't blink. She didn't appear to be breathing. She stared at *The Jungle Book* as if she believed she could make us disappear with the power of her mind.

Anita leaned down and touched her shoulder and said, "Evelyn? Let's go!" She picked up the remote and turned off the television.

Evelyn's head slowly swelled into a red ball. She screamed, flung herself backward on the polar-bear fur rug, and kicked within an inch of the glass fireplace screen. Mrs. Lancaster looked nauseated.

Anita crouched and whispered something in Evelyn's ear. Evelyn instantly stopped crying. She stood up and walked over to Mrs. Lancaster. Her head hung down. "Thank you," she said, wiping her nose on her sleeve. Her little belly poked out.

"You're very welcome," said Mrs. Lancaster with an anxious smile.

As we walked down the street, Mrs. Lancaster stood motionless behind the window.

Thirty-Eight

Carl's green military jacket flapped in the breeze. I'd never spent time with him outside of school. He and Anita, with their thin faces and skinny legs, looked like members of an alternative rock band. Evelyn held both their hands, jumped, and pulled up her knees so she hung between them.

"Evelyn, stop that!" said Anita. She staggered and lowered Evelyn's butt onto the street. I observed Carl and Anita, trying to figure out if they had ever been a couple.

Ray Ramirez was playing basketball with his little brother. He stopped playing, held the ball under his arm, and waved to us. "Hey! How's it going?" Senior class president, doing his job. The strangest thing of all was that Ray Ramirez was actually a very nice guy. He and LaTeisha were like the Greek gods — they were so far above the rest of us, they could afford to be sweet to everyone. A little further down the food chain, people were monsters. At the very bottom, with some notable exceptions, people tended to get decent again.

I'd walked down this street thousands of times, past its lawns, the walkways lined with petunias and little piney shrubs, the automatic sprinklers spinning water across the grass. The driveways were swept, the lawns were raked of every leaf and twig, and all the front doors were decorated with welcome mats and American flags. It used to look like the world to me, but now it looked like a stage set. We were two blocks from Kristy's house.

"I don't want to walk past Kristy's house."

"Detour," said Carl. We took the long way down Mountain Meadow Street.

We darted between cars across Pueblo Avenue and headed down the hill toward Tenth. And it didn't even occur to me what impression it might make for me to be seen with Anita Sotelo and Carl Lancaster until a car of kids passed. They hooted and shouted; someone threw a smashed pop can that hit Carl's shoulder. A boy yelled, "Hey, Fat-Ass." It burned for a second, but I didn't change my expression or slow down; I walked right through it. It was like walking through a wall of glass that vanishes the second you push against it. Carl said something funny, and I laughed.

We went to the Walmart. Carl and I both handed money to the checkout lady. She had saggy powdered cheeks, orange circles of blush. She winked at Carl over her bifocals. "Do you get the change, honey, or should I give it to one of your girlfriends?"

As we walked back out the automatic door, Anita frowned and chewed her thumbnail. "God, I hate cell phones. You do know that there's a bloody civil war going on in the Congo over the stupid mineral they need for cell phones and laptops, and they're destroying the lowland gorilla's last habitat, all for . . ."

"Anita," said Carl. He scratched the back of his neck and squinted. "Leave it for now. We can discuss this later."

I tore off the thick plastic packaging. The cell phone was so small and shiny. I closed my fingers over it. We stood on the curb of the parking lot.

"Now what?" I felt damp and clammy, as if I had a terrible virus.

"We've got to activate the phone and phone card. Who's got a laptop or a smartphone?"

"I don't have Internet. You don't either, right, Anita?"

Anita put her hands around her neck as if measuring it. "Nope. No kind of computer or computer access at my place." She gazed across the parking lot and pulled Evelyn against her stomach.

"I guess we're going back to Mrs. Lancaster's house," said Carl. He looked extremely tired for a second, then he threw his arms around our shoulders and we started walking.

As we walked, I laughed and talked, but mostly concentrated on Carl Lancaster's arm around my shoulders. His arm and hand molded against me. The warmth of him soaked through my hoodie. He was about five inches taller than me. I looked over at Anita—she was laughing, snorting the way she did when she was happy. Carl's face was so close to mine. He didn't look at me, but I felt him watching me with his whole body. He ran his hand over my hair, and I tripped.

Carl grabbed my arm. "Are you OK?"

Back at Carl's house, in a fast silent line, we kicked off our shoes and walked through the house and up the stairs without giving Mrs. Lancaster a chance to ask questions or offer us cookies. Carl locked the door and turned on his computer. "Leah, have a seat. Go for it."

I sat down in the blue light. His mother rapped on the door. "Carl. Carl! I'm afraid this is not a convenient time to have guests."

"We're just setting up Leah's cell phone!" Carl yelled. "Don't worry. They'll be gone in two minutes."

"I didn't mean to suggest that they weren't welcome," Mrs. Lancaster said through the door.

I typed like crazy and turned on the phone. "Just one minute . . . done."

Evelyn rolled off Anita's lap and lay on the carpet, looking up at me.

"I don't want to leave you guys." I wanted to stay forever

in Carl's room with Carl and Anita and Evelyn and the poster of the galaxy. *You are here.*

Carl and Anita nodded. Evelyn lolled against Anita's foot and stared at me with her googly eyes.

A key clicked in the lock. Mrs. Lancaster opened the door. "I'm so sorry, girls. . . ."

Thirty-Nine

We stood in a triangle facing one another. The late-afternoon light was golden and shone on Anita's face. Her skin looked ashy. She had purple moons under her eyes. "I should get home soon. I have to get up at four thirty." Anita zipped up Evelyn's jacket and took her hand.

"I wish we could hang out later," I said.

"I can't believe she used the key. It's humiliating. That is my room. I'll be eighteen in two years. I could join the army next year. I should! She'd love that! Except, I'd hate to be in the army. . . ." Carl ground the toe of his shoe into the driveway. "And I probably can't go out tonight. I have a lesson at six, then dinner, then I have to practice for a couple of hours. I've got a recital Sunday. God, I hate my life."

"Anita, can you get out?"

"I don't know." Anita shook her head and stared at the ground. "Evelyn would have to come. She's been kind of sick and probably should go to bed early." Evelyn let go of Anita's hand and swung around the lamppost in Carl's yard.

A huge cloud covered the sun and it was suddenly cold. The mountain loomed over us. Carl and Anita were both so skinny, and even standing there together, they already looked lonely. It was time for us to separate and go back alone to our rooms.

Carl put his hand on my shoulder. "I will try. I might be able to meet you at eight. Call me at seven. Do you guys want to go out tomorrow night? I can probably use the van." His mother walked behind the glass in her white living room. She stopped and adjusted one of the dried flowers.

"I'm out of here." Anita suddenly turned and walked down the street. She called back, "Call my landline about tomorrow."

I turned to Carl and felt a jolt. No one had ever looked at me the way Carl did. Calm, steady, undistracted, intrigued, like he saw possibilities in me that I didn't even know about. He put his hand on my shoulder, and I could feel him, Carl, through his warm hand. And I knew he could feel me seeing him.

I touched his hand for half a second, then scooted out from under it. "I'll call you at seven. See you, Carl!" I ran to catch up with Anita.

Anita didn't talk as we walked home. She kept her head down. Evelyn trotted alongside with her chin tilted up toward the sky. I walked them to their building.

Anita turned and gave me a tight hug, but still didn't look at me. "Good luck with whatever the hell this is about. If anything seems weird, call 911."

She unlocked the entrance door. She pushed Evelyn through. The door slowly shut behind them, then locked with a click. I wanted her to look back. I willed her to please look back and smile at me. She took an envelope and some flyers out of the mailbox, then unlocked the second door. Strands of black hair hung down her narrow back. She sagged to the side because Evelyn was hanging on to her shoulder and yammering at her. They went through the second metal door, and it slammed shut.

I walked home. A mountain of phone books had been dumped in my building's entry with the pizza flyers. I went down the stairs and walked to #3.

Cindy was wearing a lime-green uniform. She pulled a box of generic cereal out of a paper bag. "I'm going to let you get your own dinner," she said into the cupboard. "I'm sorry, but please don't ask anything of me. I had a horrible day and I need to zone out. If you want the TV, you may watch while I shower."

I went into my room, locked the door, and lay on the bed. I kicked my backpack onto the floor, and it landed with a thunk. I'd forgotten about school, even though I'd been carrying a fifty-pound backpack around all afternoon.

I tipped back my head. Light shone through the bars and the streaks of red dirt. The walls were bare now, except for Bruno Mars and Damien Rogers—no more kittens or puppies. They'd all grown up and run away.

The newspaper picture of Damien Rogers was rumpled and already beginning to turn yellow. I got up on my knees and looked at it. It was a newspaper photo of a high-school game with a guy in right field who was maybe Damien Rogers or maybe somebody else. I peeled the tape off the wall. As I crumpled the paper, my heart punched the inside of my chest.

I didn't even have to try to remember the number—my thumb just tapped it out.

He answered on the second ring. "Ashley, I knew you'd call me back."

I heard my voice tell him to meet at the Burger King by Torrance Park on Saturday night at eleven and hung up.

Forty

I opened my eyes. The lightbulb blazed over me. It was quarter to seven.

In the shower, I closed my eyes and stood swaying in the hot steamy air. I felt a little less nauseous, less dizzy and jittery. My cells seemed to be excreting nicotine the way Carl said they would. I used Cindy's body wash and shaving cream, and shaved until my legs were shiny.

I turned off the water and dried myself off with a ratty blue towel that smelled like mildew. In the steamy mirror, I saw a girl with wet black hair and pink skin. Usually, I couldn't bear to look at my body, but sometimes I did and sometimes had the secret thought that my breasts were so beautiful, it was tragic that no one could see them but me.

Corinne called my cell phone. "Finally, you bought some

minutes. I'm soooooo bored. I have to babysit. Kristy's dad made her go to the youth group at their church. It goes till like eleven! He's driving her both ways to make sure she doesn't skip." That meant Kristy was safe for the night at least.

I called Carl on the new phone.

"I can come over tonight," he said. "I told my mom I was going to be an accompanist for Mary Rogers. She's practicing for the state vocal comp. Should I come to your house?"

"Meet me at 7-Eleven at seven thirty."

Cindy was curled up on the couch. She laughed and rubbed the wineglass against her mouth. "Where are you going, sweetheart? Why don't you come watch this show with me?" she said, still staring at the TV.

"I have to go to the drugstore to get a binder for my history report. It's required."

"Stay in well-lit areas!" Her eyes glowed in the TV light. She laughed again.

"Mom, it's still light out."

It was a spring night, and the light was blue. The air was warm and soft. It was the kind of night that tore your heart out. Dogs barked and people laughed in their yards. Music trailed from car windows and faded away.

The 7-Eleven was deserted. I kept checking my phone. An old man in a blue truck pulled in. He went inside and bought a can of chew, then struggled back into his truck and drove away. I waited out front, but felt conspicuous and pathetic because it was Friday night and everyone was driving around with their friends. I went into the store and bought a blue Slurpee and ran into the bathroom when anyone pulled up out front. I almost swiped some breath mints but stopped myself. The windows turned black.

"You got to buy something else or leave," said the guy behind the counter. He was a big, sad boy with purple acne scars, the brother of a girl I knew. He'd graduated three years before.

I pushed through the dirty glass doors, ducking my head so the guy at the counter wouldn't see that I was on the verge of crying because I was the biggest idiot in the world and Carl Lancaster was a nerd and a jerk. I was stupid enough to believe that something good could happen to me.

Carl bumped across the parking lot on his ten-speed. He wore an orange bandanna around his head under his bike helmet. "Leah!"

He rode up to me and put his feet on the ground. He cracked all the knuckles on his left hand. "Sorry I'm so late. I got busted. My mother called fricking Mary Rogers's mother and asked if I was accompanying her. She went berserk. I had to sneak out. Are you OK?"

"I'm fine. You better get back home before your mom . . ."

"I had to let you know what was going on. My mom confiscated my phone. Are you all right?" He looked carefully at me. "I'll walk you home."

I walked beside Carl. He kept his head down and had a very serious expression on his face as he rolled his bike along. We walked on the same sidewalks I'd walked on thousands of times, but everything felt new. The night billowed in soft waves around us. Wind blew through my body, and all the little hairs on my arms were breathing. We didn't say anything; we just walked alongside each other as if our being together was a kind of talking.

When we got to my building, I turned to face him. "Well, Carl . . ."

He leaned over and kissed my mouth with his warm, dry lips. I put my hand on his neck, and he shivered. His helmet bumped against my head.

After a minute, Carl pulled away and buried his face in my hair and seemed to be breathing me. I was so glad I didn't smell like smoke anymore. He let out a huge sigh and kissed me again. He lifted the front wheel of his bike, turned around, and shot off into the darkness.

Forty-One

The next day was Saturday. Anita came over with Evelyn in the afternoon. We waited in my room for Carl. Anita lay across the end of the bed with her head touching the floor on one side and her feet in a box of clothes on the other. She watched Evelyn pull the books off my cardboard bookshelf. "Evelyn, put those books back.. You're wrecking them. Leah, what's going on with—"

Evelyn opened up *Green Eggs and Ham*. She turned a page and ripped it.

I said, "That's a special book, Evelyn. Hand it over." I held out my hand for the book and coughed. Ever since I quit smoking, I'd had a runny nose. Overnight, I'd developed a sore throat, and it hurt to talk. I hoped I hadn't given anything to Carl.

Evelyn stood up and threw the book at me. Her shirt didn't come down over her stomach.

Anita banged her head against the carpet. "Ugh, where's Carl? His stupid mother."

There was a rap on the door. Cindy, in her robe and a towel turban, opened the door and gave me a nauseating smile. "Leah, you have another guest." She swung the door open and squashed Evelyn behind it.

Carl slunk in and raised his hand in greeting. "Hey." Cindy stood in the doorway with glazed eyes, smiling.

"Bye, Mom." I climbed over Anita and shut the door. Carl sat on the floor against the door.

Evelyn leaned on his leg. "Carl," she said. She gazed up at him, put her little hand on his knee, and pretended to play piano. She had a few flakes of sparkly orange polish on her fingernails.

Anita pulled herself up and sat cross-legged on the bed. She rubbed her eyes and smeared her makeup. "Finally, Carl."

He pulled up his knees; he was wearing combat boots that made his feet look enormous. "I stood my ground. I said I'm sixteen and it's Saturday and I'm going to see my friends. I want my phone back. And I'm going out tonight, too. May I please use the van? I work my ass off and I deserve to have a little fun."

"My God, Carl. You actually used the word 'ass'? What did she say?"

"Her mouth got really tight and she said, 'Fine.' Then she went into the backyard and smoked a cigarette."

"Really? Patty smokes?" Anita propped her chin on her fist.

"I owe you, Carl." I coughed and quickly wiped my nose on my sleeve.

"No rush. I get paid to play a wedding next week. Are you sick?" He shyly stared at my ugly carpet. His hands hung over his knees, and his right hand tightly held his left wrist. Carl Lancaster was sitting in my pathetic bedroom, and I didn't seem to care. I was fine with it.

"Looks like we can go out tonight." Anita looked at Carl and then at me. "What should we do? Want to go down to Torrance Park for kicks?"

"What's happening with your big Kristy Baker problem? Have you gotten it all straightened out?" Carl bunched up his eyebrows. He methodically cracked the knuckles of both hands.

Anita stacked her fists under her chin. "Yeah! What's going on? Did you—?"

"I'm working on it."

The phone in the living room rang. Cindy came to the door again. She smiled down at Carl and winked. She handed me the landline. "My goodness, Leah, you are certainly the social butterfly today."

I took the phone from her. "Hey, Kristy." Carl and Anita both stiffened.

Kristy said, "Why was your phone off? We're going to the park tonight, remember? We'll pick you up at six. Dave and Rob told me they saw you yesterday with Anita Sotelo and Carl Lancaster. What the hell were you doing with them?"

I kept my gaze on the wall and thought it was probably how the earth looked from the window of a plane. The crack was a river.

"I'll call you back." I pushed the button and ended the call.

A minute before, I'd been sitting in my room with Anita and Carl, but now when I looked at them, just for a flash, I saw Anita Sotelo and Carl Lancaster. Carl's face was so thin and serious and freckled, his lips were chapped, and he had a little acne on his high cheekbones, and those long white freckly fingers. And Anita's face was kind of gray from getting up at four thirty, and also because she was probably anemic from being vegan and not getting enough iron. Her thick eyeliner was smeared, and she wore cheap, flimsy scarves and leggings and knockoff Keds.

Carl picked at the bottom of his combat boot. Anita stared cockeyed at the wall and chewed her thumbnail.

"Hey," I said. "You guys." They looked up at me, and I saw my friends again.

"I've got to go down to the park with Yertle and Corinne. We already planned it, and I can't get out of it. Just for a little while. Then I'll meet up with you guys."

And then I had to meet someone at eleven. Just for a minute.

Carl blew air through his teeth. "I can only use the van if I'm home by ten thirty. I can't be tired for the goddamn recital."

Anita had her head tipped back and watched Carl's face. Carl was looking at me. His gaze stopped at my mouth, then traveled up to my eyes. I looked at the carpet, my heart whumping.

"But theoretically, I'm OK with it," he said. "Who is Yertle?"

Anita pulled her legs up to her chest and pressed her chin against her kneecap. Her eyes looked darker, the lines of her face sharper than usual. "Fine. I might have to bring Evelyn."

"Excuse me, girls. I need to use the restroom." Carl got up and went out the door; we could hear him talking to Cindy.

Cindy said, "I understand you are a musician, Carl!"

Anita rolled over and looked at the ceiling. She tilted her

head as her gaze followed the outline of a stain. "You guys are a couple?" She sat up, crossed her legs, and straightened her spine in a yogi pose. She took some deep breaths and blew them out. "Cool."

Evelyn was sitting on my paperbacks. She paged through *Hop on Pop* and sang a song that we used to sing at the YWCA camp I went to on scholarship when I was eight:

> *"I'll sing you one, Ho.*
> *Green grow the rushes, Ho.*
> *One is one and all alone*
> *And evermore shall be so.*
> *I'll sing you two, Ho.*
> *Green grow the rushes, Ho . . ."*

Carl opened my door and stood in the doorway. Cindy was still talking behind him. He stared at my window. "Holy crap, no fire egress."

One is one and all alone and evermore shall be so. An atom. I always thought that was me.

Forty-Two

At five o'clock, Corinne called. "We'll pick you up at six."

"You're going?"

I heard her blow out smoke. "Yeah. I'm sick of Kristy and her shit, but I don't have anything better to do. Hey, what the hell, I heard you've been hanging around Anita Sotelo and Carl Lancaster again."

I opened the door to my room just as Cindy rushed from her room into the bathroom. The brother of a dental hygienist had invited her to the Hilton Days barbecue, then to a line dance at the Stoplight Lounge. It was the weekend of Hilton Days, the town's yearly festival. There were pancake breakfasts, bingo games, and country bands playing all over town. There'd been a parade down Torrance Avenue at two o'clock that afternoon. Kelsey Parker's big sister was going to be crowned Hilton Days Queen at a rodeo on Sunday.

I stood in the bathroom doorway. Cindy leaned close to the mirror and blended her eye shadow with her pinkie. She pulled back, bunched up her lips, then leaned in again and checked her teeth. She took a brush from her makeup bag and dusted bronzer on her cheeks, shoulders, and boobs. She pulled open her shirt and blew into it.

"Hey, Mom."

She spun around and posed against the sink. She was wearing tight white capris that were now dusted with bronzer, a neon-blue tank top, and new red sandals that laced up her ankle. She lifted her foot. "They hurt like hell, but I love 'em! Leah, how do I look? I stopped at the tanning salon. Do I look burnt? I finally colored my hair last night. Is it too much red? What do you think? Am I presentable?"

Her pupils were huge. Her breath smelled like Chardonnay. The corner of her mouth quivered a little.

"You look pretty."

Her face relaxed. "Really? You're not just flattering me? Because you feel sorry for me? Because I'll be forty in a couple of years."

"You're younger than all my friends' mothers. You look beautiful."

"Beautiful? Oh, Leah, you can't be serious."

"God. Yes! Now leave me alone."

"Oh, sweetie. Sorry, I'm a little nervous. A very handsome gentleman is taking me out tonight." She took my face between her hands, being careful of her nails; I could smell the polish. She pulled my head down for a tiny kiss on my forehead. "What are your plans, honey?"

She blinked like a little girl and gave me her cute, wobbly smile. She was pretending to forget that I was grounded. I'd rather she'd just say outright that it was too much hassle to be a mother. It took a lot of energy to enforce rules and curfews and groundings. It was boring and tedious to plan and cook nutritious family dinners, especially when that family didn't include a guy and consisted of a fat girl and a tired woman who just wanted to drink wine and space out in front of the TV. She got furious when I got in trouble because then she'd have to do something. "It's as much a punishment for me as it is for you!"

"I'm going over to Kristy's."

"You girls have a wonderful time. Be safe. Give Connie a kiss from me."

There was a honk in front of the building.

"Oh my God, he's here. He said he'd honk." Cindy grabbed her jean jacket, rushed across the room, and pulled a red cowboy hat out of a shopping bag. She carefully put the hat on her head without squashing her curls.

"Does this hat look stupid? It does, doesn't it? Oh, well! It's cute." She slung her red leather purse over her shoulder, took a big breath, and strolled out of the apartment.

She rattled her keys and tried to lock the door. "Screw it. Have a lovely evening, sweetie!" she called from the hallway.

Her voice floated down from the street. "Well, howdy, partner." Then the clonk of a car door. The engine faded away. I was alone.

I sat down on the edge of the sofa and ran my foot over the faded green carpet. The apartment felt unpleasantly still, like a heart that wasn't beating. I thought about how lucky I was that Cindy was never able to maintain a punishment of any kind for more than six hours. Corinne's and Kristy's parents were very strict—if they said you were grounded, you were grounded. Of course, Corinne's mom allowed her to smoke. Cindy technically did not allow me to smoke, though she had never commented on the fact that I always stank like cigarettes. When she found smoke in the bathroom and a butt swirling in the toilet, she yelled, "No smoking in the goddamn apartment, or we'll get a huge cleaning fee when they kick us out!" "I choose my battles," I'd heard her tell her sister Linda over the phone. Now I'd quit smoking and she'd never even told me to stop.

I was unable to find an expression to put on my face. It felt like my face might slide right off onto the carpet.

My knee ached. All of my bones ached. It was an ache

that started in my leg and radiated toward my stomach. Maybe I had bone cancer. I'd seen on TV once that bone cancer could be triggered by a sharp blow. I rolled up the leg of my jeans and looked at the blue bruises and the scab from when I'd tripped on Corinne's walkway. I stood up and went into Cindy's room.

I sat on the edge of her bed and ran my finger over the velveteen bedspread. I lay back and looked up at the leaves and flowers burnt into the maple headboard. When I was a little girl, I'd lie on the bed and stare at the headboard while Cindy got ready for work. I pretended that the headboard was a door to another world, and that was the world where my dad lived. It was full of flowers and leaves, but they only turned from orange to all the colors once you stepped inside.

The bed frame was the first piece of furniture that Cindy and Paul bought together. The story Cindy always told was that they were on a country drive and saw a sign for handmade furniture. They drove down a gravel road past a field full of sunflowers to a pole barn where a rancher was selling chairs, rocking horses, magazine racks, and bed frames.

We'd dragged the bed from apartment to apartment. On moving day, Cindy would get one of her coworkers' boyfriends to help us move with his truck. She'd make brownies, buy a case of beer, put on eyeliner, and tell the sad story of Paul, and how he'd died two years to the day, almost, from when they bought the bed. Besides our pathetic little

Christmases, the moving-day ritual was our only family tradition. The guys always listened to Cindy's story with blank faces while they drank all the beer.

It suddenly occurred to me that the burnt flowers and the shellacked orange wood were hideous. I could have drawn better flowers when I was six. The bed was the ugliest piece of furniture I had ever seen. Paul and Cindy had chosen an extremely ugly bed. That made me so sad I almost started crying. I rolled off the bed onto the carpet.

I lay there for a while thinking about how strange and giant things look when you lie on the floor, then got up and went to the dresser where Cindy kept her makeup, creams, and hair appliances laid out like surgical supplies on a lacy blue cloth. I pulled out the wand of her mascara, twisted out her lipsticks, sprayed perfume on my wrists and behind my ears. I rubbed seaweed moisturizer that smelled bad onto my arm. I opened her jewelry box with the little gold key and lifted the lid just enough for the theme song from *The Princess Bride* movie to leak out.

I pushed in the plastic folding door of Cindy's walk-in closet. Her shirts, sweaters, and dresses hung on blue hangers spaced two inches apart. Hanging against the wall was the peacoat with big plastic buttons that Cindy had worn for ten years. It was dingy and faded and covered with fabric pills. One of the buttons hung by a thread. "I'll never get rid of that coat. It reminds me of what I've been through. I worked three part-time jobs for an entire decade to give you new shoes and school supplies," she'd say. Then she'd stare at me and take a big swig of wine.

Her shoes were lined up beneath the coat and dresses and work uniforms. Besides her white work shoes, she had a pair of black pumps and a pair of high-heeled sandals, both ready for a big day, though the strappy sandals were sagging to the side as if they were tired of waiting. Hideous brown leather slip-ons with tassels "just for casual." The white walking shoes for the power walks she and a friend took for two weeks before they quit. There were fur-lined snow boots with blue laces that she'd owned my entire life but never worn once. And now a pair of bright-red sandals could join Cindy's collection of shoes.

On the shelf above the closet pole was the faded blue-and-white shoe box that held my baby pictures. I dropped onto the floor of the closet with the box.

My baby pictures slid around the bottom of the dusty old shoe box. The photos of me stopped at age two, when Paul died. Other than pictures taken by my friends, the only pictures taken of me since had been school pictures. We had bought the cheapest package twice, so I knew how chubby I'd been in third and fifth grade. The pictures my friends took of me with their phones always got deleted.

I was a fat but beautiful—no exaggeration—baby with fuzzy dark hair and huge saggy cheeks. Whenever I looked at the pictures, I fell into a trance. We looked so happy. I was the happiest-looking baby I'd ever seen.

I looked happier than Jimmy ever was, maybe because I was an only child, though Paul and Cindy had wanted another one. I turned the picture over—Cindy had written in her tight neat handwriting: *One year, three months, and five days old.* I was asleep on Paul's chest.

Paul had curly hair so short that it was just a ruffle on top of his head. His ears were so flat against his skull, he looked earless. He had huge dark eyes like mine. His brushy eyebrows grew together over his nose. I was glad I hadn't inherited his unibrow, though I could have waxed it. He had long cheeks and a small mouth with full lips. That was my mouth. It was weird to see a picture of someone who looked like me. No one else in the whole wide world did, as far as I knew. He didn't seem embarrassed to have a baby asleep on his chest. I was sleeping with my mouth open, with a little drop of drool on my lip, my head tipped back and tucked under his chin. He looked like a hands-on dad, though Cindy had said many times that he'd changed my diaper "exactly once."

In the next picture, Cindy and Paul stood together with me squeezed between them. Their hair blew in a long-ago wind, and fat clouds puffed across a long-ago blue sky. Cindy and Paul looked young and proud, as if they believed they were the lucky ones. I'd always wondered who took their picture. Probably a stranger who forgot about them five minutes later.

When I looked at his picture, I tried out the names. *Dad. Daddy. Pop.* None of them worked. Only Paul. He was antimatter dad, the black hole that had sucked love and money and happiness out of our lives. Maybe I'd end up drunk on a couch and never be a doctor because Paul was my father.

The few times I'd asked about him, Cindy said, "Your father was a sweet guy, but a drinker. That's all I have to say."

I first heard the story by accident when I was eight. Cindy and her friend were drinking wine in the kitchen at the apartment in Tallahassee. I was pretending to be asleep, with my eyes squeezed shut and my hand between my cheek and the scratchy couch.

He was supposed to be at work, but instead he went to a bar and drank a lot of beer and tequila. On the way home, he drove his truck into a telephone pole. Cindy started crying and said, "The poor, dumb bastard!" I'd thought she said "custard."

Sometimes at night, when I couldn't sleep, I tried to picture it. I wondered if he was alive for a few minutes, all alone in the broken glass and torn metal. Did he struggle to breathe? Did he think someone would come any minute and save him? Did a vision of a chubby toddler with dark hair flash through his mind before he died?

Forty-Three

I was outside waiting by the street when Kristy pulled up. She didn't say hi, but she turned off the music even though, or maybe because, Corinne was singing along. She bumped up over the curb as she did a U-turn.

When we got to Kristy's house, Pastor Steve was leaving. He was wearing a baby-blue polo and khakis belted a little high over his flat stomach. He was tan, and his short blond hair stuck straight up with static.

Pastor Steve hugged and rocked Kristy while she chewed gum against his shoulder. "Kristy, how are you holding up during this difficult time? Is there any way that I can be of service to you?" Then he took Corinne's hand in his left hand and mine in his right, and furrowed his forehead like he was worried about our souls. "So glad to meet you girls."

Everything at Kristy's house was just the same, except that there were daisies in the clay jug. The light of the late sun shone through the smudged windows and lit up the crumpled beige carpet. Kristy's dad puffed as he leaned over to untie his shoes. He collapsed back into his easy chair. His toes, in faded black socks, pointed straight up at the ceiling. He looked over at me with his sad eyes. "How's my girl?"

Kristy's mom sat on the couch wrapped in the orange-and-brown blanket decorated with pom-poms. "Hello, girls. We've just been praying with Pastor Steve. It's such a comfort to me. Look at what the ladies from church brought me. It's so beautiful and warm."

Corinne and I looked at the blanket, even though we'd first seen it weeks before. "Neat," said Corinne. Kristy's mom let the blanket fall off her shoulder, put her hand on the arm of the couch, and tried to push up.

"You don't have to get up, Connie," said Kristy's dad.

"Mom, please," said Kristy.

"Well, hell's bells, I can stand up if I want to." Everyone tensely watched as she rose from the couch and stood wobbling next to it.

"Girls," she said, "it's so good to see you. Thank you for coming to keep Kristy company. It's so dreary for her at home. . . . All she hears is *sick, sick, sick. Mom, Mom, Mom . . .* Corinne and Leah, come over here and give me a kiss."

271

I said, "I can't come near you, Mrs. Baker. I've got a sore throat."

"You call me Mom, Leah! Sorry you're not feeling so good." She kissed Corinne's dimpled cheek. "What's new with you, sweetheart?"

"I'm thinking of going to the culinary institute in Denver. To become a chef."

"How wonderful for you!"

Kristy rolled her eyes. She snapped her fingers and swayed as if she heard a song inside her head.

"Kristy, Dad bought loads of groceries. He's going to make his special sloppy joes for you girls tonight. Maybe you can give him a few pointers, Corinne." She started to teeter. Corinne held her elbow, and Mrs. Baker sank back down onto the couch.

"Mom, we're going to Hilton Days. We're eating out," said Kristy. She jerked her head, signaling for us to head to her bedroom.

"Kristy, are you going to the pie auction?" Kristy's mom called in a faint voice as we headed down the hallway. "I heard Mrs. Jameson—Charlie's mom—made some fabulous peach pies."

Corinne's backpack was clinking. She'd snuck into her mom and stepdad's wet bar and stolen a liter of vodka and a bottle of crème de menthe.

"We're not going to the pie auction, Mom!" Kristy yelled, and shut the door.

Corinne unscrewed the cap on the crème de menthe. She took a slug. "The coach called my mom and talked to her for an hour. Then Mom and Derrick discussed it, but Derrick said no." She wiped her mouth with the back of her hand and took another swig.

Kristy sneered and kicked back on her bed. "Keep that crap away from me. I hate it. It makes me want to throw up." She scooted back against the headboard and glared at Corinne as though she couldn't believe the idiot she'd let into her house.

Corinne put the bottle back into her backpack and zipped it up. She slowly got to her feet. "Sucks, though. I could get a softball scholarship to Western University. They have a really good culinary institute."

"Would you shut up about the stupid culinary institute?" Kristy jammed little foam pads between her long bony toes. She unscrewed a bottle of polish.

That afternoon, Cindy had come back from Walgreens with the same kind of foam pads. She showed them to me in their plastic packaging. "Lookie! I just need to pamper myself once in a while!" I'd wanted to scream, *Cindy, don't use the word "lookie." Get a life!* Just like I wanted to scream, *You are trying to destroy me!* when she brought out the waxing kit and said, "You may not be able to see it, but in direct sunlight the hair is quite visible. When I can afford it, I'm going to get you a laser treatment." She'd shake her hope jar. "You've got to plan, Leah!" She didn't mean any harm. That was the worst part. She loved me. That was love.

Kristy finished her left foot and began to paint her right big toenail. "So," she said, smiling softly, "how's Slutella and Caaaaaaaaarrrrl Lan-cas-ter?"

I leaned back on the heels of my hands and looked in the full-length mirror. A girl with dark eyes stared back at me. I shook back her hair. "Not bad."

"Oh!" she said. I watched Kristy in the mirror as she smiled at her toes and tipped up her chin. "Are they just loads of fun? What do you guys do together? Draw anime people with big eyes and jaggy hair? Does Caaaaaarrrrl play piano for you?"

I didn't say anything, and Kristy looked up. Corinne had just finished lining her eyes and watched both of us. We were all watching each other in the mirror.

"Shut up, Kristy," said Corinne. She tilted her head and smudged the liner with her pinkie.

Kristy looked up at the ceiling and said, "Wow." She shook out her curly white hair as if to remind us who she was. She snapped her headphones on and rolled onto her stomach with her feet in the air. She opened her laptop. "Screw both of you," she said over her shoulder.

Everything looked the same as it had since seventh grade. That was the year Kristy's mom redecorated the room to celebrate Kristy turning thirteen. Corinne stood hunched in front of the mirror with her flat little butt tucked in, her small feet disappearing into the frayed bottoms of her jeans. She wore a big stack of bangles. Kristy lay on her stomach, surrounded by her magic hair. She whispered the words to a song and frenetically typed on her keyboard.

We always pretended that everything was normal, everything was wonderful, as though Kristy's mom wasn't wrapped in a hideous pom-pom blanket as she died of cancer on the couch down the hall. We pretended that Kristy and Corinne hadn't ditched me for two weeks. Ditched, trashed, thrown away, erased, like I was a picture you could delete from a phone. Like I'd done to Anita.

Everything was great, even if Corinne's stepfather wouldn't let her join the softball team, though she was the best girl pitcher in the school and the coach begged. The coach said she could play varsity. Derrick wanted Corinne to babysit. Derrick had already decided that if Corinne wanted to go to college, she could study accounting at the vo-tech. She'd have job security.

Everything was fantastic, even if Cindy was getting blasted at the Stoplight Lounge. She was probably crying and telling her date the story of Paul.

And I sat on Kristy's pink carpet as if I was Leah and

Kristy was Kristy, and there was no Mr. Corduroy and there never had been an Ashley.

There was a soft knock on the door. "Girls, fifteen minutes."

"OK, Mr. Baker," I said.

Kristy twisted around and lifted off her headphones. "What did my dad say?"

"Fifteen minutes." I was tying tiny knots in the tufts of pink carpet.

"Tell him OK."

"I already did."

Kristy lay there with her bony feet waving in the air. She gave me a long, evil look. "Hey, Chubs. You really think you should wear that? Those jeans make you look kinda—"

I couldn't play along anymore. Chubs. I wasn't Chubs. "Kristy, why do you even hang around me? Do I make you feel better about yourself? 'Cause I'm fat? And poor?"

Kristy rolled over and raised herself up on her elbows. Her eyes were weird and glossy. "Chubs, you are soooo tedious."

"You can call me Leah, and, by the way, I know someone who's met thousands of people, and she thinks you're the meanest girl she ever knew. Everyone thinks that, Kristy. Everyone."

Kristy blinked. The color faded from her cheeks and forehead. She dropped against the mattress, pulled a pillow to her chest, and curled around it.

"Kristy, come on. . . ." Corinne stopped brushing her hair and looked over her shoulder.

"Lock the door." Kristy sounded like she was choking. "Lock it."

Corinne and I sat on the bed while Kristy cried. Her eyes squeezed shut, blocking out me and Corinne and the rest of the world. She hardly made any noise, but tears and snot poured down her face and made a large wet spot on the rose-covered comforter. She coughed and choked on breaths. Corinne rubbed her arm, and Kristy knocked Corinne's hand away.

Kristy pushed herself up, wrapped her arms around her knees, and rocked back and forth. She looked like a cave girl. Her hair was a crazy mess. There was a knock on the door. She went still. "Don't tell my mom," she said, and buried her face in the pillow.

"Girls, supper's ready."

"We'll be out soon," said Corinne. "Like fifteen minutes."

"I'll keep it hot," said Mr. Baker.

Kristy pulled away the pillow and let out one last shudder. Her eyes and mouth and nose were swollen and wet. Black streaks of makeup were smeared across her cheeks. She looked at me through a thick wall of tears, but there was no anger, no resentment. "Did you know they pray for me? They were praying for me, I promise you."

Corinne hugged Kristy, smoothed back her hair, and

wiped off some of the makeup with her fingers. "Come on."
She lifted Kristy's arm and led her into the bathroom.

It was the meanest thing I'd ever done.

Half an hour later, Corinne and I followed Kristy down the
hallway to the kitchen. I was in the rear with Corinne's backpack of booze. Kristy stopped beside her dad, who stood in
an apron stirring a saucepan of red glop.

"Soup's on, girls!" He held up a plastic bag of whole-
wheat buns. "Stay and have a bite to eat with us! It's my special sloppy-joe recipe. I used organic ground turkey, tomatoes
I grew and canned myself, and my special spice mix."

Kristy didn't even look. "No, Daddy. I told you we're
going to Hilton Days. Can I have some cash?" Her eyes were
still bloodshot and glassy, even though she'd used half a bottle
of Visine.

Kristy's dad stood there in his SEXY CHEF apron and held
his old wooden spoon up like a baton. His face was a red,
creased moon. The man in the moon had just had his heart
broken.

"Sure thing, sweetheart." He carefully set the spoon on
the edge of the saucepan and pulled out his wallet. "I don't
know who's going to eat all this. You girls are trying to make
me fat."

What would it be like to have a dad who pulled out a
worn leather wallet and thumbed through it until he saw a

twenty? A dad with a belly, fur that curled over the collar of his T-shirt, and a big sad man-in-the-moon face? A father who looked at you and saw nobody else?

After Kristy kissed her mom, we left. I was the last one out. The bottles clinked as I went down the steps into the garage. To cover it, I yelled, "Bye, Mom and Dad."

Then we were out in the cool blue night. Kristy unlocked the car doors, and we each threw ourselves into our assigned seats and slammed the doors shut behind us. It was like the same Saturday night over and over.

Kristy steered with her wrist as she backed out. "The smell of that shit my dad was cooking almost made me throw up."

"I thought it looked pretty good," I said.

Kristy whipped around. Her eyes were red-rimmed, but hard again, like she'd coated them with layers of polish. "You would, Chubs. Man, I'm gonna get wasted tonight."

I leaned against the webby fabric that covered the door and looked out at the driveways and lawns and lampposts. Everything was lit up. The big houses all had welcome mats by the front doors, though 99.9 percent of people really, truly weren't welcome. Mountain View Estates looked like it was made of plastic.

Forty-Four

We drove around the downtown while we waited for it to get dark. A huge plastic banner stretched across Torrance Avenue: HILTON DAYS! 125 YEARS AND COUNTING! There were dark piles of horse poop all over the street from the afternoon parade, and the air smelled like shit. When Kristy drove over a turd, we shrieked. The sidewalks were packed with crowds of families and couples. There were lots of ladies in bright red cowboy hats, though Cindy was probably the only one also wearing red sandals that tied around her ankles. Everyone moved in excited herds toward the bright lights, music, and the pie auction.

At eight thirty, we headed north on Torrance Avenue toward the park. Only the Burger King and a gas station were lit up; all the other businesses were closed and dark. There were already tons of kids in the parking lot.

Kristy parked, unscrewed the top of the vodka bottle, gulped a mouthful, and choked. She ate half a bag of Cheetos, wiped her chin, and then drank some more. "It's super gross but give me some of that." She drank straight out of the crusty bottle and got a long green drip down her chin and neck. We passed the bottle back and forth between the seats. Corinne and I both took burning slugs. Once the world lost its edges, we climbed out of the car. Kristy wandered into a crowd of boys. Corinne and I got out and stood by the car.

My throat was raw. Corinne started rapping to a dumb song someone was playing. She hooked my arm and tried to make me rap with her, but I couldn't remember the words. Jamie Lopez pulled into the parking lot in a car driven by a boy with bleached blond hair. Jamie looked ecstatic. I wanted to run over to say hi, but they squealed their tires and took off.

Corinne stopped dancing and grabbed my sleeve. Damien Rogers and his friends stood in a circle around Kristy.

Damien was wearing a white V-necked football jersey that showed off his brown neck and his thick brown arms. His hair was wet and curled around his shoulders. There were his huge eyes and his straight black eyebrows, his cheekbones, and his wide, loose mouth, the dimple in his chin. He leaned down to talk to Kristy and shook the wet hair out of his eyes.

He was with a white basketball player and four Mexican guys, baseball players with crossed arms and huge brown biceps.

I managed to ask Corinne, "Do I look OK?" before I realized what I was seeing.

Kristy scampered like a puppy inside the circle Damien and his friends made. Damien laughed when she asked his friend, "Is your name Sanchez or Tex-Mex?"

Kristy punched Damien in the chest. "You think you're hot shit, don't you? You don't know nothing."

Damien slid his hands down Kristy's arms and wrestled her. Her white hair shimmered in the light from the streetlamp. She said, "Oh, you're such a badass."

Corinne and I were sitting on the hood of Kristy's car. Corinne sighed and slid off. She rummaged around in the backseat, then came back with two Coke cans half full of vodka. She sat back down and fiddled with her bangles. Kids walked past in groups of three or four, everyone nervous and excited as they waited to see who would get shit on. I chugged the can. Heat streaked down my throat into my stomach.

The same stupid songs played. I shivered and pulled the zipper of my hoodie up to my chin. The air was swampy with exhaust, perfume, urine, and beer. My throat hurt, my stomach churned from the vodka, and my head pounded from the nightmarish sound of Damien Rogers and Kristy Baker talking and laughing. I couldn't stop myself. I turned around and looked.

Damien and Kristy scuffled around. He grabbed handfuls of her hair, and she shook it out. He hugged her from behind and rocked her. Kristy had stolen a dream out of my head.

Kristy saw me watching. She held Damien's wrists still. She said, "My friend over there—the big one—she's madly in love with you."

Everything stopped. My heart. Lungs. The world turning.

Only Damien Rogers lived. He turned around to take a look. He blinked his huge horse eyes. "You talking about the elephant? Holy crap, she's a wide ride. Uh, no thanks."

He'd made his pronouncement. The world came back to life. His friends joined in.

"Scary. Her ass alone would flatten you."

The ugly basketball player said, "She's a beached whale. She's crushing the car!"

For a minute, I was dying, or it would have been better to be dead than alive in my humiliated body. It was like I was on fire. My skin split open, and I slopped over the dirty parking lot like the Blob.

Corinne lit two cigarettes and jammed one in my hand. "Screw him. He's a jerk." I took a puff and coughed. I dropped it on the ground and rubbed it out with my shoe.

A minute later, Corinne grabbed my arm. "Jason Coulter walked up and he's talking to Damien. Oh God, he's looking over here. . . ."

A black Mustang rolled past on Torrance Avenue. Kurt King was sitting bolt upright. His head turned sharply as he spotted Kristy. He gunned his engine and drove through a red light.

"Can I borrow your lip gloss?" Corinne huddled toward me and combed her hair with her fingers. She looked over her shoulder. "Oh my God, he's coming over."

I was alone. I was completely alone as I dug in my purse and handed Corinne my lip gloss. Her eyes were bright and blind. She was looking right at me but didn't see me. I was all alone in a weird silent little bubble, even though there was laughter, a blur of voices and shouts, hip-hop thumping from car windows. I felt weirdly real and nameless, not like Leah Lobermeir. I felt like a person that no one else knew about.

Kristy pulled away from Damien. She stumbled around in a little circle. "Keep away from me, you fool!" she shouted. She leaned over and put her hands on her knees like she was about to be sick.

Kurt King would have done a U-turn. In a minute, he'd pull into the parking lot.

Jason Coulter walked over. Corinne tipped back her head and smiled up at him. He sat down on the hood next to her with his huge hands hanging between his knees. He was wearing new yellow work boots with orange laces. Corinne shook out her bangles. "Jason, what's going on?" I slid off the car.

284

Damien and his five friends were still surrounding Kristy. One of the boys snorted like a pig as I walked up, and the basketball player grinned.

Damien wrapped his arms around Kristy. He pulled her up off the ground against his body. Kristy had a strand of hair caught in her mouth and hair caught in her diamond earring. She pretended to struggle, then leaned back against Damien's chest and stared at me.

With a bored expression, Damien Rogers looked me up and down. His mouth was open a little as if he was astounded that I would approach such royalty as himself. He was so ugly and so handsome at the same time. He held Kristy against his chest. His chin was buried in her hair. Damien Rogers had his arms around Kristy Baker. Two feet away from me, and I was still breathing. My heart was still beating. The other boys snickered and shuffled their feet as they waited to see what I would do.

"I just wanted to say . . ."

I was kind of drunk and had no idea what I wanted to say. Kristy looked like a blond child as she hung there in Damien Rogers's arms. She kicked his shin, and he let her down.

I couldn't feel the ground beneath my feet. I hated Kristy—and I now hated Damien Rogers and his friends. My Damien Rogers had died an instant death. But if you kept breathing, you could see they were just dumb boys, the basketball player had tiny gray teeth and a really small head the size of a mango, and Mr. Baker and Mrs. Baker in her fuzzy pink pajamas would want me to see that. And I thought of my mom, always hoping for a Yahtzee, getting hammered downtown at the Stoplight Lounge while fat middle-aged people clapped in a line dance, and I thought about Paul Lobermeir, the poor dumb bastard, and how people make mistakes over and over.

"I just wanted to say that . . . you guys make a great couple. It's cool—one of the most popular girls from West going out with the most popular guy from Arapahoe."

Kristy blinked. She smiled.

Damien glared as if he thought he was possibly being messed with. Then he must have thought, *Why would this fat chick have the balls to mess with Damien Rogers?* He took hold of Kristy's waist with his big hands. Kristy squawked. He dug his thumbs into her sides, and she screamed.

"Take care of her. Her ride's over there." I pointed at Corinne. She was nuzzling Jason Coulter's neck.

Damien Rogers stopped laughing. He looked at his friends' faces, then back at me. "OK. Whatever. Mind your own shit, bitch."

Kurt King's Mustang pulled into the lot, and he did a slow half circle at the entrance. His tires sprayed gravel as he tore out.

Someone who looked exactly like Carl floated in a silvery

blue minivan down the other side of Torrance Avenue, but I headed in the opposite direction. I had to meet Kurt King at Burger King. I knew it was getting close to eleven because they were on number two of the Top 11 Countdown on K103. Everyone had the same station playing.

Forty-Five

Walking alone down Torrance Avenue was like walking through a movie. A few cars shot past. The road was empty and dark with utility wires overhead and lonely pools of light from the streetlamps. The sidewalk seemed to sink beneath my feet. I tripped on a broken chunk of concrete.

The Burger King was next to a closed lumberyard and was lit up like a spaceship. I walked toward the its light, its big plastic sign, the huge windows that separated me from the people inside.

The parking lot was wet and shiny as if it had been hosed off. Napkins melted in puddles of spilled pop. A girl wearing a paper hat hunched at the drive-thru window. A carload of guys pulled up. One of them barked.

I didn't see his car and thought, *He probably left. Oh, well, at least I tried.* But I walked around the side of the building, and there it was. The Mustang was parked in a square of dark space between the Dumpster and a cement wall and a chain-link fence. A security light shone onto the hood of the car. I stopped ten feet back. Kurt King sat in the driver's seat and leaned against the door. He reached out and adjusted the side mirror.

Crrreeeeaaak. His car door opened. First one cowboy boot, then the other. He pushed himself up out of the car like he was really tired. He was wearing the corduroy jacket and had sunglasses shoved into his streaky hair even though it was nighttime. He looked down at the cracked asphalt, shook his head, and carefully shut the door.

He turned around, threw back his shoulders, shoved out his hips. He tipped back his head and stared at me, not smiling, not friendly. "What are you doin' here?"

The garbage hadn't been picked up and it stank. A stack of waxed boxes leaned against the cement wall.

"Sorry. I didn't hear you." With every word, he took a step toward me. "No Ashley again, huh?" He was there, a foot from me, real and not real, a hologram.

"No."

"I saw her back there." He worked his mouth over his teeth. "I could knock those little bastards from here to there in two seconds flat." His breath was thick and hot, stinking with alcohol. I turned my head.

289

He took hold of my chin and brought my face back around. "What are you doin' here? I don't like being dicked with."

My chin was numb from the vodka, but I could smell cigarettes on his hand and something else, rancid, like old cheese. His lower lip was fat and wet with spit. My eyes felt stuck to his wet lip.

"No one's dicking with you. I'm sorry." My words came out slowly, like the air was too thick. I coughed onto his hand. I was lying. I had been dicking with him. Flares exploded in the back of my mind. But it was my responsibility. I had to fix it.

He let go of my face. "Shit. I cannot believe this. What the hell is going on here?" He moved back, sat on the car, spread his legs. He rubbed his neck, looked up at the sky. His leg bounced like a tweaker's.

I took a step toward him. "I'm sorry."

"What the hell are you sorry about? I can't even hear a word of what you're saying." He crooked his finger at me. "I don't bite. I'm the one who's being dicked with here."

He stretched his mouth and showed his teeth. Not a smile. His teeth, slick and cracked with tiny lines, and his hot vodka breath. I could smell it a foot away. He rolled his lower lip up over his bottom teeth and licked it.

He laughed as he looked over my shoulder. I turned to

see—the empty parking lot, the lonely yellow back of the Burger King with its little light and its mirror and the lit-up menu board, a broken camera dangling by a wire. No one was going through the drive-thru.

He said, "Girl, you got to tell me what the hell is going on."

He nodded as if keeping time to a song that was playing in his head. I almost laughed. Then I felt so sleepy, I could hardly keep my eyes open and focused. I wanted to close my eyes and fall asleep and stop existing. I could barely say it, I was so tired. But I had to.

"You never talked to the girl with blond hair. You were talking to me."

He stared at me with dull eyes. "I don't get it."

How alone in the world can you be? Not much more alone. Pretending to be Ashley had made me so happy. I could feel her there in the shadows, whispering to me.

The air felt cold as I breathed it in. "That girl with blond hair isn't named Ashley. There is no Ashley. You were talking to me. You need to delete that girl's picture from your phone."

He went still. I looked into the face of a man with pores and whiskers and little scars, the face of a stranger. And I was a stranger, a nothing, to him. I couldn't recognize anything in his flat green eyes.

"You've been dicking with me for a long time," he said. The skin under his left eye twitched. He hopped off the car and paced around the passenger side. He lifted the sunglasses and raked his fingers through his hair. "I can't believe this, man."

"I'm real sorry." I coughed and took a step back. "OK, so just erase her. She doesn't —"

"Where you think you're going?" He rubbed his nose on his wrist and circled me. I backed toward the car.

Strings of spit stretched between his lips. His face looked greasy. "Who the hell do you think you are? You think you can just mess with me and get away with it? You think that's OK?"

"No. I don't think it's OK. I'm sorry. I need to go." I was barely breathing.

"Girl, you got some explaining to do." He took hold of my arm, opened the car door, and jerked his head. "Get in."

"No." I pulled away. He grabbed my arm again, twisted it behind my back. I watched it happen to someone else. He opened the door and shoved me into the seat. He locked the door and slammed it. Through the glass, he said, "Bitch, don't move."

The streetlamp shone into the car. I was drunk but wide awake. My heart and brain hummed like a bird's. Everything was sharp and clear. I'd been inside the car before, but it was different. It was smaller and tighter this time, the dash was shiny and smelled like chemicals, there was a big blue comb in the cup holder between the seats—the comb hadn't been there before, and the comb was dirty; there were brown streaks on the tines—and a horse, stretched out running for its life, was in a circle in the center of the steering wheel, and a bottle of vodka was wedged between the driver's seat and the console, in the middle of the red cap was a tiny eagle with outspread wings. The bottom of the gearshift was covered with squishy black leather that almost made me vomit.

"Bitch, don't move." I watched him say it. He was walking around the front of the car with his fingertips touching the hood.

Just as he reached for his door, I unlocked the door on my side, pulled the handle, and pushed out of the car. He lunged across the seats. I landed on my elbow; my foot was pinched in the door. My blue purse that Cindy bought at Marshalls spilled—keys, strawberry lip gloss, tampons, breath mints, and my turquoise wallet with a hummingbird stitched on the front scattered across the asphalt. My phone slid under the car. I yanked my foot out, lost my shoe, and crawled backward like a crab.

He got out and came around and looked down at me with his face tilted and blank. I rolled over and pushed off the ground. His hand closed over my arm like a clamp. He grabbed my hair and dragged me back to the car. I fell and scrambled to stay on my feet, trying to keep my hair from tearing out in his fingers.

He shoved me back into the passanger seat like I was a bag of garbage. He got in and slammed his door.

"Cut the shit," he said.

He was breathing hard. I couldn't look at him. My teeth clicked against each other. I was choking on his smells, vodka and rotten sweat. His heavy, cold hand curled around the back of my neck. I wanted to scream, but my lungs were punched through with holes.

"Take off your shirt," he said.

"No. I'm sick."

"Take off your shirt." He fingers tightened on my neck. "Take off your shirt or I'll tear your head off. Quit shaking, bitch."

In five seconds, I had a thousand thoughts. Pictures. Cindy curled on the couch in her pink quilted robe with the tiny pink ribbon at the throat, the way she'd laugh hysterically when she got a Yahtzee. The big blue mountain moving closer. And Corinne and her sad mouth and her long nails going *click-click-click*, and Anita with her choppy bangs over her eyes that shone as if there was something lit inside of them. Mr. Calvino smiling at something I said in class. And Carl, the way Carl looked at me with his whole body as if I was real. How blue and clear the sky was some mornings like it went straight up to the top of the universe.

I swallowed under Kurt King's thumb. I told myself that Carl and Anita were looking for me. I unzipped the hoodie and got it off with his hand on my neck. He squeezed. I put my fingers under the bottom of my tank and began to lift. I felt air on my stomach. In the background, someone ordered a Whopper and supersize Coke.

His hand tightened; I started crying. He grunted and was on top of me. He jerked down my tank and bra, grabbed me, and twisted like he was trying to tear me apart. I screamed. One of his hands went over my mouth, the other tried to work down the top of my jeans, his fingers like strong hard worms, foreign and cold and scratching.

"Shut up, bitch," he whispered into my hair.

The back door of Burger King slammed shut. He went still.

Voices and soft footsteps came toward us across the parking lot. The clammy stench of his hand filled my nose; I couldn't get any air. I was jammed against the door. Over Kurt King's shoulder, a guy in a Burger King shirt lifted the lid of the Dumpster, and another guy threw white bags of garbage into it. *Puft, puft, puft, puft.*

The lid clanked down.

"Not a sound," he said. He slowly turned his head to look. I curled my hand into a fist and socked him in the balls.

He jackknifed over; his sunglasses flew onto the dash. I got the door open, grabbed my shoe, and dropped onto the ground. I kicked the door shut. I yanked up my bra and tank and launched up through the air to my feet.

The Burger King guys were lighting a pipe. "What the hell," the shorter one said.

Forty-Six

The first thing they asked me was "What is your name?"

I sat in the little brightly lit room for hours. I listened to myself breathing and tried to breathe as quietly as possible. I listened to the clock ticking on the wall. I looked at the drawer handles and the counters and the computer and the clock and the file cabinets and the dingy blinds that covered the window. The buttons on the big square phone blinked and blinked. They made me look at pictures in a big book, but Kurt King wasn't in it.

Kurt King almost ran over one of the Burger King guys. He was gone long before the cops came. The cop asked if "he'd done anything." I said no. I didn't have to go to the hospital. The police took pictures of bruises on my arm, the scrapes on my elbow and on the palms of my hands.

I felt strange sitting in that tiny, brightly lit room, like I was there and not there. I felt like I had left my life and then come back to it, and I was looking at it. I kept swallowing, and every time a door slammed somewhere inside the police station, my arms flew out.

A chubby, bald officer with gray shadows around his eyes talked to me for what felt like hours but was only fifteen minutes. He kept his eyes on the computer and typed. I saw when he left the computer screen open and went into the hall to talk to someone. He made a note about the "odor" of alcohol and described me as "an overweight fifteen-year-old female."

The cop who had driven me to the station came to the door. Sergeant Romero. He filled the room like a giant. He was so blue and big and clunky with his belly and boots, his belt and gun, his hat just like on TV. His breathing sounded like a roar. The backs of his hands and fingers were covered with black hair.

He shook his head, two tiny shakes. "So, you knew this guy? You talked to him on the phone a number of times? How many times would you estimate?"

"I don't know. Like twenty times. . . . He has my friend's picture on his phone."

"OK, we'll check into it."

When Sergeant Romero turned to go, he stopped with his hand on the doorknob. He didn't look at me. "I have a girl just your age. I'll be waiting out here until we find your mom."

I could still feel his hand on my mouth. I had scrubbed my mouth with wet paper towels until it was red and raw, but I could smell it.

About three thirty a.m., there was a tiny knock on the door. The door slowly opened and there was Cindy. I'd never realized how small she was. Her hair was funky. She hung on to the door knob, swaying, like she was about to pass out. She smiled and said, "Hey, munchkin."

She put her little arms around me, and we sat together in the little plastic chairs for a long time while she cried and hugged me and held my face in her hands and told me what it had been like for her when she found the messages and all the missed calls — she'd been visiting a friend's apartment and had accidentally turned off her cell — and everything that had gone through her head while she was driving to the police station, and I listened and listened and soaked up the sound of her voice, the way she smelled like Chardonnay and perfume.

She ran her thumb back and forth above a bloody scrape full of dirt and gravel. "On the way home, we'll pick up some hydrogen peroxide at the twenty-four-hour Walgreens," she said with a tiny smile. She blinked her wet lashes.

"Sure, Mom," I said, even though that stuff stung.

Forty-Seven

Cindy took sick days on Monday and Tuesday. I stayed in bed listening to Bruno Mars. She used a cookie sheet as a tray to bring me cereal and frozen French toast and teacups of orange juice and milk. She gave me Popsicles and graham crackers. I didn't eat much. I was finally losing weight. Hooray.

I didn't think or dream. I lay under the covers and let Bruno Mars trickle through my brain. I listened to the sound of my own breathing and watched the bars of afternoon light move across the green wall. I was trying to make sure that I was still alive, still me. I kept completely covered up in long sleeves, sweats, and socks. I had bruises on my arm, knees, the back of my thigh, even on my stomach and back. The bruises felt like Kurt King's fingerprints, and I didn't want to see them.

Tuesday afternoon, Cindy made me go for a checkup at the Aspen Community Clinic. We sat in the lobby paging through ancient fashion magazines. When the nurse called my name, Cindy stood up. "Mom, I'll go alone." She looked so small and worried as she sat back down. She picked up another magazine and stared at the cover.

The nurse led me down a hallway, then stopped to weigh me. I closed my eyes and didn't ask what she'd written down.

She put me in a little room and handed me a cloth gown, but I said I was going to keep my clothes on. She made me take off my hoodie, though, and wrapped the blood-pressure cuff around my upper arm and tightened it, then slowly let out the air: 120 over 80. She left me alone. I pulled my hoodie back on, then looked around the room and named everything I could. Blood-pressure reader, hand sanitizer, eye chart, examination gloves, stethoscope, speculum (yuck), ear examiner—I needed to look that one up. . . .

There was a knock on the door, and Dr. Margaret Wallace walked in. "Hello, Leah. Come have a seat by the desk. Let's have a talk before we look you over."

She was about ten years older than Cindy. She had short hair streaked with gray, brown eyes, and bright blue bifocals on the tip of her nose. She wore a white coat that matched her hair. She was as large and graceful as a ship in the tiny room.

I sat in the chair facing her and pulled the sleeves of my hoodie down over my hands.

She looked at me over her glasses. "It's good to see you, Leah. You mom wasn't real clear about what happened. Can you tell me, Leah?"

"I really don't want to talk about it."

"OK, Leah. It's your decision. You don't have to go into details, but for medical reasons, I need to ask: Were you assaulted?"

"Somewhat."

"I'm sorry. Do you have injuries? Do you have pain anywhere?"

"Not too bad. It's just bruises and cuts." I showed her my elbow, the Band-Aids on my hands.

"Were the police called? Did they take you to the hospital?"

"The police came, but I didn't go to the hospital. The guy's in custody."

"Leah, I know this is hard. Our conversation is confidential. Again, for medical reasons, in case you need testing of any kind, I need to ask: Were you raped?"

"No. And I don't want to talk about it anymore."

Dr. Wallace typed into the computer, then looked at me over her glasses. Her face was still and serious. She was silent for a minute or two.

She took her hands away from the computer keyboard. "Leah, I am so sorry this happened to you. How are things at home? Do you have good support? Do you have people you can talk to?"

"It's all right. I have a couple of good friends."

"Have you thought about counseling?"

"I don't know. Maybe."

"It's a good idea, Leah, after something this traumatic. But it's your choice. Before you leave, I'll give you a list of places you could go. Let's get you up on the table and have a listen to your lungs and heart."

She helped me get up on the table onto the paper sheet. I said, "Do you have kids?"

She said, "Two girls and a boy. I'm going to listen to your lungs. Take a deep breath." She pressed the stethoscope against my chest and my back. "Another." The stethoscope wasn't cold—that's a small but important detail most doctors forget. I knew she could see bruises, but she didn't say anything. "Very clear. Excellent."

She said, "I'm going to listen to your heart." She pressed the stethoscope against my chest. She listened. "Good. Your heart sounds strong and regular."

Dr. Wallace listened to my stomach, looked into my ears and eyes, then into my mouth and throat, and she checked the scrapes on my hands for infection and washed the cuts and put on antibacterial ointment and new bandages. She ran her thumb over a bruise on my arm.

She patted my knee. "You are a healthy, strong girl, Leah. I am very, very sorry about what happened to you. I'm glad you came. If you would like to come back, I would be happy to talk to you anytime. How's school going?"

"Pretty good. I'm getting a B+ in chemistry. I want to be a doctor."

She smiled. Her smile was huge.

Forty-Eight

Cindy went back to work on Wednesday. I checked the door ten times a day to make sure it was locked and kept a chair jammed under the doorknob. Cindy called every hour. When I heard laughter in the hallway or in front of the building, I froze. I taped my blue polka-dot curtains to the glass so there was no way to see in.

Wednesday afternoon, I got the notebook out from under my bed and started writing. The pen tore through the page to the paper underneath. Anita called that night. We just talked for a few minutes because Cindy was hovering at my door.

Thursday, Anita and Carl came over after school. Before they came, I took a shower and put on makeup. I heard the sharp, no-nonsense rap of Anita's knuckles, checked through the peephole, then pulled away the chair and unlocked the door. There they were, shocking in their aliveness, in their Anita-ness and Carl-ness. I still felt safer covered up and was wearing socks, sweatpants, and a giant green sweatshirt.

Anita curled up next to me on the couch and held my hand. She had a small but very strong hand.

Carl lurked by the door. "Carl, sit down," I said. "But first, could you lock the door?"

He dumped a thick folder on the coffee table. "That's chemistry homework. We're finishing up acids and bases. We have a test tomorrow, but Mrs. McCleary says you can take it on Tuesday. I can come over this weekend, if you want, and go over it with you. Next week we start gas laws."

Carl sat on the edge of the couch and stared at the floor. He rocked a little. His hands gripped his knees.

"What should we watch?" said Anita. "I brought Red Vines." She pulled a package out of her pocket and tossed it onto the table.

"Wait," said Carl. He took a big breath and sat up straight. His gaze skated over my face, then stopped at my eyes. The skin under his eyes was shiny and wet.

Anita's eyes were fierce and dark; she was chewing the inside of her cheek.

I said, "It's OK, Carl. Let's just watch a show."

We sat cross-legged in a row on the lumpy couch and watched two talk shows in a row. I could relax; I felt as if my friends were guarding me. The first show was about people who believed their children's autism had been caused by baby vaccines. The determined middle-aged parents sat next to their kids, who rocked and squirmed in brightly colored chairs. When the commercial came on, Carl covered his eyes with his hand and groaned. "Oh my God, this is so unscientific."

The second show was about transgender people. The guest was an eighteen-year-old girl who happened to still have a penis because her family couldn't afford the operation. She was wearing a low-cut shirt, a tight miniskirt, and heels so high I was scared for her—you can't run in those shoes. She'd been named homecoming queen at her small-town high school, where she'd never been known as a boy.

They played video footage of the homecoming crowning. The girl held the bouquet in her elbow, touched her crown to make sure it was straight, and cried. Anita watched through her fingers. "Dude, that chick's brave. If they'd found out, they would have lynched her."

We ate all the Red Vines. Anita pulled the pieces apart and dropped the strands one by one into her mouth. The show ended. Anita turned off the TV.

"Well, you guys, thanks for coming over. Cindy will be home in an hour." They didn't move.

"So," said Anita. I felt weighted, crushed by my own heaviness onto the couch. I was getting both skinnier and heavier at the same time.

"Does everyone at school know?" The thought of school made me want to sob. It was like being locked into a crowded cage with no privacy, no protection, and constant surveillance, five days a week, all day. Our punishment for being alive and fifteen.

"Not sure. I don't think so," said Anita. "Shannon the nurse knows because she asked me about you today. Be prepared: I think she wants to have some heavy-duty therapy sessions. She seemed pretty pumped."

"What the hell?" I said. "So . . . the guy's name isn't really Kurt King. It's Edgar Dithers. He was wanted for armed robbery in Nevada. They picked him up the next day. He had a stolen gun and drugs in the car. Then Officer Romero called two days ago to tell us that Edgar Dithers stabbed a guard with a fork. I'll be in college before he gets out, if he ever does."

They had his phone with Kristy's picture on it. It was evidence.

"And I don't have to go to court. They were going to charge him with assault, but they dropped the charges."

"What bullshit! *What bullshit!* They dropped the charges?" Anita let go of my hand and hammered on her knees.

Carl tightened his hands into fists. "I should go to law school and become a prosecutor."

"We were frantic." Anita swallowed. "Corinne had no idea where you were. Kristy was wasted and hanging with this total dick. We looked for you until after midnight. Carl caught some shit, of course. Stupid Patty. . . . We saw cop cars behind the Burger King, but we had no idea. I'm so sorry, Leah."

Carl sat very straight and opened and closed his hands. He was breathing very deliberately. "Yeah, me, too," he whispered. "Listen, sorry, but I got to go. I have a piano lesson. . . . God!" Carl clawed his head, then abruptly stood up. Wiping his eyes, he strode toward the door. He stopped with his hand on the doorknob.

Carl turned around and came back. He leaned down, pressed his forehead against mine, and breathed his warm tangerine breath onto me. He ran his thumb over my cheek. If I'd had a question, that was my answer.

He left. The front entryway door above us clicked shut. "I can stay till your mom gets home. Evelyn's over at my aunt's this week." Anita took my hand again and squeezed it. "Hey, I forgot! I have a present for you."

Anita dug through her backpack, pulled out a rolled-up tube of paper, and handed it to me. I untied the little string and opened up a periodic table. She'd colored in every box a different color and written the symbols in Gothic script; she hadn't taken chemistry yet. It was gorgeous and crazy.

"I used every single color in Evelyn's box of crayons. I left out the little numbers, hope that's OK. It's to help you study. For inspiration," she said. She wound strands of hair around her finger. "What do you think?"

"It's so beautiful. Thanks, Anita. I really love it." I ran my finger down the noble gases.

"Really? Do you like how I varied the blues and greens and purples . . . ?"

"Anita, can I tell you what happened?"

Her eyes were the same toward me, just sadder. "Sure," she said.

"I can't talk to Cindy about it. She gets too upset."

"Of course," Anita said. She held my hand in both of hers and sat very still.

It was like taking off a bandage and looking at a scar for the first time. You unwind and unwind the white bandages, and get closer and closer to the hurting part, and the last bandage comes off, and there it is out in the air and the light, still raw, hideous, gnarly, and gross-looking, both worse and not as bad as in your imagination, and you look at it and start to figure out how you're going to live with it.

Forty-Nine

Cindy brought home a book about teen sexual assault from the library, but it was mostly too painful to read. The book was so worn, the pages smudged and dog-eared and the saddest parts underlined in pencil and purple pen. *Me exactly!* was written in the margin in little-girl handwriting, the dot of the exclamation mark a round ball. I stuck the book under the bed.

Time for school. Cindy drove me and waited in front while I climbed the steps and went in the door. Even though it was seventy degrees out, I wore jeans and a long-sleeved sweatshirt.

I had an overdue assignment for Mr. Calvino. It was ten pages long, handwritten, single-spaced, with footnotes, and titled "High School Social Hierarchies and Oppression in Hilton, Colorado." In the introduction I wrote:

Dear Mr. Calvino,

This is the assignment for the last instructional unit. I went over the word limit. It's also my submission for AP language arts. You can give me an F if you want, but I will not read this to the class. You are my intended and authentic audience.

In the school's front hallway, Sergeant Motts was breaking up a fight—he gingerly stuck his nightstick between two girls who were ripping at each other's hair. "Come on, girls! Behave like young ladies!" I walked by and handed Cindy's note to the office lady—she wrinkled her nose and read it through her bifocals. She handed me a pass and hunched back over her computer keyboard.

Shannon the nurse rushed out from the back office. She skidded to a stop when she got up to me. "Is it OK if I touch you?" She gave me a shoulder hug. "Let me know when you can take two hours off in a row, and we'll have a nice long talk. My schedule is completely open!"

Then the bell rang, and I was swept along. No sign of Anita or Carl. My default position of invisibility, except when ridiculed or attached to Kristy and Corinne, still held. No one saw me. No one noticed me. I had been gone one week but could have been gone a month or a year—it wouldn't have mattered. Either no one knew what had happened or no one cared.

Kelsey Parker and friends swept past in shredded jean cut-offs, flip-flops, their long hair in topknots—they'd changed outfits for the season. I wasn't even a blip on Kelsey Parker's blue-contact-tinted retinas. But watching her, I noticed for the first time that Kelsey Parker was knock-kneed, and with her hair up, she looked narrow and snaky as an egg noodle and maybe even had a touch of scoliosis. Kelsey Parker in twenty years: huge inappropriate hair, a frozen expression, back problems, the top real-estate agent in Hilton.

All those shiny faces, shiny with sweat, makeup, and acne cream; shiny with hope; shiny with faked excitement. Except for the stoners, everyone tried to look so happy and be so loud, as if they were at the center of a nonstop, movable party. And everyone, even the stoners, tried desperately to make sure they were attached to at least one other person, and preferably three or four, because you must never, ever be seen alone.

And here came LaTeisha Morgan and Ray Ramirez, arms intertwined, cheeks brushing as Ray leaned in closer to hear what LaTeisha was saying, and they actually did look happy. I wondered if they'd break up after Ray went to college. He had a full scholarship to Notre Dame.

I walked alone up to Corinne. She was standing at her locker with Jason Coulter. "Just a sec, Jason," she said, and pulled me a few feet away. He rolled his eyes and turned his back.

"Got to make it quick. God, you were sick for a long time, girl. Sorry I haven't called. I've been really busy. So, everything's good?" And there she was, Corinne, with her dimpled cheeks, and the faint lines in the freckly skin between her green eyes, and her serious mouth that she'd frosted with lip gloss. She had an enormous piece of grape bubble gum between her teeth and cheek.

"We're going to prom," she whispered. "Mom bought me a dress. Guess what? Jason's going to Western University on a baseball scholarship. He talked my mom into letting me play softball. He convinced her. She stood up to Derrick. I get to practice with the team the rest of the year. Jason's little sister is watching the boys for a couple hours in the afternoons. Next week, I get to start pitching in games. Will you come watch? I had to cut my nails off." She wiggled her fingers at me, blew a bubble, and popped it with her tongue. "You won't believe this, but I quit smoking."

Jason Coulter turned around and crossed his arms. He tilted his head. "Come on, Corinne."

She put on more lip gloss and blew into her cupped hand. "How's my breath? I got to go but I'll see you."

"Where's Kristy?"

Corinne stopped turning and looked at me. "Mrs. Baker died last night."

Her eyes got big and wet-looking. She suddenly stood on her toes and waved. "Kelsey! See you at practice!"

Fifty

Cindy held on to the steering wheel like it was a lifesaving ring. She'd sprayed on way too much perfume.

"You should wear your hair like that more often," she said. "It's very sleek."

I was wearing an old-ladyish black dress Cindy had bought at a consignment store and the pumps we got when I was thirteen for my aunt Peg's funeral. I'd had insomnia and then woke up late, and hadn't had time to dry or straighten my hair, so I'd put it in a ponytail. I never wore my hair in a ponytail—it looked ridiculous, but who gave a shit? I was going to Mrs. Baker's funeral. I wondered if her doctors had tried hard enough. Maybe there was just no way to fix her.

"You look lovely! You're wearing the earrings I gave you!" Cindy turned her head and smiled in a hopeful way.

I laced my fingers together and stared straight ahead. "Thanks."

"Leah, it's so good of you to come with me to Mrs. Baker's funeral. It will mean so much to Kristy, and it means so much to me—"

"Of course I'm going! She was like a mother to me."

Cindy suddenly looked stricken and tilted up her chin. "So, you thought of Connie as your mother?"

"God, Mom!" I lowered my window. Cool air blew across my face and hair, and oxygen entered my lungs. "I said 'like a mother.' Like a mother. Let it go."

Cindy's face went still and blank. She swallowed and almost drove through a stop sign.

She hit the brakes, and we both flew forward. She smiled her tiny bitter smile as we drove through the intersection. "Well, Connie was an awfully nice lady. She did anything and everything for Kristy. She was able to be there for Kristy twenty-four/seven, as I have not been able to be for you as I've had to earn a living. I'm sure you do wish she was your mother—"

"Come on. Please. I just meant I loved her. Not more than you. God, I'm so tired." I sighed, leaned on my fist, and looked out the window. "And by the way, you look lovely, too, Mom. I like your new lipstick."

We drove down Tenth Avenue past the Safeway, the 7-Eleven, the EZPAWN, then along Costilla Street on the outskirts of the downtown. We passed the Stoplight Lounge. In the morning light, the trash-strewn sidewalk, purple glass lanterns, and fake river-stone facade looked extremely tragic, and I suddenly thought that maybe death was a bar like the Stoplight. Maybe Kristy's mom was going in right this minute. She'd push the door open and shyly look around the dim room before spotting Paul Lobermeir at the far end of the bar's counter. She'd scoot between the tables. "Excuse me! So sorry, dear." She'd hold out her hand and say, "Are you, by chance, Paul Lobermeir? Leah is the living picture of you! My Lord, your daughter is a lovely, smart girl." Then she'd sit in her fuzzy pajamas on a stool right next to Paul. She'd tell him how I wanted to be a doctor. And Paul would introduce his friend, the woman on the stool next to him. She had long black hair, tea-colored eyes, and a huge, movie-star smile.

We drove through the downtown to a neighborhood in the red hills on the outskirts of Hilton. The funeral home was a blank yellow-brick building, long, low, and windowless, as if to prevent leaks from what it contained. The only decoration was the fancy lettering on the sign: PETERSON'S MEMORIAL CHAPEL.

"No one's outside. I hope we're not late." Cindy checked her tiny gold watch.

Cindy hurried toward the doors. She took little biting steps in her high heels. I tried to walk while pulling up and untwisting my panty hose—I was wearing a pair of Cindy's.

The crotch wouldn't go much past my knees, and they had torn in three places — I'd stopped the runs with nail polish. As we got closer, we could hear a voice murmuring.

"Oh my God, we are late!" said Cindy.

I actually reached for her hand, but Cindy hugged herself and tucked her hands into her armpits. I pulled open the door and we looked in. There was an entryway and double doors that opened to a room full of people sitting on folding metal chairs. At the front of the room was a shiny coffin covered with flowers. Pastor Steve was wearing a white-and-purple robe and stood by the coffin. As he talked, he opened and closed his hands as if trying to catch something out of the air.

We tiptoed into the entryway. A guest book with gold-leaf-edged pages was open on a podium. Cindy signed it and handed the pen to me. "You have to sign."

In my best handwriting, I wrote, *Leah Anne Lobermeir.* I set down the pen. I was alive and I had a name. I followed Cindy into the room full of people. An usher with a tragic frown silently unfolded chairs for us.

I lowered myself onto a chair and made a big squeak. It was so quiet. The air was thick with the smells of flowers, cologne, perfume, toothpaste, and another smell, awful and sweetish.

People shifted in their chairs and softly coughed into their fists. Pastor Steve looked at the ground. There was a long silence. He raised his face and pressed his hands together. "I knew Connie very, very well. I was a witness to her long, courageous battle. . . ."

After that, I only listened to snatches of what Pastor Steve said—"hard to understand" and "we can only trust" and "a better world." What I was seeing took up all the space inside of me. There was no room left for words. A woman with a strange, bony face lay stiffly in the coffin. She was wearing pink lipstick and a yellow wig.

Kristy's hair was in a tight braid that hung down her back like a white rope. She sat next to her dad in the front.

Pastor Steve pressed his hands together. "Let us pray." After the prayer, Mr. Baker stood up to speak, but his big round face turned red and he started to cry. Two older men helped him sit back down. Kristy looked for a second at her dad and then turned back to the coffin. I grabbed Cindy's hand. She was squeezing a wet tissue.

A couple of ladies, friends of Mrs. Baker, stood up to talk about her. One of them sobbed and could hardly talk, and the second woman made a speech that went on for ten minutes. She didn't cry but talked slowly with a weird bright smile. I couldn't hear either of them. It was like watching TV with the sound turned off. I closed my eyes and prayed for the service to be over. Cindy squeezed my hand and let it go.

When I opened my eyes, the crowd crystallized into people I knew. There were teachers from school. Señorita Johnson. Mr. Calvino. The assistant principal, Mr. Widmer, was sitting in the fourth row next to Shannon, who turned around and smiled meaningfully at me. She was still desperate for me to come in for a therapy session.

In the third row, Jason Coulter was sitting with Corinne, her mother, and her stepdad, Derrick. Both Corinne and Jason sat with bowed heads. Their heads tilted at the same angle, and their backs curved together. They were a perfect match and looked like they were engaged and would probably get married and have a baby much earlier than anyone expected, and then I imagined Corinne in divorce court at age twenty-five, though hopefully she'd be a chef by then. Corinne was going to wear a strapless jade-green dress to prom. She showed me pictures on her phone.

Everyone said "Amen" and the service ended. For a minute, no one moved. Then people began to whisper and hobbled to their feet.

Kristy turned around in her chair and stared at me. We acknowledged each other like survivors of a terrible battle, and she looked away.

Within a minute, people surrounded Kristy and her father. Her dad stood up, but Kristy stayed in her chair. The ladies crowded around her, stroked her head, and kissed her cheeks. Kristy sat like a stone princess in the middle of the mob.

I stood up. "I'll wait for you outside."

Cindy stiffened and frowned. Her face crinkled up into a thousand tiny lines like paper cuts. The wrinkles had appeared in the last two weeks. "I don't want you to go outside by yourself."

"Mom, we've talked about this. I'll be careful. I won't go anywhere."

"OK, honey. I just need to speak to Kristy's father." She sat up straight but wobbled a little as she stared at the people surrounding Mr. Baker. She reached up and touched her cheek. "We had the same flowers at my mom's service. My mom, my dad, and Paul all died within the space of five years. My goodness, that was something!"

For a second, I saw a young woman, just a few years older than me, alone in an empty apartment, with a dark-haired toddler playing at her feet.

Without looking at me, she took my hand. Her thumb absentmindedly stroked my fingers, then she squeezed them. "You're my girl," she said.

Mr. Calvino turned around and gave me a sad smile.

I was the first person to leave the building. The world was white with sunlight. The sky was a dirty blue.

I walked up the sidewalk. I hadn't been outside, alone, in a couple of weeks. My heart thumped, and my brain started to fog up with anxiety, but I made myself listen. A thread of wind wound through the trees. A dog's bark echoed down the empty street. It sounded like a dog barking in a dream.

It felt wonderful to walk, held back only by saggy panty hose. I hadn't walked in a long time. There was just air and sky. I wasn't trapped inside a funeral home or a school or an ugly apartment. Cindy would be a while. She'd have to wait in line to hug and console Mr. Baker.

I walked up the hill, looking back every minute to keep sight of the funeral home. I passed a house with Christmas lights feebly blinking around the front window. A ceramic rabbit with floppy ears sat on its hind legs in the weeds. A dead orange Christmas tree strewn with tinsel lay in the side yard. A chain-link dog pen held only a dirty blanket and a knot of rope. There was nobody but me.

At the top of the street was an overlook with a view of the mountain and the town. A few days before, I'd watched a nature show about how mountains were created. Mountains were made up of rocks, just plain old rocks, pushed out of the earth by violent forces.

Down below, Hilton glittered like it was built out of mica. In the east, past all the housing developments, Hilton ended, and the dry yellow plains began. A cloud passed over, and its shadow moved across the neighborhoods.

I stepped off the cracked sidewalk and stood on the dead grass at the edge of the cliff. Wedges of red rock stuck out of the cliff face, and at the bottom there was a slide of dirt. People threw trash down the hill—a mattress, box springs, a high chair, shoes, dead computers, rags of clothes. I could imagine a girl lying there like a giant doll, lip gloss smeared, teardrop necklace lost.

I cupped my hands around my mouth and shouted, "Hello! Hello! Hello!"

I would climb down in my blue scrubs. I would make sure that she was breathing, then listen to her heart. I'd hold her hand and say, "What's your name? You're going to be OK."